WHO SHOT YA 2

Renta

Lock Down Publications and
Ca$h Presents
Who Shot Ya 2
A Novel by Renta

Lock Down Publications
P.O. Box 870494
Mesquite, Tx 75187

Visit our website
www.lockdownpublications.com

Copyright 2018 by Who Shot Ya 2 Renta

First Edition October 2018
Printed in the United States of America

This is a work of fiction. Names, characters, places, and incidents either are products of the author's imagination or are used fictitiously. Any similarity to actual events or locales or persons, living or dead, is entirely coincidental.

Lock Down Publications
Like our page on Facebook: Lock Down Publications @
www.facebook.com/lockdownpublications.ldp
Cover design and layout by: **Dynasty Cover Me**
Book interior design by: **Shawn Walker**
Edited by: **Lashonda Johnson**

Stay Connected with Us!

Text **LOCKDOWN** to 22828 to stay up-to-date with new releases, sneak peeks, contests and more…

Submission Guideline.

Submit the first three chapters of your completed manuscript to ldpsubmissions@gmail.com, subject line: Your book's title. The manuscript must be in a .doc file and sent as an attachment. The document should be in Times New Roman, double-spaced and in size 12 font. Also, provide your synopsis and full contact information. If sending multiple submissions, they must each be in a separate email.

Have a story but no way to send it electronically? You can still submit to LDP/Ca$h Presents. Send in the first three chapters, written or typed, of your completed manuscript to:

LDP: Submissions Dept
Po Box 870494
Mesquite, Tx 75187

DO NOT send original manuscript. Must be a duplicate.

Provide your synopsis and a cover letter containing your full contact information.

Thanks for considering LDP and Ca$h Presents.

Dedications

I dedicate this book to every nigga that's ever questioned, God! Every nigga that's got out the mud cause the only blessings they ever had was the ones they created. Most importantly, I dedicate this book to the ones that thug with me. Papa—it's a race for that Purple Heart, big bruh. It's' our reason for livin'!

Renta

Part One

When one knows how to make love to their thoughts he becomes a God of his nature. As playas, we sometimes become so enchanted with the Rubies in our vision, that we disregard the clarity of a diamond. Yet, only a boss can tame his nature and make sound decisions in the waters of temptation. Who's to say one is inadequate rather than merely not trained? Every man wasn't molded to be a boss so for him to be who he was created to be is not a flaw, but an edge to every hungry nigga's game. If there were no squares; who would the wolves prey on?

Let me give you this jewel the streets blessed me with. See, I was raised by a dope fiend and a mean selection of game niggas and bitches. Yet, not to say I don't have a pure section of self, because in the midst of being groomed for perceptive perfection. I was also being taught a vital law of the land—loyalty! Selective loyalty because not everybody deserves that portion of you. There is a rule amongst the breed—it's a law, one must always stand on because when you forget, you become an animal.

You can't play—con—or not give a fuck about everybody! You gotta reserve love, loyalty, and respect for some people. Jewel, a game nigga once told me, "Assata, if you have a woman you love, yet you know she is a hoe. How can you blame her for what she is rather than never forgetting who she is? Your heart fell for her on its own, she is just being her. She may change her stance, but it's her walk that she can't change. Yea, a hoe will change for the right cat, but it's only the breed of a nigga that can understand the value of her pussy versus the virtue of the woman herself.

It's up to you to decide which you'll invest your heart, sweat, and time into. If you fall for her—put a baby in her, etcetera—etcetera, then the union crumbles and another nigga snatch her up and treats her the way she deserves to be treated like a slut, versus the way you treat her. You can't be fucked up. She is—who she was from the first day you met her. Your love or the fact she is your baby mama, doesn't change the fact she's a—well, let's just say a free spirit!

Master your thoughts—become a fox mentally and a wolf in the terms of observation. The fox is crafty, it knows when to be a predator and how to escape the reality of being a prey. The wolf, on the other hand, is bred from a pup to be a predator. Yet, it knows how to be one. The wolf's most keen sense is his observation. Through observation, you'll see the weakness of your bitch and or team. The smallest crack in your game will allow the serpents to slither through the opening that shoulda been closed.

It's a known fact, wine ages with time—the longer it sits the more it rots! The more it rots the better it tastes. My nigga, sometimes good shit comes from bad thoughts. Even Abraham Lincoln knew that—that's why he signed the Emancipation Proclamation."

Chapter One

Betrayed
~Nutz~

"James Swanson—this is your final warning—turn off the vehicle—toss the keys and any weapons on your person out the window and step out of the car, cautiously. Get on your knees with your hands behind your head. Failure to comply will result in immediate gunfire—I repeat—failure to comply will result in immediate gunfire! You're surrounded—there is no escape—"

Those are the words the agent spoke through the megaphone but in my head, I heard. *'Get the fuck out the car so we can murk yo dumb ass, black lives don't matter!'* Only thing I can think is *there's no way out.* Exasperated, I laid my head against the steering wheel—all sorts of shit rushed through my mind. *I wondered how many niggas locked up behind them bricks has sat in this type of situation and laid it down? I wondered how many of those boys vowed to hold courts in the streets rather than be judged by twelve? Thought after thought fired through my mind.*

Destiny stirred beside me—the animal within me was telling me, I should put one in her melon and just go out legendary. But, on the other hand, this bitch maybe my only way out. I lifted my head up at the sound of the ghetto bird; two armed men stood locked and loaded at the doors of the helicopter as it circled around me.

"Wha—wha—happen?" Destiny rasped through split lips.

Her eyes were unfocused as the sounds of the helicopter intermingled with the fool still speaking through the bullhorn. She looked down at her exposed chest, the wire was snapped and blood tainted her skin. Once her eyes met mine, the bitch did some real white girl shit, she screamed at the top of her lungs. I pointed the tool in her direction and the devil spoke through me.

"Bitch, if you don't stop all that pussy ass screaming. I'ma push your next daydream all over that seat," I hissed, nudging her head with the barrel of the pistol.

The menace in my stare quieted the silly bitch. However, she knew I was 'bout that action, so I ain't have to repeat myself.

"I'm not gonna ask yo' fake ass why you did it. I don't even give a fuck. What I do need to know is what all they know?" Destiny trembled in her seat searching for answers. "You know what it don't even matter, this what you gonna do tho—you 'bout to get yo' punk ass husband on the line. I'm talking like *now*, bitch!" Spit flew from my mouth as the cocaine in my veins heightened my senses.

Tears ran a race down her face as she wedged herself against the door and cowered in her seat.

"James, please listen to me—please," she begged. "I—"

"Bitch, I'm not gonna ask you again. You set me up, fam! I kept it all the way 'G' wit' you and you bit me. I've done all the listening I'm gonna do with yo' fake ass," I growled, laughing at my own stupidity.

Irony is a bitch, the same get out of jail free card, I used to get my brother out of a jam, is the exact same one putting the nail in my casket.

It's crazy how lust can drive a man to recklessness. I was so busy trying to put my dick into something, that I allowed a snake to slither into my camp. I should have known shit was 'bout to get ugly when the punk bitch wouldn't give me the pussy. My thoughts were interrupted when Destiny reached for the door handle attempting to make her escape. I laughed harder as the child safety locks enable her plan.

"Let me out! Let—me—out—plee—please," she broke down.

Like a maniac, my laughter stopped and my face became a mask of square fuckin' business. "I usually don't give second warnings but then again, I usually don't let a bitch get one up on me either. So, the day is filled with new shit, huh?" I used the tip of the gun and wiped away a stray tear. "Look, Des, or whatever the fuck your name is—you got me in some deep shit and you 'bout to get me out of it." I used my free hand and reached over grabbing a handful of her hair, forcing her to stare at the predicament she caused. "It's either that or I'm gonna sign those indictment papers them white folks gonna give me with yo' blood! Either or—you gotta pay up. In blood or with your help—your choice," I hissed.

Destiny looked at me wide-eyed, I could tell she was wrestling with her options. I understood what love did to this female and Destiny was just the pawn in a vicious game of chess played between good and bad.

"Destiny, you're so blinded by your emotions for that pussy ass attorney. You can't see that he doesn't give a fuck about you. If he did, he never would have fed you to a hungry crocodile-like me." Destiny struggled against my grasp, but I only held on tighter.

"Wha—what do you want me to—to do James? I mean—the—they have us surrounded. They know, I am here—they know you have drugs in this car and you're armed." Tears streamed down her face ruining her mascara. "Jus—just please don't make this any more complicated than it already is. I don't wanna see you get hurt," Destiny cried.

Her words infuriated me, causing fire to ignite in my eyes and my finger to twitch on the trigger. "Call—your—husband! I'm not sayin' it no more!" Lava spilled from my lips. I watched her shaking hands as she reached for her purse. "Don't be stupid lil' one you know I'm surgical with this shit, matter fact—"

I released her hair, reached over, and snatched the purse out of her grip. She jumped so high her head damn near hit the roof. I kept the pistol aimed in her direction, as I poured the contents of her purse into my lap. The sneaky mu'fucka had a .22 she obviously was going for if I woulda been dumb enough to allow her to. I picked up her phone and pushed the rest of the contents on the floor between my legs. I made sure to kick the pistol under the seat away from the desperate bitch.

I handed her the phone while laughing at the clown that had repeated the same shit about surrendering for the hundredth time. As if they were gonna let loose into a car with the Federal Attorney's wife. The stupid mu'fuckas had to know I was onto her. I bet the pussy ass D.A. lost his head when I snapped the wire.

"Sa—Sa'Mage?" The sound of Destiny's voice snapped me out of my thoughts.

I reached over and snatched the phone from her, without warning. "Hello—hello? Destiny, can you hear me, baby? The voice on the other end panicked.

"Hey baby I'm home," I sang into the receiver.

The silence on the other end of the phone was profound. I took the phone away from my ear and glanced at the screen to make sure the line was still connected. The heat that exploded from the phone let me know he was in fact still there.

"You little piece of shit! You better not lay a finger on her or I will—*"*

I'm thinking *yeah—yeah—yeah mu'fucka—how this cat gonna threaten a wild man with nothing to lose?* "Shut, yo' bitch ass up," I screamed into the phone as spit flew everywhere.

I had already made up my mind how this story was going to end. May as well try the last card that lady bad luck had dealt me. "Yo' bitch ass played a nice game of chess house nigga, but the thing you couldn't have anticipated is the mind of a madman once self-preservation kicks in." I turned my head slightly in Destiny's direction to keep her in my eyesight. "Now, I know, you don't give a fuck about this bitch. That's one thing we got in common, but the difference between us is that you can't show it."

To show him how serious I was, I took the phone away from my ear, and backhanded Destiny with the pistol. Her hands shot to the newly open gash, as she screamed in agony. "You hear that— you hear that, house nigga! What I need you to do is get your boys to *back the fuck up* and let me through. Nobody is to follow me and once I am clear, I'll drop yo' bitch on the other side of the road unharmed and be along my merry way. If not—" I left the promise hanging in the air, so the sucka could come to his own conclusions.

I heard him as he took the phone away from his ear. Through the windshield, I watched as he walked over to a tall white cat standing by a van. A few seconds passed and what seemed to be a heated debate ensued. It went on for roughly two minutes. I watched as Kendricks' put the phone to his ear in exasperation. The deep breath he took, told me I was not gonna like what he was 'bout to say.

"Listen, James—I—I need—" No love resided in my heart as I cut him off midsentence.

"Naw, you listen, homie! You got twenty seconds to clear this bitch out or you can call the meat wagon and tell 'em to make reservations for two cause this bitch is 'bout to die, and after that, it's gonna be some real John Dillinger shit."

Destiny rocked back and forth and cried softly, as a river of blood poured from the gash in her face. "Now you can test my 'G' or save your wife, neither matters to me. Her life is in your hand's homie, think quick cause the coin is flippin' in the air, once it lands on heads or tails your life will be altered just as mine has. I glanced over at Destiny and watched as she tried to stop the wound from bleeding. "Twenty seconds ain't long, fam especially when life and death has to be determined somewhere between the numbers one and twenty." I disconnected the call and focused my gaze on Destiny.

She rocked back and forth mumbling incoherently, she was so lost in whatever conversation she was having with herself, that she didn't even flinch when the muzzle kissed the side of her head, that's when I tuned into her words—

"Lord is my shepherd, I shall not want, he makes me lie down in green pastures—" Unbeknownst, to her the phone had just been picked up on the other end.

"Hello—hello—Swanson? Listen—I need more time—" *Boom!* The cannon exploded in my hands. Destiny's scalp along with her prayers crashed through the passenger window. "Twenty," I growled, into the phone before the car begun to shake from the numerous shots of high-powered artillery.

The last thing I remembered was my brother's last words before he washed his hands with the game. *"Mu'fuckas ain't loyal no mo', fam. Every bitch you've ever given your heart to will be in the wind, the very minute you sign your name on that dotted line. I'm telling you, fam! Let's change the story, homie."* I shoulda listened to bro!

***

~Assata~

I once read that if you allow a man to choose arrogance over being humble, the true nature of his heart will spill from his tongue. I've learned that envy—jealousy—and greed was a poisonous concoction, and when a mu'fucka digest its essence, the infliction that comes along with its bitter taste is deadly. An enemy is a snake in the cage. That's how it should be viewed at all times! See the serpent has been a man's enemy since the day Eve gave her ear to a slick talkin' nigga. The serpent, who told her the power of her pussy and caused her to sew fig leaves together to cover herself from the eyes of her very own man.

Yea—you can say that the man covered himself as well, but it was after Eve told him how powerful his dick was. See, this reversal of roles disrupted the natural order of things, so it introduced humanity to snake shit. It was the first recorded time a man ever snitched. *Genesis 3:11-12—the first time a woman reflected her man—Genesis 3:13—the first time a man was introduced into his natural self—a God! Genesis 3:22/Psalms 82:6.* The serpents game was so powerful, he reversed the roles between man and woman as, Eve lead her dude to not only defile his garden, but also his God!

The ones we allow to close, the family and friends we bring to the table to break bread with. The very ones we feel comfortable enough to fall asleep around, these are the most poisonous snakes that grace our castles. It's cause they're so close—so silent. This is the virtues of the serpent. Imagine having the very nigga you entrust your secrets to. The same man you'd sign ninety-nine years for, picture what it feels like to have that same cat cross you over a bitch or a few pennies. Imagine him aiming at your thinking cap over a misunderstanding he coulda got understood.

When you fuck with a nigga he deserves the benefit of the doubt, right? Can you boys imagine the woman you've taken outta tennis shoes and introduced to the appeal of stilettos? The woman that knows the combo to the safe. Yea, that same bitch you repped in front of the world—fuckin' a nigga you consider family?

The thang that flows through your mind is. "How the fuck that happen?"

I'll tell my G—when you forget about the last time you trusted a man? When you took the snake out of its cage and allowed it to crawl around the house. That's how it happened—the last female you allowed into your fold that didn't know how to control her pussy. That's how it happened, fam. You allowed your vision to be clouded by the word *'real'* and forgot the diamond necklace at home.

Yeah—the necklace is the scars that taint your neck from all the times suckas tried to slice your throat. The diamonds are the experience that comes with betrayal and costly mistakes. It's always the ones we call friends that bite us, fam, but I guess if Sammy the bull could do it to Gotti anything is possible! Real niggaz get raw deals.

***

~Six~

Before my lower lips kissed the tip of his manhood something in Assata changed. I saw it, felt it. Before I could insert him inside of me, my equilibrium was stolen, and somehow it had become hard to differentiate between consciousness and subconsciousness. The motherfucker had just hit me like I was a fucking man! *What the fuck?* In the brief moments of trying to blink the disorientation and pain away. I couldn't seem to wrap my mind around what could have possibly caused him to flip out like that. Assata stood over me with death in his eyes.

"Assata—ba—baby, what! What's wrong?" I stammered.

The look of pain, betrayal, and clarity was a deadly melody exuding from his stare. He held up a half-smoked black-n-mild and my blood froze inside my veins.

"When did you start smoking wineberry black-n-milds, Six? I must have missed the memo or something lil' one, cause I've never seen you smoke. As a matter of fact, it's only one mu'fucka, I know that rock with these nasty sumbitches. The math equation I'm trying to break down shouldn't equate the two of y'all in the same room together," he growled, as he tossed the black-n-mild at my feet.

"The only way that expression could even be politically correct is if I've been dancing with snakes and bitch I ain't never been a fan of reptiles unless they were on my feet." He reached down and grabbed a handful of my hair.

Assata yanked me to my feet, my scalp felt like it was on fire. I tried to get to my feet as fast as I could before the crazy son-of-a-bitch snatched a patch out of my head.

"A-ssaa-tta!" I screamed in an attempt to plead my case.

My back slammed against the wall, his hands wrapped around my neck and with the constrictions of a boa constrictor. Asphyxia sang its tune as stars danced before my eyes. My left eye stared down the tunnel of what must have been a *100-caliber* pistol! Every word that slipped from his lips was punctuated with a different aggression.

"What—tha—fuck—is—up—Six?" His eyes were red as coals, I could see my funeral in his pupils.

"I—ca-can't—breathe," I rasped.

Assata seemed to snap out of an evil induced vision, releasing my throat with an air of regret. Yet, he kept the hideous gun aimed at my head. As if the weight of the world was on my shoulders, I folded over and hungrily suck in a lungful of air. One never knows how precious oxygen is until they're deprived of it. I felt like I was hyperventilating as a tropical storm raged through the small island on the left side of my chest and at ninety-nine miles per hour, it pushed itself up and out of me until a river raged down my face. My every mistake—my stupidity—the harm I'd done, it all busted out of me like water did the levees in New Orleans.

"I'm sooo sorry, Satta!" I never meant to hurt you, baby, I—I—oh my God," I screamed, as regret shattered me into a million emotional pieces.

I love this man—deeply, but I had done shit to him, I knew we could never bounce back from. In hindsight, I could see the shit that drove so many females that loved a street nigga to the point of doing shit they never imagined. Assata backhanded me causing me to scream out, I held my face as it was stricken with pain.

"God ain't got nothing to do with this, fam. If you knew me like you know, you know me—you better catch vomit at the mouth and give me the real." Assata punched a hole in the wall as he took deep breathes. "It's some nightmare on Elm Street shit going down. Ain't trying to go to sleep and meet the Boogeyman," Assata said, then grabbed my face forcing me to look at him. "This the bidness, ma—I ain't fucked up about you giving the nigga pussy cause ain't no rewinding that, but—"

"See, that's why I fucked him," I erupted. The look on his face became mask with danger, but he gave his undivided attention. "You've never given a fuck about me, Assata Lamar!" I threw caution to the wind and slapped his hand away from my face. "I gave you more than my pussy, dude. I gave you my heart and all I've ever been to you is a warm mouth to stick your dick in and a piece of convenient pussy!" Tears streamed down my face as I slid down the wall into a puddle of melted shame—hurt—and confusion.

In a hurricane of mixed emotions, I told him the absolute truth. For the next half hour or so, I gave him the closure he deserved. No matter how painful the truth was, he deserved it. Deep down, I understood that being an emotional creature caused me to do shit that didn't justify the means. I shoulda never fucked his potna. I buried my face in my hands out of shame. I now understood that it did not get me retribution, only some good dick and a lower sense of value. Assata stood over me breathing hard.

"Out of every nigga, you coulda fucked, Six, why a cat I thug with—huh? You helped kill a nigga I would give my spine for—you-you—" Unexpectedly, he busted out laughing, then the dam broke and allowed his pride to melt into liquid that burned down his face.

I stared at him confused like, 'what the fuck'? My expression only seemed to inflame his laughter.

Assata leaned down so that we were face to face. "You played a nigga so good, I became the exact typa nigga I despise, a sucka!" He laughed harder and louder. "Crazy part 'bout it, shawty, I really gave a fuck about your filthy ass!" He had the speed of a striking cobra when he struck me across my face with the butt of the pistol.

My world tilted, as blood poured from my left eyebrow. He must enjoy that S&M shit because again he grabbed a handful of my hair.

"Urrruugggh," I screamed, as he yanked me to my feet and crashed the tip of the gun through my teeth. Death has to be better I think to myself!

"Fuck, is he at, huh? Bitch if you lie, you'll die for days—I'll murk your slut ass—revive you—then kill you again! On gang," Assata shouted.

Blood leaked from my mouth as everything blinked in and out like a picture show. The only thing that held me up is the hair he clinched so tightly in his hand.

"Answer me," he exploded—then—his face went slack. Suspicion set aflame in his eyes as they searched mine, no doubt finally putting the pieces together. Assata let me go and gravity pulled me back to the ground hard. As rain fell from my eyes, my mind couldn't conjure up any rational reason why I was still breathing.

"Kill me—" I whispered, as he rushed into his clothes. As Assata headed for the door, he didn't even look back as he said—

"You're already dead, Six." Then he disappeared into the night.

Chapter Two

He had perspiration leaking into his eyes as he ran blindly through the dark woods. The underbrush was dense, with every stride escape seemed more and more unattainable. Many welts and scratches canvased his young flesh from his face on down to his legs as vines and withers showed no mercy to his ambition to get away. Yet, he pushed forward, something with a thirst for his blood—something sinister and dark, stalked him relentlessly. His reality and nightmare was separated by a mere tear of consciousness flickering between the two like a slide show.

Moments of familiarity—Belle's face—him and Nutz as kids—a feeling of boarding a plane—voices—but what never changed no matter the scene, were the woods—and the feeling of being pursued. So, he ran and ran like his life depended on it! Unexpectantly, he cleared the woods only to find himself ankle deep in muddy water—a swamp! The bare trees scattered into the night, erected from tainted water that was stained with patches of grass and thick green algae. He paused for vital moments—breathless. His eyes scanned the darkness from the perpetual swamp to the direction that death. While in high pursuit, dread consumed him.

It was either plunge forward through the unknown or await whatever fate was sure to come from behind. "Decisions—decisions," An evil child-like voice said, giggling in his head.

A sudden movement in the darkness forced his hand and without further thought, he stepped further into the icy water.

"Berg," a familiar voice sang sweetly to him. He knew the voice, but there was no way possible it could be rational. "Beerrg—heeelllp meee!" The voice followed him.

Ice-Berg forced his way through the sludge. It seemed as if he was sinking in the thick mud. Then something or someone, entered the water behind him and with a quick glance, he tried to see through the darkness and the fog that had somehow become so thick, all he could make out were silhouettes and shadows dancing under the pale moonlight. Still, he knew it was out there and coming straight for him.

"Why, brother?" The voice whispered in his ear.

As he became startled from its proximity, he snapped his head forward, that's when reality lost its battle with the nightmare. Tisha, his sister, materialized before him with a demonic smile contradicting the love in her eyes. Blood and brain matter stained the heavenly white dress their mother laid her to rest in, and a patch of her skull was missing where the bullet he'd taken her life with entered and exited.

"What, aren't you happy to see your baby sister?" She sang stretching her arms out to hug him.

Ice-Berg was so terrified, he backed pedaled in an attempt to put distance between them. But in his haste, he didn't notice the numerous snakes slithering at his feet. He fell backward into the cold water and instantly dark arms pulled him under. He was suffocating, his lungs were filled with putrid water. As he attempted to claw his way to the surface, he couldn't understand how the water, he stood in had become so deep. Finally, breaking surface he tried to regurgitate the nasty water that felt like worms in his stomach.

The sky had turned an evil purple and as his eyes found Tisha's. Time tumbled backward as maggots crawled out of her mouth and she tried to force words that sounded like a cult chant. Involuntary, he screamed as mud-slicked hands snatched him back under the blackness. He fought and screamed until he broke surface again. Ice-Berg swung with all of his might in an effort to battle what he couldn't win against.

***

"Ice-Berg," a feminine voice called to me.

In my insanity, I didn't notice that the voice no longer belonged to my deceased sister. All I knew was that evil was here for me in the form of one of my greatest regret. A pair of strange hands held me but failed to restrain my left arm. I swung as hard as I could with a yearning to save myself from the unknown.

"Fuck—the fucker just sucker punched me!" A gruff voice declared in agony.

The sudden outburst caused me to pause and crack my eyes open. Four, maybe five unfamiliar faces stared down at me. A sudden bright light shined into my eyes causing me to squint, as slender fingers probed my face. My right eye was forced open as exhaustion fell over me almost immediately. I had no more energy left in me, so I merely observed, as whoever these strangers was assessed me. The light clicked off and through the haze of my mind, I tried to recall the events that led up to me being in this strange place. From somewhere above the haze, a blinding pain surged through me, my shoulder and stomach was being probed and the pain was excruciating. Yet, I had no energy to cry out.

"How is he, doc?" A feminine voice penetrated the cloud of darkness.

The answer to that million-dollar question was lost as the murky waters pulled me back under, but this time I surrendered to its embrace without a fight. The last thing I see before my lights dim to total blackness was Belle's face.

***

~Jazzy~

I stood perfectly still perfectly still, as chills crawled up and down my spine. "Why, Gus—why Shy? I—I thought y'all were brothers, D.B.D remember?" I still held onto the phone as I slowly turned around to face a man, I once respected—a man, I once embraced as family—my brother's killer.

He stood in the doorway with a black pistol aimed at me, but from the look in his eyes, I saw the confliction—the uncertainty. This man had a hand in raising me. He'd watched me grow from a girl to a woman. But now that the cat was out the bag, I wondered how much weight history would carry, when the nigga's secrets could end his days in the form of either the chain gang or a bullet with his name on it placed in the equation. A storm of memories reflected in his eyes in tears that refused to fall.

He replied with a sad smile. "Brothers," he whispered. "You shoulda left well enough alone, Jazz. Shoulda just stayed in Cali—the dead needs no company, lil' sis. Now look," Gusto shrugged his shoulders like I made him do this. "You've put me in a compromising position, fam—D.B.D. I took that shit literally, Jazz—I loved my niggaz from a cold heart," He pounded his chest with his free hand. "I've killed and bled for them niggaz, how did they repay me?" Gusto stepped closer to me.

I could smell the hint of black and mild on his breath as he looked me dead in my eyes. "Listen close, lil' sis, this tale I'm 'bout to give you is the reason I had to smoke one of the dearest nigga's to me—your brother—it's also the reason, you'll have to be buried next to him."

***

~Ice-Berg~
Flashbacks

Belle screamed as I squeezed round for round from the Glock .40. Life and death was being determined in that room, as the short burst from their guns sprayed the bed. I dropped to the floor still blastin' this mu'fucka right before the lights went out. My room was a war zone as gunfire illuminated the darkness. I heard one less gun as something heavy fell to the floor. One down—two more to go. I rolled myself against the wall away from their aim, they're out of their element.

Click—click— "Fuck!" I screamed, as two things placed the odds back into their favor. First, I'm outta bullets—secondly, pain exploded everywhere!

I didn't know how many times I was hit, but I did know it was the worse feeling I had ever felt. A sudden chill blew through the room—not the typa breeze that came from wind sneaking through an open window, but the typa cold that came from something like those steel cabinets at the morgue that they kept the bodies in to stop them from decomposing quickly. Suddenly, words were spoken from the darkness that sent chills down my spine.

"La Santisma Muerte chu are great and merciful. You protected me from evil and accepted me without judgment. Oh, holy death, accept this right of blood offering as my sacrifice to you—" I heard Belle praying to Santa Muerte, who is a saint. I learned that drug cartels and men that accept death as a gift rather than the end prayed to.

"What the fuck!"

"He's dreaming again," I heard someone say from somewhere far away.

"Belle," I moaned but there was no answer.

Yet, I felt something sticky, thick, and warm splash on my body. I wanted to wipe it away, I wanted to get up, but I just couldn't muster the energy to do so. Yet, I could still make out the sultry voice of the woman, unfortunately, she was speaking in another language. The only words I could make out were puzzles within a bigger enigma. Dragons blood, reapers blood, valerian root, and vandal root. Along with something about The Leviathan!

"Fuck, Leviathan," I repeated in my head.

I knew that word, but what was it? Then it hit me, The Leviathan. It was in the Bible! A sea monster, a serpent. In Satanism, it was a demon of the fire which could be controlled by the witch or warlock and brought into the world to fuck shit up!

***

~Jazzy~

"You ask me how I could kill our brother? He killed me first," Gus spat.

The pain registered on his face showed how much he hated himself for how shit turned out. But the betrayal he felt wouldn't allow him to see beyond what he couldn't change. He couldn't see that the ending result was just as much his fault as it was theirs. No one forced his dick into that woman. I honestly, didn't understand what would be the purpose of intentionally giving him the virus? Yet, a confused mind was one of the most complicated to convince and that was one of the main reasons I knew, I was about to die. Maybe unconsciously, I had prepared for it since the day we buried Shy because I felt no fear—only anger. Heat bubbled inside of me and before I could control myself, I slapped him.

Gusto laughed menacingly as he grabbed my hand and snatched the phone from it.

"You know Assata gonna murder you, right? You're a fake nigga, Gus—you killed your own dawg cause you couldn't control your dick! My brother loved your hoe ass and you killed him! You could kill everybody you know. In the end, you'll still be dying," I hissed.

His face contorted into an evil smile, that one could tell was strained. "See, Jazz, I've always respected your, 'G'. You're not afraid to speak your mind regardless of the situation, but lil' sis we must all die one day. Who we meet up with in the afterlife matters not. God or the Devil—Assata? Gusto placed the phone in his pocket and made the tip of the Glock kiss my forehead. "He'll now know what it feels like to live hanging off of the edge of life. He will die daily just as I am dying," he said with a look of satisfaction.

In confusion, I ask for clarification. "What do you mean?"

Gusto laughed and replied. "I mean exactly what I said, Assata is somewhere not controlling his dick as you say. As we speak he's dying and enjoying it!"

***

~Six~

'Dying wasn't nothing like I expected,' I thought as I laid in this cold tub and allowed my life's blood to spill from the slits on both of my wrists.

I had prayed and inscribed a letter to my parents as well as to Assata. I wanted them to know that this wasn't their fault. The words I wrote to Assata played in my mind, as my life drifted away with each drop of blood.

My Baby,

It took me twenty-eight years to truly understand, that love can't be taught by reading a book. Our story started so beautifully, Satta—the good girl and the beast. I can apologize for crossing you until the last drop of my blood splashes against this floor but being the type of man that you are. Your heart will only understand what would take a lifetime to show. Baby, we both know that in this lifetime that's not possible. So, I've decided to try in the next life. Hopefully, we meet there one day. I never meant for shit to get so blurry, bae, but I guess when the good girl falls for the beast, she never anticipates one moment to the next. I love you, Satta.

Maybe, one day you'll be able to see that the only reason, I ever went against the grain is because that love I harbor for you is tainted when it is not reciprocated. A woman loves deep, Satta. She loves deep enough to kill for you, deep enough to kill you, and at times deep enough to kill herself! I've done all three in the name of loving you, baby. Although, it may sound crazy to many, to the ones that love that deep it's perfectly sane. Lol! It's the true meaning of loving someone to death. No—I'm not crazy, bae just the good girl, who fell deeply for the beast. In the end—I just want you to remember the conversation we had by the lake before shit got crazy?

The answer is, Yes, Assata I believe in destiny. Yes, I believe in love! I do and as I conclude this letter, I want you to always remember. Even though a man creates his own destiny, that same destiny can be altered when he begins to believe in the things he once didn't. Be happy, baby, but never forget yo' rida, signed in blood.

Your lady, Six

***

~Jazzy~

'Dying—enjoying it?' In my mind, I was thinking what the fuck was this nigga talking about? I assumed the confused look on my face was evident because the nigga seemed amused. My mind was running wild, out of nowhere my heart began to ache. My hand shot to my chest, it felt like I was having a heart attack. Maybe Gusto felt as though, I was finally realizing that death is certain, or maybe he was just ready to get it over with. Resolve etched into his facial, as he made that sad smile again and told me it wasn't personal.

"Send my love to Shy, fam. Tell him we're even," he said, as he pulled the trigger.

Boom—boom—boom—

The tool burped in his hand. I felt no pain, as I fell to the floor. My head hit something sharp as my world tilted. I didn't know how many times I was hit but I did know, it was the worst feeling I had ever felt. Then there was a deadly silence. Yet, even in death I still couldn't shake the feeling of emptiness, and right as my light dimmed, it hit me! Something happened to Assata!

***

~Assata~

I mashed the pedal to the floor as I gunned the whip to get to Jazzy before everything I love was taken away from me for sins I was innocent of! All this time this nigga has had them alphabets. I honestly, didn't know how the fuck he got 'em. It honestly, never mattered to me cause that was my dawg! Yet, the shit Six just dropped was some deep shit. I didn't eighty-six the punk hoe, cause I got love for the woman. I'm a man that has seen the craziest shit in life, and when it comes to women, I had always understood what the heart of one contains.

A woman loves deep and is just as vindictive when she's hurt. Women are emotional creatures that will do whatever it takes to make her man feel the way he makes her feel. I tapped the break slightly, then I came off Loop 288 at a suicidal 80mph. Something out the corner of my eye caused me to glance at the car pulling up beside me. Doing almost a 100mph shouldn't nobody be moving at the same pace unless they were following or chasing me. Shit! I swerved into the next lane as a masked gunman let loose with what seemed to be a Mini .14.

My window shattered, but if I was hit I couldn't tell. Like magic, the burna was in my hand and the clip hangin' out that bitch was a full thirty rounds that made me feel like I could shoot all day. If I was 'bout to meet the reaper, I was coming with company. A burst of rounds swiss cheesed the side of my shit, I eased up on the gas, so I could work this bitch efficiently. Fuck duckin' down in the seat trying to hide from death. I had one hand on the grain and the other I used to finger fuck the tool. I took my eyes off the road for just a blink, I glanced at my attackers, niggas hung out of a black on black GMC with blue bandannas covering their face. Fuck! Slugs jumped out the side of the P.89 as I went head-on with death.

I musta rocked the right mu'fucka cause the SUV swung quickly in my lane. I stumped down on the break to prevent colliding with it. It veered off somewhere, I couldn't tell because I was fishtailed and that was all she wrote. All I remembered was the feeling of the whip flipping so many times I lost count, but I do remember the stillness after it landed on the roof. I remembered the dizziness, the blood, but most of all, I remembered someone pulled me from the car.

I heard a feminine voice say. "Get the gun out the car." Then shit went black. "Say, Shy, I'm on my way dawg!"

Renta

Chapter Three

We Need You—Wake Up
~Jazzy~
Weeks later— November 1, 2018

The constant beeping of the EKG and all the other machines he was hooked to, sounded like seconds being counted down as God made a decision about his life. It was a time, I had to fight to hold on to hope and sanity. However, my grip on both seemed so fickle. It had been weeks since I was found in my house unconscious, drowning in my own blood from a head fracture. It had also been weeks since they found Assata naked outside of the hospital. He was apparently, dropped off by a fleeing vehicle.

So much to say, yet so many jagged pieces that didn't fit together. I honestly didn't know what happened, except that Gusto was found dead under an underpass with three fatal shots to his back. He must have thought, I was dead the night he came to kill me. Thankfully, when the gun fired I hyperventilated and passed out. From what Mar told me I hit my head during the fall busting it wide open. What I burn to know was—*who shot Gusto? Who saved my life without wanting to be acknowledged? Also what happened to Assata?*

They found him naked on the ground of the hospital. Once my girls found me at the house bleeding all over the floor, they got the ambulance ASAP! They'd stood beside me through the entire ordeal. Marcella kept me informed about what was being said in the streets, but I didn't pay it any mind because people in the hood don't know how to mind their own business. I stood over my baby and I allowed my fingers to trace the bandages wrapped around his face. It broke my heart to see my baby, laid up in that cold ass room with all those tubes and IV's running in and out of him. He hadn't as much as stirred since I came to his room. Still, I didn't leave his side for anything besides to shit, piss, and go home to shower and get a change of clothes.

I cried and prayed for him so much I wondered if Allah could hear me.

I leaned over him with my lips inches from his ear. "Please, bae—wake up! I miss you, sooo much," I whispered. "We miss you, yes I said *we*. I'm prego, Satta. You're going to be a father. So, you see baby, you have to wake up," I cried, as I laid my head on his chest.

My tears soaked the hospital blanket and all I felt was helplessness. That was one of the hardest things for a woman to feel regarding her dude.

***

~Assata~

I didn't know how long I had been laid up in the hospital, but I had been mentally awake for days. I had heard everythang going on around me, especially Jazzy. The worse part 'bout being comatose was not being able to respond! While listening to lil' one cry and pray over me. It hurt like hell, not being able to heal that shit. Each time shawty mentioned, God I wanted to tell her He didn't exist, but then again, who was I to rob her of her anchor to sanity? I had fought and fought to snap outta this coma shit, but my body just wasn't rocking with my mind at that moment.

So much shit played through my mind. Shit had to change if I was gonna bring a seed into this world. I couldn't risk its life or Jazzy's by rockin' the way I did. But shit the mud was what I was familiar with. I found myself drowning in the waters of my experience. I had to mentally relinquish the hold on what I had become so attached to. Familiarity is a beautiful consciousness when speaking in terms of your gal or someone you love, but it's a two-edged sword. It was also a disease! When one becomes too familiar with a certain way of life, fear of the unknown stagnates their growth.

How can one become the master of the universe when all they know is their universe? I was gonna murk them pussy boys that tried to take me under. That's on gang!

***

~Jazzy~
9:30 a.m., December 16, 2018

I woke up in the same cramped chair, I'd been sleeping in for the past month and a half. For some strange reason, something felt off. It was that feeling you get when your peace is invaded? As I tried to adjust my eyes to the gloom of the room, I was scared to death by Medusa! I screamed unconsciously and recoiled into the chair.

"Goose! Get away from that young lady, right this minute! Nobody wants to wake up to your ugly face, dammit," A middle-aged woman admonished. Once she stepped in front of Medusa, I saw how well kept and beautiful she was. She looked down at me studiously. "You must be, Jazzy?" she said with an extended hand.

I was skeptical but didn't want to be rude, so I took her hand and gave a slight nod of affirmation, that I was indeed who she said I was. For some reason, I felt uncomfortable in her presence even though, I didn't know who she was.

I assumed it was etched on my face because she smiled her pearly white teeth at me. "Oh, forgive me chile, in my sixty-five years of living I sometimes get ahead of myself, my name is Lovey." She glanced over to where Assata was assumed to be at peace. "I guess you can say I am this knuckleheads mother, well—the closest to a mother he's had since my baby sister, his mom, was killed in Florida." She then turned and for the first time I notice the other man standing beside Medusa—well, now that I could see clearly, it was not Medusa, just a slim cat with long dreads.

The other guy resembles Assata vaguely the differences were evident though. "These two hooligans are Assata's brothers. The one with that hair is his eldest brother, Goose, from San Antonio and the short quiet one is Pain, he's from here. We heard what happened to my baby when these nice people contacted me about Assata's accident. With a weary face, she glanced over at Assata. "The car is in my name—hell all his things are in my name. So, they contacted me to tell me about the car and my baby."

Curiosity got the best of me. "And me, how did you know who I was, Mrs. Lovey?"

She flashed that motherly smile again. "Baby, I know everything about my baby! He tells me everything. Beyond that baby, I know your whole family, Jazmina. Good people, she reached up and patted the side of my face tenderly. "Matter fact, your mother was over at my house not too long ago."

I cringed when she said that. My mom was a full-fledged addict and our relationship was strained. I despised the weakness of the woman that gave birth to me.

I jump from the soft contact of Lovey's hand against my face. "You must forgive her, chile. God is the judge of this life and there's a reason, He gave you the mom that He gave you. Maybe if she wasn't so weak in your eyes, you'd never have the strength to be so strong. Never shun small beginnings." She leaned closer to me, her eyes explored mine. For some reason, I felt naked, literally! "Chile, you're pregnant?" she said matter-of-factly.

Chills ran up and down my body. '*Is she psychic or something?*' I thought.

As if she could read my mind she said, "Lovey's been around for a long time, chile. When a woman lives as long as I have, she knows things!"

Goose stepped forward, I didn't realize how intense his eyes were until this moment, as he focused his attention on me. "Listen, I know you've been through a lot. I am not trying to add more to your plate, but we need to know everything that you know about my lil' brother's beef. Anything is helpful." The veins in his neck expressed how he felt to see his little brother laid up with tubes down his throat.

"I honestly don't know what happened." I looked at him with a look that said, '*Come on you know your brother!*' Assata has millions of niggaz that wanted him dead, but none that I could think of that would have the nuts to try.

Lovey reached up and grabbed a few locks of his hair to move him from in front of me. "Boy, can't you see this chile has been through enough. Save that mess for after she's eaten some real food and slept in her own bed," Mrs. Lovey scolded.

I could tell, he was not feeling that idea, but the respect he had for Lovey took prestige over his gangsta. The look in his eyes was a direct indication of our future encounters. The dude Pain had yet to speak, but his stare was intense and it made me a bit uncomfortable. Lovey walked over to Assata and rubbed her hand over his face in a motherly gesture. You could almost feel the love she has for him. We watched as she closed her eyes, bowed her head, and acted like she was praying, but it was something deeper than that.

It was as if energy was being traded between her and Assata. Deeply spiritual and scary. "He'll wake up, he's just tired. God isn't through with him yet," she said opening her eyes.

I could see the tension ease in both brothers as if her prophesy was spoken by God himself. Just as peace entered the room, Lovey looked to Pain then to Goose. "And neither is the Devil."

That's when the machine, Assata was hooked up to started going crazy!

***

~Assata~

I heard Lovey speak over me. My big mama always had a power about herself, that some would confuse for evil if they didn't know her. But, she was the sweetest woman, I had ever known. Our family came from Opelousas, Louisiana back in the late seventies and migrated throughout Texas. Lovey was the eldest of eleven kids and her gift has been harnessed over the years so much that she scared people. Her hand against my face was electric. I could literally feel the energy she was transmitting into my limbs. I could feel my blood surging through my veins. Even though I couldn't see my surroundings, I could almost picture the knowing looks on Pain and Goose's faces, as well as the confusion on Jazzy's.

Somewhere between subconsciousness and reality, me and the old lady met in a collision of chemistry. Whatever that shit was that gave birth to a woman's love for her child. It was like, I was walking through a thick mist of fog. Nothing else existed, but this galaxy of awareness that only she and I existed within. I stumbled blindly through the mist until the fog opened to a clear stream flowing backward. It was surrounded by still maples and wildflowers. There observing me from a small clearing sat Lovey. Her smile was radiant as she watched me.

She stood to embrace me. "Chile, what I tell ya hard headed butt about them streets? Now look at chu—someone has you laid up in this here hospital, looking like the dead warmed over." She held me at arm's length and studied me.

Her stare was powerful—she loved me—feared for me but knew that the blood in my veins was spiked with the DNA of her late husband—a fighter! A street nigga! After a long pause, she gave it to me as raw as a brick of Columbian Cocoa.

"Assata—you must stop this mess. You's lucky one of them bullets ain't sent you to be with yo' mama!" The fire that ignited in my eyes told her, her words fucked with me. Yet, with a sad smile, she continued. "You see, chile, you may outrun a bullet, but you can't outrun God? Even though he watches over fools and babies alike. He makes no mistakes when he wants something rather it be their health, attention, or life!" Lovey turned away from me and walked over to the bank of the river. She stared down at the turbulent waters as she allowed the waves to kiss her feet. "When he talks yous better listen, chile, cause he speaks out of love and anger alike." The frown on my face made her giggle at my stubbornness.

I picked up a small stone and tossed it into the river, as I wondered how could a body of natural water flow backward? "Lovey, you know you raised me to fear God, but God don't give a fuck—" The sharp look she gave reminded me of the strength in her arms when she used to work them switches on my black ass. "Sorry, Lovey, you know I didn't mean to be disrespectful. But, Big Mama, if there is a God up there—if He knows everything before it happens. Why He let it happen? I don't get dude, Queen."

My statement must have been one she anticipated, because she too turned her attention to the river, with a knowing smirk. "Baby I am not God. Some things I can rationalize, but again—I am not God, chile." Lovey reached over and grabbed my hand, pulling me closer to the riverbank. She pointed at the water and there I saw my reflection, except, it wasn't me in the present time, it was me as a child.

My pulse quickened. "You see, Satta, God is like a road of love, but a highway of pain. No matter which you choose to travel first, you'll eventually end up doing a hundred miles per hour on the other as well, because they lead to the same destination. How do you cultivate love without fighting through the pain? What would give you the motivation to survive the pain if love wouldn't be obtained?" Lovey turned to face me. "God is a mysterious one, and religions have been created based off of so many different perspectives. Some people follow Jesus to get to Him—some follow the teachings of Muhammad—and some even follow Satan! The point is no matter who or what you believe in, it becomes God! A man without something to believe in is a man destined to fail."

She then turned to me with a penetrated look and ask me a question that was so simple, yet so hard to answer. She placed both hands on either side of my face. "Assata—do you care if you live or die?" Her eyes searched mine, as I asked myself the same question. For some reason, I couldn't seem to come to a solid answer. At least not the typa answer, a nigga would give to his moms.

I came from a place where summers were short and the winters seemed to last forever. On the conas that me and my niggaz thugged on, dying wasn't a thought. It was simply a matter of time! A roll of the dice that a nigga really couldn't control. Her eyes looked sad as she realized I couldn't answer her question. Lovey nodded her head in disdain—or maybe she was having a trip down memory lane.

She whispered, "So much like your Grandfather—he always said you'd be the lion." With the same sad eyes, she rocked my galaxy, as she began to fade from my world. I reached for her—my heart became heavy—I needed understanding. "The lion is brave,

Satta, but even the king of the jungle can be run from his pride or die trying to defend it! This young woman of yours is with child, but before you become a father, you'll have to know the answer to my question. Since you don't, the child will pay for the sins of his father." By now, Lovey was barely a mist.

I was lost, I chased an apparition of my Queen. Then something dawned on me, she said his, it's a boy. "Please, Lovey—come back," I raged but all I heard was the sound of the machines I was hooked up to and the doctors that rushed in.

"Everyone out of the room. The patient is going into cardiac arrest!"

Chapter Four

A New Day on My Block
~Tomorrow~
A month later—January 16

The sun beamed down on the block the Kreek as we called it was just like any other hood around America. It had hoes trying to snatch a bread winna, fiends doing some of everything for that next high, and niggaz chasing that check! It didn't matter how that dolla came, with blood on it or if it came from their moms' purse— money was truly the root of all evil. The streets gave me the name Tomorrow, a fifteen-year-old nigga outta the ruts. I been out in this jungle my whole life. My mom's a fiend and if I didn't get it by crooking, my lil' sis and brother's stomachs would touch their back.

I wasn't trying to hear it, period. "Dice on me, Clack." I heard my nigga Dino yell at the pitch-black nigga from Hic Street. I knew it was 'bout to be some shit from the look the nigga gave homie. "Nigga, fuck the dice on you, cuz, you broke bad two shots ago? Fuck outta here with that crumb shit," he hissed.

That nigga must got a drum or something nearby! Willow Creek and Hickory Street are arch enemies. Villain and Piru niggaz out the Kreek and Hoovas across the park on Oak and Hic Street. Southeast Denton ain't big at all and everybody knew every fuckin' or everybody was related! That how is how small the city actually is. Yet, no matter the relation or size of my city, niggaz died everywhere and being disrespectful in the next niggaz playground would have yo' thinkin' cap leakin'.

I guess this nigga Clack thought cause he was an O.G. Capps relative he got a pass, but maybe he ain't heard that us young niggaz go dumb. Dino looked from the sucka to me. I know my nigga like the back of my hand. I guess Lil' Jackie musta read the signs cause he was the only reason Clack's bitch ass wasn't on his way to talk to God—or the devil, right now.

"Hold up, fam." He puts his hands up to caution Clack. "Dice is on that young nigga. You crapped out two rolls ago!"

Clack frowned before he exploded. "Nigga, you on that home-boy shit, Lil' Jackie cause you know this nigga people."

"Bitch ass nigga, you got one more time to use that pussy ass word, and it's gonna be cuz you did that I paint this mu'fuckin' concrete wit' yo' blood—Blood," I seethed as I clutched the banga. The tension was thick as I watched playboy daring him to try my 'G'. I may be young but niggaz knew my get down.

"You niggaz gonna kill each other or get this money?" A feminine voice cut through the electricity.

Reluctantly, I took my eyes off this bitch boy and set them on something way more appealing. I stared at a pair of pedicured toes on up to some butter pecan thighs. I allowed my eyes to roll over her essence until they landed on her dark hypnotic eyes. The bitch sorta resembled a thick Yara Shahidi, but she was darker with more spaz to that ass. Armani stood bow-legged, with her titties perky in a skin-tight, midriff tank top that complimented, the off-white mini skirt hugging her juicy ass hips. The belly ring glistened in the sun, as she stood with just enough jazz and attitude to take the malice outta the testosterone that was dancing in the air.

"I don't give a fuck who the dice is on. I'm trying to get at this money. So, you boys play nice and do rock, paper, scissors or some shit to see whose roll it is," she smiled seductively at me then at Clack's bitch ass.

True to form, the pussy ass nigga Clack held his hand out to hand her the dice. Just like a wienie ass nigga, he'd rather lose his life over the dice when it came to a nigga but offer a female he never kissed, let alone fucked everything he was just willing to die, kill, and create a war behind. I laughed as Dino snatched the dice out the niggaz hand and in the same movement whipped that tool on him.

"These dice ain't worth yo' life, homie, but I've killed for less. So, it really don't matter, it's yo' call, folk." The look in Clack's eyes told a tale all in itself, but the thirst for his blood swam in Dino's eyes like a vampire.

We all knew Clack wasn't no tuna—it was not in his blood, but homie wasn't dumb enough to try to have a drawdown with a hunnid doc holidays, at least I hope not anyway.

"What's poppin', folk, we gonna play with these cubes or play with these tools?" Dino questioned as if he was asking about a game of ball rather, than asking a nigga to decide his fate.

The fire in Clack's eyes burned down to embers as he gave a slight nod indicating he was gonna keep his life.

"That's what's up, fam but I'm not stupid, my boy. I just upped this burna on you. I know you, wit' it, Clack so before shit gets ugly—hand yo' tool to Lil Jackie." Clack's face balled back up automatically, but before he relit that fire, pussy extinguished it, again.

"Clack, baby boy, you're way too young and handsome to be on this kid shit with this young boy. He may not know better but you do," she said, then stepped to the lame with her hand out for the pistol.

Dino looked kinda salty about her downplaying him, but I gave him a look that said *'chill'*. Even though, I'm one of the youngest niggaz in my hood. I came up hard and fast with my wolves. Just like any other hood in the wilderness, it's shark-eat-shark—dawg-eat-dawg! I'm up on the seductions and trickery of these hoes out here. I learned from the best—a dope fiend! The skepticism on Clack's face spoke volumes, but some whispered words in his ear, from those juicy ass lips rocked his wienie ass to bed as Armani reached under his shirt and removed the bulge that was evident. But, not before she caressed his dick and turned to hand Lil Jackie the steel. Before she turned back around, she winked at Dino letting him know it wasn't personal. The bitch knew how to assuage a man's ego. The smile on my niggaz face told me, he had just gotten macked!

"Now can we get to this bread? I'm trying to see if I can tap you boys' pockets before y'all kill each other," she giggled.

I'd yet to say anything beyond my irritation of Clack's constant use of that vulgar word— *'nigga'*. Dino dropped twenty on the ground and shook the cubes for his shot. Even though, I was his back I didn't bet against my man's so Lil' Jackie faded the bet. He got popped out the gate!

"Big ups to my Fo's and Tray's—Folk nation in this bitch!" Dino boasted.

Dino was a Gangsta Disciple but he was from the cona. He'd left for a while, but when he came back they blessed him with Folk bidness. Niggaz was fucked up but them boys wasn't tryin' to see Dino get on his dumb shit! Dino was on a roll but true to form, lady, lucks slutty ass switched on fam, and he crapped out with two hunnid on the wood. Him and Lil Jackie family, so he ain't sweat it, but no nigga that's a true man wants to lose. Dino was fucked up. By now the dice game was in full swing.

"T, what's up?" someone yelled.

I tried to recognize the voice over all the noise. I eyed the crowd and spotted 'em as they headed in my direction. It's Ms. Maria, my niggaz Shy's mom. I saw the wolves swallow her up before I could get to her. Niggaz surrounded her with all types of sizes of dope trying to outdo the next nigga. Not one nigga gave a fuck 'bout her being the homies moms and who was I to cast a stone. I helped feed her habit as well. Maybe not, in the same manner, those niggaz did, but in the end, it was all the same.

"I got them two for tens that'll make you sin!" I heard one of the niggaz sales pitch.

I smiled, *'you gotta love a hustla'*. I had to force my way into the throne of hungry niggaz. Some of them gritted on me, but it is what it is.

I spotted Ms. Maria. "Excuse me, that's who I'm shopping with," she pointed me out.

I could tell niggaz wasn't feeling that, but she wasn't the only smoka in the hood, so niggaz wasted no time getting back to bidness.

"Whew," she exclaimed. "These knuckleheads don't respect shit anymore."

I stared at her in disappointment. I hated seeing my nigga mom out here bad like that. Niggaz didn't give a fuck about her being a homies T-lady. They'd let her degrade herself in some of the vilest ways with no regard for the love Satta and Shy gave the hood. Me, I gave Ms. Maria her fix to keep her off these crooked streets. I was trying to help her salvage the little bit of dignity she still had. I gave it to her without accepting her money. I'd want my hood to do the same for me even though, I know these same niggaz I rode, stole, and killed for served my Queen an ill hand.

Still, I didn't blame 'em. We were all hungry and just cause I respected the game didn't mean the game deserved respect.

My face balled up immediately. "Damn, Maria, what I tell you about being out her like that? You know Shy wouldn't be cool with you being out here bad like this!" I frowned at the skimpy sundress she was wearing.

Even though she was up in age and a smoker, the woman still had that sex appeal. "I know, T, but I've been calling you all morning and yo' shit keeps going to voicemail," she whined.

I took the bidness phone off my hip and frowned at the black screen. I tried to power it on but no deal! I could only imagine how much money I'd missed since the battery died.

"And stop trying to use my son's name to make me feel bad. Shy is dead and he's not coming back! Now are you gonna help me out or do I need to go elsewhere?" she said, making me want to knock her lipstick crooked.

She knew I wouldn't chump her off to one of these savages, but she was dead ass about turning to one if I couldn't feed that monkey on her back. Without another word, I walked towards the trap. I knew she followed me even before I looked back. I wondered if Shy's fucked up with me for serving his Queen?

***

~Jazzy~

It had been a month to the date since Satta's been laid up in that cold hospital room. It took Ms. Lovey days to finally get me to leave his side. When he woke up I wanted to be the first face he saw, but the truth was my faith was all fucked up. I had never been the type to question Allah but then again, I had never known anyone that was in a coma. I did my research and found out that the doctors were correct, it was a 60/40 chance that Satta would awaken outta the state he was in and even if he did, there were numerous misfortunes that could wake with him, loss of memory, paralysis, mental illness and more. The fucked-up part was that the sixty percent of him not waking up is stronger than the forty that he would.

Even though, the doctor said it was all up to him. I knew that they couldn't give us any promises because they didn't rely on faith, as we had. They only placed their stamp on medicine and their ability to operate! My heart called out for Assata. My body craved him—my body craved period! Lately, my mental capacity had been lost in a world of questions and what ifs. *'What if Assata didn't wake up? What if I moved on thinking he's not gonna wake up and he does? Would he fault me? Was that betrayal— so on and so on.'*

As I was thinking those things and preparing for a much-needed hot bath, my doorbell rang. Fuck! Why did it seem that every time I was about to wash my ass somebody showed up? In frustration I headed for the door, wearing but my t-shirt and panties. I wondered who it could be. No one outside of my girls and a few family members knew where I rested at. Quickly sliding on a pair of shorts, I headed for the door.

As soon as I got to the living room, Marcella's cheesing face was the first thing I saw fogging up the glass. I couldn't help but laugh at her goofy ass, yet the bitch's timing was nerve wrecking. I unlocked the door, ready to give her a piece of my mind, but the surprise was on me. As she stood there with that silly ass grin on her face, a six-foot fantasy come true stepped from the side of the door.

"*Shotta!*" I shouted in surprise.

My mouth hung to the floor as I tried to find the words to speak rationally. Shotta was my ex-dude. I met him when I was at UCLA, he's a street nigga with intelligence. We started kickin' it—well we fucked a few times and somehow became inseparable while I stayed on the west coast. Once I got the news of Shy's murder, I packed and left like a thief in the night, and even though a woman was supposed to be dignified at all times. I had to step down a notch and deliver the news to him over the phone. Now—here he stood! All six foot- two inches of him. His skin the color of malt liquor, and those long pretty lashes over his bedroom eyes. The only flaw about his nature was the chest length dreads he kept done in a cute pattern. It was not that they didn't fit his swag, it was just that I was not into the dread head thing. Never have been!

"Sup, babes, you had to know I'd show up. I can tell that you're glad to see me," His cocky ass said with a slight smile that revealed the adorable dimples I used to lust over.

"And how might you come to that conclusion? That I'm glad to see you, I mean?" I arched my eyebrow in anticipating his answer.

He laughed, "How else can I tell, J? I always told you your body couldn't lie to me." His eyes then trailed down to my chest—and it hit me—how my nipples use to get hard from his presence.

I blushed as I crossed my arms over my chest. I turned my gaze to Mar, there was no need to ask how they got in touch. When she used to visit me out west Shotta introduced her to his cousin and as far as I know, they never stopped communicating.

"Mar, what you on, I mean—you know the deal. So, why would you be so messy—so disrespectful?" She opened her mouth to explain, but I put my hand up stopping her. "Bitch save it, there's no excuse!" I rolled my eyes at her before turning my gaze on Shotta. "Shotta, I told you we needed to cool off. I mean—this poppin' up to my house without an invitation ain't cool. You know I got feelings for you, but I also have someone I'm seeing, and we already had a misunderstanding with this same type of fuckery. Mar knows that!" I frowned at her.

The smile slipped from his face an anger took its place. "Yeah, she told me about your little friend, but I'm here to get what's mine. Look, Jazmina, I've let you play house with homeboy long enough. Now I'm coming for what's mine. He's placed your life—"

"Shotta," I interrupted him. "What you not understanding? I'm not yours—really, I've never been." I felt a headache lurking behind my eyes—pinching the bridge of my nose. I exhale a deep breath. "Shotta, you shouldn't have come here. Yea—Mar may have told you about him, but what she couldn't have told you was that he'd kill you for coming for what's *his*!"

***

~Tomorrow~

After I made sure Ms. Maria was straight, I found myself back at the dice game just in time for the dice to land on Snake-Eyes crappin' some skinny pocked face out. I squeezed back in next to Dino, I saw my boy working clean. The stack of bills in front of him told the tale.

"Finally," Armani exclaimed. "You niggaz acting like y'all ain't wanna give a bitch a play at the dice."

I watched, as she took the dice and dropped her short sexy ass down into a crouch, with her legs spread eagle. That fucked me up. It caught the whole squad off guard. All I saw was raw hairless pussy lips pouting out at a nigga. Them bitches was so fat it was like somebody hit a pause button on the hood and the only movement was the lil' bad ass kids running wild, and the sound of music blasting from niggaz systems.

"Damn, you niggaz, gonna keep staring at this pussy or try to get at this bankroll, I got right here?" She flashed a knot that was as big as a small pocketbook.

If she wasn't the big homies, Tricky's relative I'd relieve her of all that shit, like right now. The nigga Clack snapped back to reality first.

"Bitch, you doing that shit on purpose. A sucka would fall for that weak ass shit, but not the Clackalac!" This lame ass nigga thought he'd said some playa shit.

Armani didn't respond, as she dropped fifty her first roll, and just as I thought, the clown Clack matched her. She shook the dice real good, so niggaz could hear them clacking together and released them as if she was born to do that shit. I watched as one landed on the tray and the other spun before it settled on a pretty four.

"Hit dice!" She did a lil' dance before she picked up her Lucci. "I'm feeling lucky today boys. I'm getting the house on my next roll," she said, as she dropped five crisp hunnids on the wood and all eyes landed on her.

Niggaz underestimated females when they played a man's game, but what most niggaz didn't take the time to realize, was that some women were schooled by game niggaz, so their game was just as tight as ours.

"A'ight—I see that's a lil' too steep for you po' hustling niggaz—" she reached down and picked up two of the bills then caught the eyes of each of us as a challenge.

"Man, I got that bet, ma," a nigga from the block named Ja'Ray called.

"Naw, nigga, I got my back," T-Money interjected, as he dropped three crisp ones on top of the three already down, but Armani wasn't impressed.

"Hold up, daddy," she said to T-Money. "You can't speak on my money." She turned her attention to Ja'Ray. "I want that fade too." She dropped three more hunnids in a separate stack.

In my mind, I'm thinking *'come on, fam.' How the fuck a nigga not gonna sense something fishy jumpin', when a bitch bettin' threes on her first roll?* That was how boys always ended up being food. They take their eyes off common sense and allow bravado to lead them into the lion's mouth. Ja'Ray smiled at T-Money mischievously like, *'nigga you ain't runnin' shit.'* That shit musta gotten under homey's skin cause his dumb ass spoke up quick.

"We may as well shoot the other two bills, sweetheart. I mean— since you're so sure about your issue and all."

I laughed at fam. I grew up with the nigga, but he was as green as grass. Armani dropped the two on the six already down and lame brain followed suit. He dropped a band of three hundred on the first roll. Bitch didn't even have a point yet. As she shook the dice, our eyes met in a clash of acknowledgment. Every bet she made, I side betted with the clowns that was just as stupid as Ja'Ray and T-Money.

These was my dawgs but shid, as I said earlier it's dawg-eat-dawg when it came to getting that bag. If Armani was an outsider, I would have gladly rocked her to sleep but since she was one of S-E-D's finest. I'ma eat off her plate. She let the dice roll and as them bitches tumbled, I watched the niggaz watching the dice as they rolled to a stop.

"Naturals," Armani screamed, as she raked up her loot. She then snatched up the dice as T-Money reached for them. "You niggaz are as good as this pussy!" she mocked as she rattled her femininity.

All eyes zeroed in on her lower lips, all except mine. I watched admirably as she replaced the crooks, trick dice, with the actual ones.

"Bitch let me see them dice," T-Money fumed. She merely dropped them at his feet and as he inspected them, she frowned. "What, you tryin' to accuse me of cheating?" she screamed. She threw a hundred at him and another one to Ja'Ray. "There, I'm buying my way out the game. You niggaz sore losers," she said, as she stood and strutted away.

T-Money was still inspecting the dice for flaws.

***

Goose sat inside his white-on-white Benz truck observing the scene from afar. The day had been profitable and the best part about it was he didn't have to kill nobody. He watched the dice game and laughed at the clowns getting taken fast for their chips. Whoever, lil' mama was had a game 'bout her only a game nigga could detect. He watched as she played the crowd with seduction and he saluted the awareness of the shorty that peeped her but kept his lips sealed.

"What you thinkin' 'bout, bruh?" Pain asked.

Turning his gaze to his younger brother, Goose couldn't shake the feeling that had been nagging him since he got the call about his lil' nigga being gunned down.

"Somethin' ain't right with this whole shit, bruh. There are too many loose ends that lead nowhere, and Ms. Lady lil' bruh rockin' wit' tellin' me some spooky shit 'bout some nigga wit' aids trying to whack him. We need to get to the bottom of this shit fast. I got shit to tend to back in the Tone, but I ain't leaving till whoever tried to take Assata out is eliminated—them and their entire bloodline!"

Pain simply nodded his head as he twisted up a Kush stick. There was no need to verbalize his intentions cause his tool barked for him, but there was one thing that ate at his mind and he needed to run it by fam.

"Goose—what you think about the girl, Jazzy? You think she had anything to do with it?"

Goose turned his attention back to the activity in the hood. "For her sake, let's pray she don't," he whispered.

Pain leaned his seat back to get comfortable. "Or it's night-night for lil' baby," he seconded.

***

~Ice-Berg~

My eyes popped open to a light so bright, it seemed like my head just cracked open. My head was pounding, it felt as if I was about to throw up. Nausea spun through me like a hurricane in the middle of the Pacific causing me to snap my eyes back shut.

"Arruugh," I yelled, as I grabbed both sides of my dome.

As soon as my hands made contact I knew something was wrong—terribly wrong. I started feeling around my cranium, I was confused by the thick padding wrapped around my shit.

"Chu, mas take it easy, Papi. Chu no position to move so—so fos," she said, from somewhere beside me.

Instant recognition serenaded me causing me to pause and crack my eyes open into slits trying to brave the powerful light. Belle sat next to me, looking poised and exuding sex as if things never got crackin' in my room. I was at a loss about how many days—hours—or minutes has passed, from the looks of shit, I had missed quite a lot. The bed I was in must have been a freaky mu'fucka cause it was massaging my back and the mattress molded to fit my form. The room I was in, was aglow with the sunlight pouring through an open window, that allowed fresh air to flow through the room causing the drapes to dance lazily in the breeze. A vase of fresh wildflowers was next to my bed, but that didn't explain why the fuck, I was here or what the fuck was going on.

I intended to say just that, I turned my attention to Belle, but as soon as I opened my mouth to speak, fire rushed through my lungs and my words escaped my lips in a whisper. Fear bathed me and I guessed she saw it cause she did this calming gesture with her hands while filling a glass from an ice pitcher. She handed it to me and looked at me with a gentle smile.

"Drink—chu feel mosh better. Chu been through a lot and me know tu wan explanation. So, drink and ask chu questions."

I sip the cold water gingerly, without taking my eyes off of her, and as it slid down my throat, relief was a beautiful companion. "Wha—what's—going, B—Belle? Wha—what's happened—to—to me?" I croaked.

I guess some shit was better left under the dirt cause the shit she told me, fucked me up so bad I damn near passed out. She said I'd been out of it for thirty days. That night in my room shit got ugly, I was hit three times, once in the shoulder, once in the stomach, and once in the thigh. Two of the henchmen that came with Russia were laid down, but Russia got away. She said she got me out of there and we'd been in Guayaquil, the largest city in Ecuador.

She said my face has been plastered all over the news in connection to a drug enterprise and the kidnapping of a federal attorney's wife. Fuck! The F.B.I and the D.E.A wanted me, and I was number ten on their most wanted list. The next bomb the bitch drops on me put me out for the count, as hurt raced through my veins like it was my life's blood itself. Nutz was dead—killed! My heart turned cold at once, froze over like the Atlantic. Dead—my nigga, my baby brother? My mind tried to put the pieces together, that's when she fucked me up like a mental patient! Literally, she told me, that she'd had a private doctor to do reconstructive surgery on my fuckin' face. She changed my identity to help me elude the laws back in the states. She said, she knew my drive and knew I'd never find peace here. She finished by telling me the spookiest shit ever!

"Santa Muerte saved us that night in chu room and we owe her what we've promised instead of me husband's blood, it will be ours that becomes the sacrifice for the Holy Death. Chu mos go back and kill our enemies or we will both die!"

Renta

Chapter Five

Wake Up—We Need You
~Twisted~

As I walked into the trap on Ruth Street, it was like walking into one of them white boy's meth labs somewhere out in the middle of the country, except this shit right here had straight hood niggaz with millions on their mind. As soon as I hit the kitchen, my mans Lil' Joe handed me a face mask. I watched as four naked bitches capped and bagged that 'Boy' up as my loc's observed and directed. 'Boy' is what we call heroine out here in the streets, it's the strongest and most addictive narcotic ever discovered.

The streets know me as Twisted, Hoova Crip nigga off Hic Street, and the lil' cousin of Ice-Berg and Nutz. My right-hand is Lil' Joe also Hoova. Ever since my loc Ice-Berg disappeared from the face of the earth, we've been running shit. The spot pumped that *'White-Girl'* at first, but I'm assuming someone fucked up the shipment and added two bricks of *'Boy'*, and since then—well—the streets been jumpin'.

"Sup, Cuz?" Lil' Joe locked the hood with me and our fingers connected into two capital C's.

"Shid, grooving loc, what's crackin' over here?" I inquired, as I watched the packaging of my shit. One of the girls looked up at me with lust dancing in her pupils.

"Sup, Tessa?" I acknowledged lil' one.

We'd fucked around a few times and lil' baby was a troopa. Even though she fucked with them niggas on the otha side of the hood, she kept it funky wit' me. She was a jazzy lil' bitch, the only reason I ain't wife her was cause the bitch had me skeptical of her get down. Any bitch that rocks wit' the enemy of where she's from has the potential to be a snake. So, for the time being, I just watch her and prep her to be Queen one day. That's exactly why I checked her and Joe, not on no sucka shit, but it's levels to this shit. I'd already told both of 'em, I didn't want her in none of the spots, but for some reason, she thought she needed to hustle.

"Fuck, I tell you, 'bout bein' up in the spot, Tessa?" I gritted, as my eyes bore down onto her. She frowned as she stood up and her titties saluted a nigga as she walked over to me.

"Nigga fuck I tell you 'bout tryin' to demand shit when you ain't put a claim on none of this?" she said, rubbing her hands down her body.

I looked at Lil Joe before I said, "Bitch go get yo' clothes and go sit in the car before I wring your neck!"

She rolled her eyes dramatically, but that ass turned and did what the fuck I told her to. She knew I believed in smackin' a bitch when she failed to know her place amongst men. She also knew that I hate defiance. I was suddenly, snapped outta my thoughts by the sound of Lil' Joe's laughter.

I turned my heated gaze on him. "Fuck so funny, Cuz? I told you not to let her in the spot, homie. This ain't no place for my bitch. What if I let your gal in the spot and let her get naked?"

The laughter never left his voice as he responded. "Cuz, my bitch is right there," he pointed to Mena, a dark-skinned girl from the hood. She was naked as a newborn and as her eyes found mine. I diverted my stare from her succulent titties.

"Cuz, a bitch gonna do what she chooses when you're not around. That's why I don't sweat it but on the set, if you woulda told me you got tags on shawty. I wouldn't have disrespected yo' game like that, Hoova. You make it seem like she's just anotha hoe, so I saw nothin' wrong with lettin' her hustle," Joe rationalized.

Even though I was still heated, I knew my nigga was speaking the gospel, so I let it go. "You got that ready for me?"

Joe's didn't speak another word, as he turned and walked over to the cabinets.

He pulled out a backpack and tossed it to me. "Fifty large."

I turned to make my exit and caught Mena eye fuckin' me.

I shook my head, "Say, Cuz, yo' bitch being a slut indirectly. But how can you blame her, when you got her in a position revealing all that's pose to be for your eyes only?"

I kept laughing as I smashed out, but not before I heard the unmistakable sound of hand against face. Cuz could talk that playa shit all he wanted, but no nigga wanted his hoe to be a hoe outside of the bedroom.

***

~Jazzy~

I walked into my house after spending the day at my baby's bedside, I was exhausted. Me and Lovey had built a beautiful bond, and there was no more questions whether or not I was strong enough to stand by my man. Lovey told said she couldn't blame me if I chose to move on with my life, and neither would Satta. She didn't know Satta like I do, he would blame me.

"Chile, a woman has to determine what loyalty means to her. If you choose to leave this man, it matters not how I feel or what I think, nor Assata. If a woman can find peace with a decision she's made no matter how foul or dishonorable it is, then she is a woman that doesn't walk by morale, but a woman who lives the life of a generation. A generation that slices the throats of the ones they vowed a lifetime to. Sugga, only thirty percent of women are who they say they are, the other seventy percent are exactly who they don't say they are. I know you're part of that thirty percent, and if you choose to move on. It wouldn't be for any other reason, then this man right here not waking up before you die. You're a woman, Jazmina, and you are a rare breed, baby. Pressure is always harder on women like us cause we love deeply."

I smiled at the memory of that conversation, as I stripped out of my pants. Gotta love women like Lovey. As I pulled my shirt over my head, I headed for my room with a burning desire to find my sleigh bed. I decided I would shower after I got a few winks in. At least that was the plan until his voice spun me in the direction of my dining room, that's when shit got real.

'*Smack!*' Life became blurry, as my body turned with the impact of the slap. Before I could gather myself he was on me. He slammed my back so hard into the wall, that it caved in and I was pinned inside it.

"Bitch, you know not to disrespect me like that—ever," he raged with slits for eyes.

Tears spilled from my eyes as all the promises he'd made about never putting his hands on me again, was broken for the millionth time. The millionth time, that he vowed this would never happen again. Shy dying wasn't the only reason I came back. I had to beg this nigga to let me attend my brother's funeral because he didn't trust me outta his sight. He's the same nigga that told me if I didn't return he'd find me and kill me.

"What, you thought you could run away from home, huh? Bitch, I own you," he spat, as malice did the tango in his eyes.

"I—" I sniveled— "I hate you so much! I'll never belong to you again—you-you promised not to do this again!" I had raindrops falling from my eyelids.

I could see the tornado in his eyes die down just a little bit. His dreads were laid across his face making him look like a sexy ass madman. Only if sex appeal could override abuse, I'd fall back in love with him, but since it couldn't, I merely stared at him with the deepest hatred.

"Miss me with all that broken promise shit, J. You make me do this shit to you. I told you to bring yo' ass back home, but you tried my gangsta anyway. You even tried to play tough when Mar was here. Now you don't sound so tough," He smiled sinisterly, as he used his knuckle to wipe my tears away.

His head was tilted to the side and the insanity laced within his words told me, he meant every—single—word.

"Baby girl, you know, I'm 'bout that murder shit. So, take my words as serious as you took your brother's death. You have twelve hours to have yo' shit together and be ready to get back West or I'ma kill that nigga you been visiting at that hospital. Then I'ma whack the old bitch that be there more than you. You're coming back home, or you'll be the death of him. I almost got him on that freeway. But if I must say so myself the boy is a gunslinger," he revealed the missing pieces.

The pieces of the puzzle I'd tried to put together, well, those mu'fuckas had just fallen in place. I felt chills running down my spine, as I came to the harsh realization, I was the reason Assata was laid up in that cold room. The devil had followed me to the people I love, now the man I had always envisioned being mine was in a coma.

Immediately guilt spilled from my eyes. "You—you will never take me away from him. Why, Shotta, why would you want a woman that can't love you? Why won't you let me be happy?"

He gave me the deepest truth an animal could ever give a person. "I guess, I'd rather see you dead, than happy with another nigga. You got twelve hours, Jazzy, play with me if you want. Please don't be stupid, love, let's leave peacefully. Nobody has to die, ma, but they will if you test my shit," he said, as he took his pistol from his waist and aimed it at my head.

The first thing that came to my head was Assata's poem, *'Ocean of Grief'*, when he said, *"I can't say I'm happy for you—in fact, I wish I knew magic, so I could conjure up something tragic for you!"* I wondered if somehow, he'd learned magic.

***

~Assata~
Four Months Later

What's the use of a bulletproof vest if the nigga aiming at your thinking cap was the same nigga you allowed close enough to your thoughts? They say that the best way to determine the value of ones potnas was to bring money or a bitch into the equation. Money can cause a hungry niggaz stomach to blindfold him to his morals. I learned that a bitch with a little bit of ass and titties will drag the serpent outta a nigga that lacks the ability to control his dick. That's the weakness that stole the definition from a man. A nigga must see beyond loyalty and what sounds real. Loyalty is the fibers of a righteous man's foundation, yet the actual foundation is his beliefs, his morals, and his limitations.

A man with no beliefs has no balance. A man with no limitations will do anything. How can he trust the next man when he can't even trust his very own limits? That's why I fucks with a cat based on his beliefs. If his beliefs are righteous, how can his loyalty be tainted? If I questioned somebody, I've already allowed into my cipher, that meant I needed to tighten the fuck up! My decisions affected my life. My bitch's life, the wellbeing of my seeds, as well as my whole structure and fam. A man gotta make good decisions cause if the vibrations become hazardous to the shit he loved, he becomes a dangerous man.

The type of nigga that will accidentally kill himself by way of his very own decisions. I gotta be a boss cause my castle—my woman—team—and child depends on my decision making. That's what I was thinking as Lovey lit candles all around me and placed her hand against my forehead. My limbs sparked a flood of her spirit and I could feel the ole lady stepping into her love. It's as if a gravitational pull guided my feet until I was stumbling through the fog. It's as if my feet had a mind of their own, as they led me like a navigational system.

Unexpectantly, I stepped from the fog and into a bright sunlit cemetery. Its familiarity paused me cause without having to be told, I knew where I'd end up. So, that's where I headed, I spotted Lovey at the tombstone laying down a fresh vase of roses. As I walked up behind her, I read the engravement on the marble headstone— *'Ruth Ridge, A Mother, Sister, and Daughter-1967-2002, Always in our Hearts.'*

"We never know when it's our time, chile. Sometimes God comes at a time none of us expected and maybe that's why the bible says He'll come like a thief in the night. How you doing, baby?" She said, without the slightest indication of her knowing I stood behind her.

This was one of the many tricks she'd mastered over the years. I didn't take my eyes off my T-lady's tombstone, as I nodded my head like Lovey could see me.

"Maybe—but I think if there's a God, he's just a thief period. He's too cool with the devil and sometimes while they're playing chess, he sacrifices some good people in order to win a game that he could win in one move. I'm coolin' Lovey, how are you, beautiful?"

Turning to face me she smiled at how I viewed shit. This lady raised me to be a man, and to never hide the true me from nobody. So, I gave it to her from my gut. The raw truth of how I felt. She's the typa woman that respected the real in a nigga.

"Chile, you've been mad at God ya whole life, but I can promise you, if you wouldn't have Him in your life it woulda been you buried under all this dirt, instead of Him taking your mama to get your attention. You're not God, Assata, no matter what you've read in them crazy books," she laughed softly at my facial expression. "What, you didn't think, I'd be snooping around your house, while you've been here in this dark place? Boy plaaease—I'm a woman, chile," she said in a sista girl way, with an arched brow.

I loved this lady. I laughed at her silliness but knowing her like the back of my hand, I saw the storm in her eyes. Something wasn't right! "Lovey—why did you come here, mama?" My question seemed to strike a nerve because she cringed slightly.

"Why would something be wrong, chile, can't I just want to spend time with my baby boy?" She smiled, but it didn't reach her eyes.

"Lovey," I whispered, as I gently took her face into my hands. "You're my world—you've stood beside me through the good, bad, and the ugly. We don't fake nor keep secrets from each other, mama—tell me! Tell me what's happened, Queen." The resolution was a powerful element, as she placed her hands on top of mine.

"Assata, you have to answer the question, you have to baby."

I was confused, as I looked at her, searching her eyes. "What question, Lovey? What are you talkin' 'bout, Queen?"

She smiled bitterly. "Do you care if you live or die, chile?"

For some reason this time she asked just felt different. I thought about all the shit I'd done in my life, the few people that had actually loved a nigga. All of 'em I thugged for—my nigga Shy—he gone—gotta live for him. Jazzy, even tho, she fucked over me wit' Nutz, I still fucks with her. My big bro Goose—the nigga will kill the world for me. I couldn't die on him. My other brother, Pain? Damn, and

59

Lovey? All this shit sunk into my soul and slipped from my tongue in the form of absolute truth!

"Yes, Lovey—I think, I do care."

Lovey looked at me quizzically and shook her head amazed. "You think? Well, rather you do, or you don't matter not at this moment. Things has changed, chile, and people need you, their lives depend on it." She then turned to my mom's tombstone, "Wake up Assata—you have to wake up—now," she demanded, as she began to fade away.

"Nooo—not yet, Lovey—I need more than that! Who needs me mama—who?"

"Wake up baby—we all need you! Wake your behind up!"

***

~Ice-Berg~

She unwrapped the gauze from my head slowly. I hadn't seen my own face in almost two months. Yet, I'd obtained all of my energy back. The wounds healed nicely even though, I gotta deal with this shit bag from the hit I took in the stomach. But, shit coulda been worse though. Anticipation and fear exuded from my pores as she got to the last wrap. All sorts of shit rushed through my head. What if the surgery didn't sit well with my face? What if the hoe got me lookin' like Gary Coleman's lil' brother? The breeze that fell over my face let me know that it was free from the cotton cage, it's been hiding behind for the last six weeks. I studied her facial expression as a slow smile blossomed into her features.

"Chu are a brand-new man. You are handsome and beautiful all at once. We will be victorious, hmm," she said, as she walked over to the dresser and picked up a handheld mirror.

As she walked back over to me she said something in her native tongue and held the mirror out to me as if it was a relic so precious we had to be very cautious with it. Fuck all the theatrics, I needed to see my face. I snatched the mirror from her and she laughed softly at my impatience. I had slow determination, as I lifted the mirror to my face. A sharp breath got stuck in my throat as me and my reflection faced off.

These mu'fuckas had me looking like a gangsta version of Ginuwine. Except for the voice and skin tone, I looked just like a pretty boy ass nigga. The mu'fuckas even changed the color of my eyes to smoke gray, dark niggaz ain't got these type of attributes unless they're cut wit something. Plain and simple, these folks had me looking like a whole 'nother man. I didn't even recognize myself, so I knew the authorities wouldn't either. Even if, I was standing next to the Americas Most Wanted pictures they have of me posted all around the states.

A crazed smile eased onto my face. My first order of business was gonna be retrieving the reins to my empire. Fuck it, new identity—new chance, and nothing to lose. Them white folks murked my brother, somebody gotta answer for that shit, and I knew just the mu'fucka to start wit! If it wasn't for him, none of this shit would have happened. It's time to bury the bullet and I got a whole drum of 'em to bury him with!

"Chu have chu work cut out for tu. Me know chu going to reclaim chu position of power. But chu mos remember chu promise to the Holy Death—chu mos give her the blood of mi husband or it will be our blood that spills."

As she said this my mind took me back to the weirdo shit that was happening while I was sleep. The Leviathan, dragon blood—reapers blood—valerian root—vandal root?

"Belle—what the fuck is reapers Blood? While I was sleep, I heard a woman speaking of the Leviathan!"

She looked at me almost surprised, yet after a few moments of evident consideration, the resolve washed over her face. "A spell! Mi mama placed a smell on you. A spell of protection—" she paused again, then continued. "A dark spell that will help you in your pursuits but will taint your soul." Our eyes lock in a showdown of questions, answers, and frustration.

"How did Russia make it out of there alive? How did we survive?" I questioned, but somehow already knew the answer.

Belle smiled, "Devils shoestrings," she said.

I had confusion painted all over my face in the form of a whole bunch of, *'what the fucks'* and even more *'Bitch you better elaborate.'*

Interpreting my facial expressions correctly, she didn't hesitate to answer. "A root from honeysuckle. It grows in wild fields and forest. It's used for protection, some people bathe them in gin and bury them in the ground, or the door to your room. It trips the devil, stops him, and gives him pause, if only for a moment!"

Chapter Six

Life Loses Its Meaning
~ A Face in The Dark~

I've had my eyes on the chess board since things took a change for the worst—well in some cases—cases like mine. It's changed for the better if I must say so myself. A few pieces had to be taken off the board, but sometimes it's best to play with pawns instead of utilizing your power pieces because it gave you more sense of the game. It gave you a feel of what it felt like to fight with a sword instead of a gun. A lot of shit almost went down a few months ago when Jazzy's clueless ass almost got herself killed. What type of bitch lives alone and doesn't lock her door? I'm saying if a mu'fucka wants to get in there's more than one way to skin a cat, but damn, don't make it easy for them.

Yet, that's neither here nor there because I helped her cheat death. I even staged it to make it look like Gusto was slayed in his car. The only reason I intervened with the reapers plan was because I needed Jazzy to help me carry out my plans. *Assata!* That sexy motherfucker was the plan. In his situation, I was kinda late, but the motherfucker handled his own, like a real nigga suppose to. I just cleaned up his mess and got him to the hospital before he bled to death.

I have to admit stripping him naked was the best part of it all! His dick thought uncircumcised was beautiful! But never mind his dick, I have bigger plans for our baby boy, Assata. First, I had to make sure he stayed alive long enough to bring those plans to fruition.

***

~Armani~

The night-club Dreams was packed to capacity. Everybody was in that bitch, from the raggamuffins to the bad bitches. It was easy to spot the boss niggaz and even easier to distinguish the lames acting like bosses. I even saw this wienie ass nigga go to the bar and pay the bartender for two empty bottles of Ace! Like, where they get those niggaz from? How I saw it was if a female gave you some play simply because you can drop twelve or fifteen hundred on a bottle, she's just as lame as the nigga who bought the empty bottles cause a niggaz pocket don't determine the nigga. It only made him look like somethin', but in actuality, he might not be shit, except another nigga with full pockets.

Me and my girls were up in the V.I.P doing our thang. It was turnt all the way up in this bitch and the whole Kreek was on deck! Niggaz were drunk and out of control. Tomorrow and his ace, Dino were over in the cut lookin' devilish as ever. Them two lil' niggaz was always up to something, but I like Lil' Tomorrow's badass. Any bitch with eyes could see that he was gonna be a boss one day. The potential was evident. Dino, on the other hand, hell I thought he'd be dead before he turned twenty-five. I wasn't trying to jinx lil' buddy, but he was a monster and it was only a matter of time before the inevitable transpired.

Tricky and the high life Villain Circle was live and direct. They were celebrating the homecoming of some nigga named, Lil' Heavy. I heard he used to do his thing back in the day but got cased up when the fed boys came to town back in 2003. It's now 2018 and the nigga was just seeing daylight. Damn, fifteen years, I bet that niggaz nuts is smoking.

"Gurrlll, look at all this money in here. A bitch can't even keep my eyes on just one nigga! Got me feeling like a slut," my girl Marcella screamed over the music.

Her and our third wheel, Tessa clinked their glasses. I leaned over and corrected her silly ass. "Bitch, that's because you are a slut," she dipped her middle finger into her drink and stirred it before pointing at me.

I met Marcella and Tessa a year ago when I first moved here from Dallas. Marcella went to the University of North Texas and that's the reason I moved up here to this little ass city. How I worked them niggaz at dice made me no hoe, I'm just a hustla by design. I revealed my pussy to do what needed to be done. But none of those niggaz knew what this juice box felt like. Sex just don't move me the way it moves the average bitch. I have a daughter that depends on me to teach her how to be a woman and I take that shit seriously.

"Excuse me, ladies, these are for you from the gentlemen at the table over there." The waitress pointed at a table over in the corner.

"Uh oh." I saw those Ruth and Hic Street niggaz up in there.

This shit was a molten pot waiting to spill over. Twisted and the goons made it rain. The young niggaz were Crip crazy over there, as they chunked up their sets and repped their shit. Twisted saluted Tessa and went 'bout his business. I guessed he sent them drinks to let her know he's in the house so don't act up. The nigga was looney. Well, that was my thoughts until the nigga Lil' Mac blew a kiss at me and held up a bankroll. I laughed at his silly ass. Yea, he was cute, but I'm not fuckin' with the opposition at all!

I told Tessa all the time that that shit ain't righteous, but since she was from Ruth Street, she was like fuck it. She moved to the Kreek a few years ago and that's how she and Mar got cool, but as I always say, bitches will either be the strength of the empire or the destruction of it!

"Damn," Marcella said, as she elbowed me to get my attention.

My eyes followed her excitement until I found what had the whole VIP observative and curious. There was some Ginuwine looking nigga walking into the spot, dressed in a white Givenchy suit, with baby blue pinstripes. The silk baby blue shirt he wore underneath the jacket, had the top three buttons undone, revealing a red gold Cuban link that had chunks of diamonds embedded in it. But the eggshell white Mauri Gators was what set off his attire. He moved with the etiquette of a boss and the first word that came to my mind was *the plug!*

I watched as he spotted Twisted turning up bottles with a frown on his face, he attempted to approach the table, but before he could take three steps in that direction, them shootas barricaded him with their tools in hands. The Ginuwine looking dude seemed unfazed, as the light shined on his bald head. He put his diamond encrusted hand in the air and did this circle like motion, seconds later shit got real movie like. A small army flooded the V.I.P packed the typa heat that could melt iron. There was something fucked up 'bout them, their posture was barbaric, but the main distinguishment was the big ass tattoos on their faces. Some of them were bigger than others, but the words *MS-13* were unmistakable.

As the music stopped and playboy's aura received the respect it deserved, he smiled shining a gold tooth. "Dig, we can do this the easy way or the hard way. But either way, it's done, I'm leavin' with that nigga in tow," he said, pointing his finger in Twisted's direction. "I came in peace and that's how I plan to leave." He then turned his eyes to Twisted and continued. "Cuz, we got some unfinished bidness to talk about and it can't wait."

Lil' Joe stepped forward with his cannon in his hand. "Shid, Cuz, if you got something to say spit that shit out. Cause he ain't going nowhere without us. If he do it will be over my dead body!"

The man in the suit laughed. "Cuz, taking him over your corpse is the easy part, can't you see the thirst in the eyes of my shootas?"

All eyes turned to the gunmen. Now that I was more alert, I saw that those cats weren't black, they were Mexicans, but darker. Each and every one of them looked hungry for blood and willing to turn this club into a bloodbath, just on the word of this bald-headed, grey-eyed man. I was so confused because he was as dark as a room with the lights cut off.

"Joe Milson, nigga, I know your whole family lil' nigga. Don't make me go dumb—y'all can come with cuz. I wouldn't have it no other way."

Joe frowned his face up surprised. "Say, homie, don't be using my government like we familiar. Wait, how the fuck you know me, anyway?"

At that time Twisted stepped up beside Joe and stared at the stranger with a studious eye. "Nigga, we don't bar you or yo' shootas, we are shootas. We gone step outside and see what you talmbout, but don't make no more threats or Lil' Joe's body won't be the only body getting stepped over." He stared into the stranger's eyes.

The bald guy was unfazed by the proclamation, he whistled and like trained soldiers the ese's left the same way they came.

The stranger looked as serious as death. "I got a message from ya big homie, Berg." He turned and made his exit, never looking back to see if Twisted followed.

Twisted and Lil' Joe looked at each other and followed without further debate. Long after they'd left, the D.J. still hadn't started the music back up. Mu'fuckas was still wondering if they were 'bout to die—including me.

***

~Assata~

Somewhere deep in this dark place, a wound of lightening raged across a pitch-black sky. The illumination showed a chipped road leading somewhere unknown. *"Wake up, we all need you!"* Lovey's words played inside the walls of my head like a favorite song one can't get outta their mind. The sky was lit by another streak of light and that's when I saw the sign that pointed to the road. It said, *'Wake Up'* with an arrow pointing straight out. It didn't take a scientist to know what time it was. I decided to do what the Lion, Tinman, Scarecrow, and Dorothy did, I followed the chipped road.

Out of nowhere, but I shoulda expected it rain began to fall from Heaven. I had no shelter or shield from its essence, yet I braved it and kept pushing forward. It seemed with each step it fell harder. There was no wind, but somehow the rain came down slanted and heavy. Somewhere from up ahead, I saw a speck of light. It looked as if, I was standing in a pen tube, staring from the back of it and out the opening that the cartridge slides into. Another sign appeared to my left, it pointed in the direction of the light.

I fought my way through the storm that was now a mixture of hail and rain. I ran my hands over my face to clear it from my eyes, something strange caught my eye—red, blood red! My hands were covered in it, but how? Am I cut—nosebleed? Through the confusion, I looked down at my body and for the first time, I noticed that I'm naked and my chest—my feet—me, I'm drenched in the thick blood. I held my hands out in a cupped fashion and watched as it filled with thick red blood. Then—the hail—wait—not hail, bullets, 7.62s—AK47 bullets!

I heard the splash of the rain—blood, as it hit the ground. The clinking of the shells as they bounced off the stained concrete. I picked up my pace from a jog to a straight out run. From the darkness, the sounds of the automatic gunfire resonated, as a powerful blast of lightning-caused me to look up at the sky, which caused me to stumble into a free fall. I was helpless to prevent it, so I thrust my hands out to lessen the impact, but it did no good, I sank into the two-foot inches of red liquid and tinted brass.

A shadow passed over me causing me to turn on to my back, shid—if I'ma die, I wanna face off with my killa. The shadow wasn't a shadow at all, but something even crazier. Above me, in the sky that was now blood red, lightning danced as I stared at a real live picture in motion of the day I tried to whack Nutz. In a flash of light, the scene changed to my first kill at fourteen. Through glazed eyes I watched as with every squeeze of the burna, a different kill played in heavens floors. It was as if the sky was a big ass plasma feeding me the animal side of my nature. The shells jumped from the different tools I had used and fell to earth like snowflakes. They sounded loud, but I felt nothing even though they bounced off me as I bathed in the blood of the ones I'd slayed.

I felt nothing, Well—that was until shit got wicked. The next scene stoles my breath. It was my mother in a dark alley arguing with some faceless nigga. Shit got heated and he struck her—*hard*, over and over again until she crumbled to the ground—D.O.A! Tears mixed with the blood on my face as I gritted my teeth against the sudden pain inside the spot where my heart was 'pose to be. Then Jazzy looked down upon me. She was trying to say something, but I couldn't hear her. I focused on her pretty lips, as I read them, I formulated six words that she seemed to repeat as many times as the faceless nigga struck my moms.

"Save me—baby, I need you!"

Then a stranger with what looked to be snakes in his head appeared, but I couldn't see his face. He snatched her into darkness that I couldn't enter. My blood was boiling, my limbs twitched, fire was in my veins, and right as the sky faded to a pitch-black state, I saw Lovey. She was crying, she was scared, she was—

"Aaarruugghhh," I screamed in rage.

I popped out of the blood with murderous intentions, shit looked different. The many sounds rocked me as I tried to get my bearings, and as sweat poured from my pores, one thang was certain—this scene right here wasn't no dream or nightmare. This was *real life*! The monster had risen, and murder was in my eyes.

***

~A day later~

Goose and Pain looked on as Lovey listened to the doctor trying to explain, how a coma patient just disappeared in the middle of the night. She didn't look surprised nor alarmed, but the doctor interpreted her passive look as concern. He'd repeated the same shit three times.

Lovey placed her hand on his shoulder in an assuring gesture. "Sweetheart don't worry yourself of God's work. My son will be okay. Just like a dog, he will always find his way back home. God has his hand on that boy and God knows what he's doing. So, don't worry about my Assata—no sir. Your hospital is safe from any ramifications. You have my word."

The doctor stared at her skeptically. "Bu-but, he may be in danger. It's impossible for him to—"

Lovey patted his shoulder softly before turning to look at Pain. He grabbed her hand and led her away.

Goose then stepped to the doctor with a backpack. "Doc, I think we need to step into your office." Fear fell over his face in a moment of panic. Goose instantly recognized it. "Naw, Doc, it's nothing to be alarmed about, but I'm sure your staff wouldn't understand a black man handing you a backpack with eighty-grand in it—would they?"

The doctor looked from him to the backpack, once their eyes met again, one thing was evident—money spoke the same language anywhere.

***

~Assata~

I eased the door open as silently as possible. I knew I had to look crazy, being barefooted and in this skimpy ass hospital gown. As I closed the door behind me, I felt naked without my tool. I felt like every second was being counted off by the devil without it. I closed the door behind me, the silence was as thick as a bitch with ass shots as I felt my way around in the dark. I knew this house like I knew my own, so it was nothing to find my way around without light. I wasn't sure if I'd step into a trap or not so I walked light so I didn't disturb the devil if he was sleep. Slowly but surely, I checked every room, every closet—everything. I saved Jazzy's room for last.

The door was closed and as I stood before it a sick feeling swam through my veins. I couldn't quite put my finger on it, but something wasn't right, yet still, I eased the door open and quickly stepped outta the way just in case someone was lying in wait and sent shots my way. Now sure that the house was empty, I flicked the light on. The room bathed in a dim glow as I inspected my surroundings—everything seemed normal, but the bed looked as if no one had slept in it in days. I stepped further into the room and sat down on the edge of the bed. I had to figure out what the fuck I was going to do.

I didn't know what happened the day them fools tried to put me under, but I remembered being pulled outta the whip and some hoe talkin' 'bout getting my burna. So, that told me that somebody wanted me to live—but most of all—somebody didn't want me to go to jail. They cleaned up behind me. Who though? Where the fuck was Jazzy at? Then—as if it was a bad dream—the reason I was speeding to get to her festered in my mind, Gusto. What happened?

Jazzy was there to see me at the hospital so she's safe, but—hold up—I musta been moving too fast and missed it.

Now the envelope in the middle of the bed was evident as truth itself. My gut spoke to me even before I reached for it. "Don't read it," it told me. But curiosity killed more than a cat. My name was inscribed in cursive across it in Jazzy's handwriting. I opened the envelope and pulled the letter out, and life lost all of its meaning.

My Assata, Feb 14

I don't think there is ever a good time to say good-bye. Never a good time to tarnish a love like the one, I have for you. So, I won't say nor do either of those things. But, I will give you what you deserve— the truth! Baby, I haven't been 100 with you. Yes, ninety percent but the other ten percent sometimes outweighs that whole ninety, right? Baby, please don't hate me—my love for you is the air I've used to keep my sanity. You've touched a part of me Assata that no other man has or ever will. I won't allow it! I honestly can't imagine a better man to leave my heart with.

So, that's what I'm doing. I'm leaving my heart with you, Assata so that no other man will be able to possess it. Take care of it, my baby, and do me a favor. Don't take yours away from me—I need it to live—to breathe—to know! To know that no other woman will be able to say she has it. To know that I still live. I guess you're wondering what the hell is going on, huh? So here it is—you remember the girl Karla that used to be my roommate? Well, she has a brother name Shotta and we fell for each other while I was out west.

I was confused and lost, Satta. You was out in the streets and— well—you can imagine the rest. I came here for Shy's funeral, and instead of merely losing him, I also lost my heart—to you! So much so, I was willing to leave behind all that I had back in Cali to be with you. Long story short, he came for me, bae—and I realize now that I love him. If you're reading this, it means you're out of the coma—at first, I was lost—but in the end, I knew you'd come back for me. Big smiles, baby—I love you! Please don't come looking for me. Let love be as it was. I'll die loving you baby!

Listen, I want to end this with my heart—do you remember the story of Mohammad going to the mountain? I need you to go there—to the mountains! Remember what he did for his family—his wife? What she did in return? I need you to hear me, Assata! It's not time to get mad at God nor question my decisions. Forever, is in the mountains my baby—you just have to climb up there to get to it. Remember me, Assata, the little girl with the pigtails that used to sneak out to check on you when your nine- year old ass was out under the street lights. Gus is dead, baby—he killed Shy! Go find your heart Assata—I'm rooting for you!

Your Bonnie

Part Two
~Assata~

It doesn't matter if it's an enemy or strategy you must know the exact measure of brains and brawn to use in order to succeed in your conquest. In this game of chess that some perfect, yet some play so thoughtlessly—it's imperative that you observe with keen eyes the depths of your foes ego and greed. Even for a master of a craft it sometimes can be too easy to miscalculate a certain move if he's too busy focusing on his insecurities rather than his audacity. A meek decision is the reflection of a nigga with no heart—no nuts! In order to become great, you must learn the power of an audacious execution.

"Chess—strategy and observation. You must be sharp! A king knows better than to fall victim to poor decisions and or gluttony. Even during a feast, he insists that everyone around him eats until they're full—drink until they're drunk. Even to his Queen, he says "Eat, my love, this is a moment to celebrate." This is his rib. He's molded her to fit him, to think like him, and to protect him. So, if she's not his reflection by now, she's the block that will destroy the pyramid. The one who will betray him in due time.

So, he must test her well. He sips his first cup of wine and pretends to be full. The only mu'fucka he prevents from partaking of the festivities is his general. The one that he trusts with his life. He leans over to him. "Don't eat—don't drink. The meat is a poisonous snake and the wine is its venom. It's proportioned so that there is enough poison in each dish to kill if one overindulges," he whispered to him.

Then together, they watch as every mu'fucka falls face first in their plates. Dead—dead from the mere essence of their own greed and lack of observation. The king glances over at his Queen, love, trust, and loyalty it all radiates from her eyes as she holds up a small portion of meat. "I'll never let you down, my King," she says. Then she places the meat in her mouth and chews it. A smile creeps onto the king's face. "Observation my dear General, if they would have simply taken a glance, they would have noticed that the meat was blue, and the wine was black."

Never take your eyes away from the chess game, because even though she's essential and can maneuver all over the board, sometimes even the Queen should be sacrificed, especially when she's not trustworthy!

Renta

Chapter Seven

Murda—Temptation
~Pain~
Eight Months Later

I stood over a nigga named Qua with blood in my eyes as I held the fifty caliber between the windows of his soul. We had his bitch ass tied and duct taped to a chair in his living room. He was steady trying to tell me something but the tape covering his mouth had his words sounding like one of them Christian people speaking in tongues. Sweat poured from the boy's body as fear escaped his eyes. He knew he was 'bout to go to sleep, eternally. Blood spilled from the cuts and gashes he incurred from the ass-whoopin' I put on him with the butt of the .50.

I'm cut-throat to the bone when it comes down to my enemies but all in all, I'm a good nigga, that's the only reason I snatched the tape from his mouth, allowing his bitch ass to speak his last words.

"Pain—Pain," he screamed so loud I almost reconsidered my decision letting him speak.

"Look, you bitch! If you scream one mo' time. I'm gonna knock yo' muthafuckin' brains all over this bitch's dress," I growled, as I nodded towards his baby moms tied up next to him.

"Cool, my man—sho you right." He took a deep breath and continued. "Look man—I swear that shit that happened to y'all's brother had nothing to do with Hic Street! If it did, I'd know about it, Cuz."

'Boom—'

The tool burped in my hand and his left shoulder exploded spraying his baby mama with speckles of blood. Muffled screams ensued from her tapped mouth, but I didn't even give the bitch a glance. Dino rushed over and up-righted the boy. He cried incoherently, and I couldn't blame him. The whole corner of his bidness was somewhere floating in the atmosphere.

"Don't be disrespectful—watch your mouth, homie—you don't see none of your homies here," I said, then felt Goose tapping me on the shoulder.

"Let me rock with him, lil' bro," Goose requested.

I stepped back and allowed my fam to work. It never amazed me how a crocodile could be so diplomatic as this one.

"Look homie—I can give two fucks 'bout this lil' gang shit you, country boys got going on. Somebody gotta pay for tryin' my lil' nigga. Now you can either let us know who the trigga men are or sacrifice your whole family for some niggaz, that will fuck yo' bitch as soon as you're off the shelf." Big bro was a dragon with eyes of fire, as he stared at Qua maliciously.

"Look, man, I'm telling you the honest to God truth—I—don't—know—shit! If anybody would try to start a war in the hood without lacin'—aww shit," he screamed, as Goose jammed the butt of the AR into his open wound.

Forcefully, he wedged it in the niggaz shoulder until a quarter of the barrel was buried inside the boy's shit. Damn, he was better with me—at least I woula just dome called him and got it over with. Real shit tho—it was plain for all eyes to see that this boy was tellin' the truth. Niggaz like Qua wouldn't sit under pressure like this. He'd have been told on his mama if she was the one responsible.

"Pleaaseee, okay—okay! I know, I'm—oh God—I know, I'm 'bout to die but please spare my gal and kids. This is my—my karma—not theirs," he cried through the sniffles and deep breaths.

I locked eyes with Goose, I could he was in a dark place, as he barked orders at the boy. "Shut the fuck up nigga! Your karma is—their karma! You and your faggot ass homeboys tried to whack my lil' brother, and these streets ain't gonna be safe till it's painted with the blood of the guilty—starting with you!" He then turned his eyes to the niggaz two seeds, a boy, and a girl.

The little boy must have been about three or four and the little girl was about six. Dino stood next to 'em with a monstrous .44 in hand. Tears fell from the beautiful little girl's eyes as she held her younger brother close to her adolescent body.

"Is tat a gum in your hand mister?" she asked curiously.

Goose looked to Dino. "Dino, get them outta here, fam," Dino smiled but complied.

I guess big bro did have a heart. Seconds pass after Dino left the room. I awaited the signal from big bro, but he merely stood over Qua and stared down at him. His eyes were clouded over as dark reflections set flames in his eyes.

"I think we need to make a statement, Pain." He put the AR down, removed the velvet satchel from his shoulders that I'd been wondering about since we set out on this mission. Then he reached inside, and with a slow antagonizing display, he pulled out the sharpest, shiniest scalpel I had ever seen. It was the length of a midget's arm, with what looked to be a snake carved out of some typa gold for a handle. I looked at him like he was crazy. I mean, I knew we had been apart for a minute but— *"What the fuck?"*

I jumped back as the blade swooshed through the air in a wide arch before finding shelter halfway through Qua's face. Bloodshot out everywhere. Goose's hands and face was tainted with its essence, as he stared at his handiwork. Vomit rushed up my throat, but I fought to hold it down. I'm a 'G' through and through, but this shit was some real Hannibal Lecter type shit. As a testament, Qua's bitch began to choke as her dinner rushed up to her esophagus, but it had no exit due to the tape over her mouth. Her chair rocked wickedly as her body fought to relieve itself of what would surely be the death of her in a few minutes.

A mushy sound could be heard as the blade was pulled from dude's face. He looked like a sliced tomato split into two sections and barely held together by the spinal cord, that the blade didn't slice through.

'Whack—whack—whack!'

Blood squirted everywhere as vertebrae and cartilage was severed, with each swing, fam punctuated his words.

"Somebody—gotta—pay," Goose growled.

I turned my head after the first piece fell from homie. Silence permeated the room. I looked to Goose curiously, to see what the bidness was, big bro was outta there! He was drowned in blood and some other typa matter that I couldn't quite pin the color of. He looked demonic as he smiled—gold shined from behind blood-stained lips.

"Since we ain't got all the pieces to the puzzle yet, we'll just send pieces of this nigga to his big homies until they piece the shit together for us." He then said the craziest shit ever. "Help me bag this boy up, lil' bruh."

I turned my eyes to ole girl, but she was already outta there. I aimed the .50 at her and let off two shots to her face, just in case. I turned my gaze back to big bro.

"Fam, you know, I love you, but—" that's as far as I made it before gunshots were heard from the direction where Dino took the kids.

***

~Other-Side of Town~

A small Toyota bent the corner of Hickory Street. The tinted windows were pitch-black under the glow of the moon. It was 2:15 a.m. and the activity on the block was still at an all-time high, as the natives pumped narcotics between houses, up and down the street, as well as along the corner that led over to Oak Street. A group of rowdy youngsters stood on a porch freestyling and whatever else to keep warm from the frigid breath of the night. A youngster named Mookie did a beat against the wood paneling of the house as his loc Archie blessed the spectators with his skills.

"I'm sick with it/need an asylum/niggaz test my shootas we'll whack him, and whoever standing beside em/drop em wit' the barracudas, on my mama they'll never find em/just me and ridas/Hic Street finest, I was bred where the weather be/colder than a polar bear pussy, better check my pedigree/I'm doing it for them niggaz that kame ahead of me/reppin for my block till the opposition bury me/raised off can goods/same conas that Kapp, Dre, and Lil Man stood/ name not Luther, but I'm a king of a grand hood/hood infused wit' narcotics/lil niggas watchin'—plottin' for their training day— Denzel Washington/so tell me what you know 'bout it/moms bein out late/lil brotha and sista need me so my life on the line to make sho the fam straight."

Niggaz went dumb as the homie came from the gut wit' it, but it was one lil' nigga that knew it was real out there so his eyes were glued to the activities of the block. He saw the small car as it eased to the curb and instantly his hand went to his waist. He tapped his potna Tutta and nodded his head at the car. This was a drug-infested cona, so it was no reason to be alarmed, especially when the passenger window rolled down and the female driver leaned over.

"What's up? You niggaz working or just warmin' up that porch. I got two hundred to spend with whoever has the best dope," she yelled, scratching her arms as that monkey rode her back. "Come on, now, I'm sick y'all—I need my medicine!"

The porch turned into a zoo as niggaz pulled packs out their ass, from under their nuts, and some other crazy places. As they rushed the car, the only thing on those boy's mind were adding that two hunnid to their stash. Only one could get the bite, though.

Mookie beat everyone. "Sup, ma—I got that shit Frank Lucas had across the water! You'll nod for years," he said, as he flashed a handful of heroin capsules. By now six or seven dudes were at the car screaming their sales pitch. "Hold up—hold up, damn," she screamed over the pandemonium.

She reached over and gave Mookie the two hundred in exchange for ten capsules, causing agitation and disappointment to the unlucky. "Awww—don't look so sad y'all—my smoking partner is in the backseat. He may want to spend a little bit."

Hope sparked in the eyes of the young wolves. "Where he at? I can't see dude," one of the young niggaz said, as he placed his face against the back window for a better look.

'*Boom!*' His face disintegrated as the window exploded. Blue ta-ta-ta-ta-ta-ta. The Draco spat fire like a dragon, as the blue bandanna wearing figure operated it surgically. From side to side and in a sweeping arch, attempting to annihilate everything moving. Archie ran full force with survival on his mind. Tutta who was running beside him, flipped forward like someone pushed him hard from behind—the reaper was here and hungry for souls and homie's name just so happened to be on a 7.62.

Several shots from the porch caused the reaper to change course. The lil' nigga that spotted the car from the jump was working his burna like a man. If there was a reward for holding it down, he'd had earned it, but the reaper didn't give a fuck about bravery. He just wanted what he came for. The block was waked now—shots rang out from everywhere.

"Get us the fuck outta here, Tracy!" the reaper screamed, as the small car jerked forward and barely missed a shirtless gunner takin' aim at the windshield.

He jumped out the way as Tracy gunned the compact car down the street, fishtailing onto East McKenny in a life-threatening escape. The back window exploded as the car hopped the curb onto East McKenny. Luckily, the main street was almost deserted as they flew through the red light and made it to safety.

"Slow down, Tracy—we peace, ma. We good—we—damn," he said, as he pulled the blue flag from his face. "Pull over right her, fam—we gonna have to foot it from here."

Tracy's nerves were shot as she pulled the car over into a small cul-de-sac, sweat beads flooded her face as she stared at her shaking hand.

"Assata—you owe me extra for that, boy—you said you just wanted to scare those boys. Boy, I know y'all's mamas. I can't believe you-you owe me," she said shakily.

Assata laughed, "Come on Tra—you know, I got you, lil one—I 'preciate the get down too. My fault I didn't keep it muddy with you out the gate. I didn't need you all shook up and shit," he said, as he got out the car.

Tracy used her shirt to clean the steering wheel before following suit. She smiled her stained teeth at him. "Boy, Moose would beat yo lil' ass if she was still here, let's get out of here before we get jammed on a humbug and get the needle. I want my money when we get back to the Kreek," she laughed, as she walked passed him.

She made it four or five steps before Assata called out to her. "Hold up, fam—I got your pay, right now."

"Good! Now we can separate, we don't—" she began, as she turned to face him.

The gloved hand tightened on the CK arms .45—his trigger finger steady, and with a light tap fire rolled from the tip of it, exploding her face like a watermelon dropped from a two-story window. Her body tried to catch up with her spirit, as she stumbled backward, and finally crumbled to the street with her remaining eye open. Assata glanced forward, then rushed back to the car leaving behind no witnesses except God.

***

~A Face in the Dark~

My legs were spread eagle, as a six foot even Adonis sucked my pussy as if it was his favorite entrée. My hand held the back of his head, while I suffocated his face with my pleasure, as I grind my pelvis back and forth on his lips.

"Suck—ohhh— this—umm pussyyy," I moaned, as I squeezed my left nipple, turned on by the sight of my juices saturating his face. "Suck it—ssuuucckk it, you mu-oh-mutherfucker," I screamed, as the damn broke between my legs and my waterfall came down thick—warm—slow.

I pulled his face away from my lower lips and forced him on his back. Then I pulled him to the edge of the couch so that his ass cheeks were barely on the cushion. I straddled him by way of planting my feet on either side of him and squatted over his dick. I reached down and began massaging his thickness as he palmed my breasts and pulled my right nipple into his mouth. I slid down onto his delicacy and squeezed my lower lips into a vise. The amazed look on his face told me, my little trick was a delicious surprise.

I eased all the way down to the base of his cock and my pussy lips kissed his nuts before easing up slow and droppin' all my weight down onto him. There was no barrier between pussy and dick—just wet—hot—penetration. My mind carried me to the object of my fantasies, Assata! The way I watched him put his gangsta down last night had my kitty on fire. He was an animal and as I rode his dick, I closed my eyes and imagined it was Assata's dick I was taking so savagely. I went faster and deeper, as I bounced this ass like I was trying to win the twerking queen contest. I felt his hands on my ass trying to control my wild movements—but he was out of his league.

"Oh shit—ma—I'm—damn, ma—I'm 'bout to—Aaaughhh," he screamed, as his passion erupted from his nature and got trapped by the rubber barrier separating his flesh from mine.

I still rode him into a frenzy, while thoughts of Assata had me crazed with passion.

"Oh—Jesus—fuckin'—Christtt! Ass—Assata, I'm 'bout to—to—A-sssaat-ta," I screamed, as my ocean below created a hurricane around his pole.

I felt his shit at ease instantly, confused, I cracked my eyes open as the tremors subside. When our finally met, evil stared back at me.

'What the fuck?' I thought. I'd just given this motherfucker the best nut of his life and he looked disappointed—angry even!

"Who the fuck is Assata, bitch?" he hissed.

No—I didn't—I couldn't have—did I? "How do you—" I began, but then it hit me. Assata's name musta slipped while I was lost in the moment. Oh well, this motherfucker, ain't my man!

"You need not worry about who the fuck he is! Don't get stupid, homeboy, you're already flirting with death for fucking the boss-man's lady." I matched his tone.

The storm in his eyes faded as he was snatched back to reality

"In that case—" he said, as he turned into a monster!

He pushed me off of him, turned me around, and rammed his dick in my asshole for good measure.

"Yes, you crazy, son of a bitch! Fuck me like Russia isn't your boss!"

***

~**Tomorrow**~

Me and the squad rolled up to Club Dreams thirty deep. I can assure you everyone was strapped and ready for action. We were *made* niggaz, so we passed up the long ass line that bent all the way around the block. Niggaz screw faced us like they had a bad taste in their mouths, but they knew we was piped up.

"What's the business bitch ass nigga? You looking like you wanna have a showdown?" I heard my nigga Spyda spaz on a muscular black nigga with a Rick Ross beard.

He chewed on a toothpick as he met Spyda's stare without fear. We all stopped, sixty pairs of eyes bore down on the nigga. Dino was thirsty to get it poppin' which fed the movie that's 'bout to be made. Tricky stepped up being all diplomatic and shit.

"You niggaz at ease—this dawgs night—we here to support the homie so it ain't gonna be none of that bloodshed unless truly necessary." He turned his low gaze to the black, muscular dude. "Say, homie, this your lucky day. Thank whoever you pray to cause tomorrow you may be food. This is your warning—be easy, bleed!" He then turned his back to him and just like the other twenty-eight of us with the exception of Dino, the hoodie he had on read. *'Kreek Nigga Beware of Dawgz!'* Reluctantly, the rest of us turned to follow, but my eyes stayed on the sucka. He saw me analyzing him and laughed as if he knew the world's biggest secret. I stored it in the back of my mind to be on the lookout for the nigga. Something wasn't right with the homie. I caught up with the gang only to step into a heated convo between the bouncer, Bear, and Tricky.

"Fuck you mean, naw? Bear, you know, me and my niggaz ain't partying without our bangaz. Look—" Tricky pulled out a big knot and peeled a rack from the stack. He tried to hand it to the bull neck, football playin' built ass nigga, but he pushed it away.

"Naw, Trick, yo' bread ain't no good tonight. Last time I let niggaz in with heat, the club was mobbed by an army of crazy ass Mexicans and some bald head nigga. Gold Tongue ain't feelin' that typa shit in his club, and I ain't losing my job over you niggaz bullshit. Y'all can either leave that shit in the car or parkin' lot pimp, but ain't nothin' happenin', homie," Bear demanded.

Defiance glowed in his eyes as him and Tricky drew the line in the sand. "Nigga, who the fuck you talkin' to like that? You ain't sold that shit!" Dino upped his clappa. Ever the dramatic one, he wanted to get it poppin'.

I stepped up before Tricky had a chance to. "Naw, Dino, Trick is right. This Assata's night, we gonna rep for, fam tonight. Some of us just gonna have to parkin' lot pimp with the bangaz to make sure shit don't get ugly. It ain't shit."

Bear looked at me with respect and a bit of relief. I looked to him with truth and a whole lot of resolution. "Say Bear, if something pops off while we're naked, if I breathe to see daylight, you're a dead man— that's on H.L.V!"

***

~Assata~

"A'ight, mu'fuckas, I see the house is filled with drunk mu'fuckas!" The host, Blue, screamed in the megaphone. "A lot of y'all may remember me from John-John's hosting poetry night. But as we all know, shit got funky a few weeks ago and the owner, Pop, had some real legal issues that forced him to close the establishment. For all you mu'fuckas that's been living under a rock, the fed boys came to town, and well—y'all know what's up, and if you don't, it wasn't meant for you too. Damn, look at this mu'fucka," he pointed to a slim light-skinned man that sat close to the stage. "You musta been one of them mu'fuckas that's been living under a rock?" The crowd laughed at his jest. "I bet when Malcolm Little said, *"we didn't land on planet rock, planet rock landed on us—* you was like, yeah—that nigga tellin' the truth. Look at you— lookin' like, who the fuck is Malcolm Little?" he paused to sip from the amber liquid in his cup. "Malcolm Little, is Malcolm X, mu'fucka!" The club was in an uproar.

Dude laughed along with everybody else, but the slight red tint to his skin told the tale of his embarrassment.

"A'ight, a'ight—tonight is poetry night and we got some bad shit in store for you ladies and gents. So, without further ado, let me call a real queen to the spotlight. Y'all give it up for Earth

Freedom," he said, as the lights dimmed, and the smooth jazz band played a real funky instrumental.

Free stepped onto the stage with her usually wild hair, braided into two big braids twisted to the back. She was a true redbone, that knew how to exude the right amount of sex appeal, and not over-shadow her self-respect. The black skinny jeans hugged every curve and cuffed at her ankles revealing the Charlotte Olympia peep-toes that adorned her feet. Her D-cup breasts looked like they defied gravity in the YSL made shirt, that allowed the gold droop necklace, that was accentuated by a chocolate Vivian Diamond to plunge be-tween them. She smiled that sexy smile, as she did her ritual with the microphone, caressing it from top to bottom.

"Peace, my people, it's always a pleasure to be able to exploit my passion to y'all." You could tell the hood was on deck because instead of snaps and mellow applause, niggaz whistled, made com-ments about her curves, and wild out altogether.

Not letting that faze her, Free took it in stride. "Tonight, I'm doing a piece, I like to call *'Merely Perfect Strangers'*. Y'all vibe with a queen." Her eyes were half mass as she held the mic with both hands without takin' it out of its cradle. *"Why is it, that every time I see you, you look as if you've lost your best friend?*

As if you went to sleep and woke up to realize, love wasn't real, but before you fell asleep—you was in your best trance?

Yet, to those that doesn't know any better, they merely see your contagious smile—

The name of your shirt—the price of your best pants—

I see beyond that God and if you allow me to pass you by, con-tinue to live that lie, you may miss out on your best chance.

I see what's inside of you without sonography—

A raging hurricane that twists to reach out and grab me—

Until I'm swept into a beautiful destruction—

An ocean of pain—anger—and seduction—

Surrounding an island called 'the heart' that merely needs a beautiful reconstruction.

I want to give you my loyalty—that's gotta be worth something

Picture us in a locked room doing things that surpass the embodiment of fuckin'—

Climax without the physical need of touchin'—learn each other, until we're so hot that we burn each other when we finally start touchin'—

On the point of combustion—baby please—pay attention—no interruptions.

I want to Bonnie and Clyde for you, revolve around you three hundred sixty-five days of the year, the approximate time that it takes the earth to revolve around the sun—

I'll be your rida, put the bullets in your guns—

Your survival—breathe air into your lungs—

Your freak—ride that dick til' you speak in tongues—

Your rib—if you go to jail, I'll stand beside you, even if tomorrow never comes, but first—we gotta meet each other because right now, we're merely perfect strangers."

The crowd went silly, as she blew a kiss and walked away throwing the peace sign in the air.

"Yeah, that sexy mu'fucka right there, makes an ole nigga contemplate adultery," Blue yelled over the excitement.

"A'ight now, Blue, don't make me cut you," An attractive middle-aged woman yelled from the side of the stage.

"Oh shit," he said in mock surprise. "I forgot Angie was here, y'all give it up for my beautiful wife. Baby, you know, that was just a jokie joke!"

The club ignited with laughter once again. Even Angie had to laugh at her husband's silliness. He put a hand in the air and did a calming motion.

"Y'all, mu'fuckas settle down, I got something real nice for the ladies."

Many whistles could be heard throughout the spacious club. "Bring it on, Blue—we waiting, baby," A chubby sista screamed from somewhere in the back.

Blue laughed, "I bet yo' hungry ass is waiting—waiting on the night to end so you can make it to the nearest IHOP!" The club was a volcano as it erupted with drunken laughter. Big girl was comfortable in her skin, yet she still gave him the finger. "Naw, love—Blue loves the ladies. I see you over there putting on for the plus size women. But dig this next act, is a very dear friend of mine and I love to see him work. Most may know him for putting it down in the streets, and some may know him from gracing the stages of some of the hottest night spots, and—some may know him from his hoeish ways—look at you," he pointed to a cute sista by the bar. "I ain't even said his name and you lookin' like, I hope it ain't Tyrone." The cuties companion gave her a curious look, as the club exploded in humor. "Naw, homeboy, I'm just bullshittin', don't get home and Ike Turner yo' gal. Anyway, without further ado, y'all give it up for my godson, Assata!"

The love was pure as I made my entrance. I was fresh as always, the Ferragamo slacks sagged slightly from my waist, but they hung over my black Gators perfectly. I was shirtless underneath the black vest that was complimented by a blood red back. My ensemble was completed by a forty-two-inch cable, that had a Draco AK.47 that looked like it was made with glass for a pendant. A black bandanna was tied around my head to add to my thug appeal.

"What's the business world?" It sounded like a dog pound, as niggaz started barking and throwing up sets like they was auditioning for the next Westside Connection video. Even some of the Crip niggaz gave it up, but the ladies set the standard.

"Say, Blue, fuck you always setting my shit up behind, Free's? You know that's not right, fam—the lady makes it hard to catch a break!"

Blue merely smiled as he raised his cup of Remy.

"I ain't done this shit in a lil' minute, fam, due to a storm that's been blowing through my universe as of late, but I'm fighting the good fight. Death ain't want me yet, so tonight I want y'all to thug with a gangsta, as I give you a piece that I've dubbed, *'Ghetto Boy Stranded'*." After the crowd simmered down, I released a typhoon of pent-up thoughts and pain.

"Who'll cry for the ghetto boy—the lil' ghetto boy that never had the chance to grow?
The lil' ghetto boy that never had the chance to know—

To know what it's like to have pops show up to my game—
To know what mama had on her mind as she stuck the needle in
her veins—stood under a pale moon with a smile on her face as she
danced in the rain—
Who'll cry for me? That boy inside that never had a chance to
grow—
That lil' nigga that got lost somewhere inside of me that you'll
never get the chance to know?
I guess some niggas are best left buried within a cemetery of
secrets—
A black diary that's held tightly by that lil' boy that's buried
inside me so that prying eyes won't be able to read it.
I was once told that love isn't so far and all I have to do is
stretch my arms to reach it—
Yet, I am scared because my heart is made of glass, and if it's
dropped it may shatter into a million pieces.
I'm a castaway—trapped on an island of broken promises—
Surrounded by a sea of forever that didn't last longer than to-
morrow did.
Loving you is like a soldier on the battlefield, holding a dying
friend that he'd fought beside his whole tour.
Listening to their last words—a sickness to which you wished
you had an old cure.
I wonder who will cry for the lil' ghetto boy—the boy that's
locked inside of a Pandora's box.
Shid, you ain't even gotta cry for 'em—just try to find the keys
to pandoras locks.
May you can't—maybe no one will, love—feel—or cry for the
ghetto boy that's trapped inside my spirit—
Don't sweat it lil' ghetto boy—I'll cry for you—I'll just do it in
silence, so no one can hear it."

***

~Armani~

The boisterous crowd was wild with awe and emotion. Whoever this nigga was he'd just brought down the house. He was dark chocolate, with a swagga that was his own. I couldn't take my eyes off of him. Tattoos peek from under the thin vest he wore, he had puppy dog eyes, that seemed to see everything roll over me in seconds. The corner table that me and my girls were seated was to the left of the stage in perfect view. I crossed my legs and sipped a chilled glass of Perrier Jouet. I could feel my juices making me sticky. The Jeffrey Dodd slip gown that molested my every curve, allowed air to make love to my skin, enhancing the experience to the point I felt like I was naked in this dark room—just me, and this—dessert of a man.

"Damn, bitch," Tessa snapped me from my fantasy.

Confusion eased onto my face as I tried to gather my senses.

"What? Why the fuck are you yelling in my ear, like I'm deaf?" I spazzed on her.

"Well, bitch, you must be I've been trying to get your attention for the last thirty seconds. You've been bouncing your leg so fuckin' hard you knocked over my fuckin' Cosmo!" She pointed to the stain on the cloth that she musta used to clean up my mess.

I so embarrassed, as I tried to salvage my dignity, by saying I had to pee but didn't want to miss the poem. All six pair of eyes landed on me and were stained with skepticism. "What? It was a good poem," I chuckled.

***

~Assata~
Last Call For Alcohol

"Hey—Assata! Assata—wait up," A feminine voice called to me from behind.

I turned to see what the bidness was and came face to face with beauty.

"Ummm, hi—I know we've never been properly introduced, so I thought this would be as good a time as any to meet the infamous Assata." She stuck out her hand. "I'm Freedom."

My diamonds peeked from behind my lips as I took her hand and brought it to my lips. Damn—she was as soft as I imagined.

"That's peace, earth, and as you know, I'm Assata. It's a pleasure to finally meet the woman of every hour."

She smiled revealing deep dimples. "I didn't know gangsters could be so charming."

I gazed into her soul before giving a response. The anticipation was beautiful as our eyes danced. "Maybe you just have the wrong definition of a gangsta." Lil' one was tickled at my 'G', my eyes were tryin' not to drop to those come suck me titties.

"Say, Satta—come on dawg, we trying to smash out, big homie," my lil' nigga Tomorrow yelled, as the squad surrounded us.

The alarm was evident in her posture as thirty-something Blood and Piru niggaz pulled up in force.

"Well—I guess we'll allow fate to bring us together again," she said, as she took a quick glance at the goons that looked as if they were part of Al Queda.

Before turning her attention back to me with questions swimming in her eyes. I took her hand for the second time tonight. I eased the tornado of curiosity and fear, spinning within her internal.

"Peace, queen, you're forever safe with me. But more importantly, real niggaz don't wait on fate to dictate how shit plays out. So, tonight you riding with a gangsta, we'll skip fate, and make our own rules."

Chapter Eight

Missing Him Is Better Than Getting Him Killed
~Jazzy~

"What the fuck, Jazz?" Charla screamed as she pulled the glasses from my face.

My eye were swollen shut from the fight me and Shotta had the night before. The punk motherfucker hit me with a closed fist because his jealousy caused him to see shit that wasn't actual. The night started well, he'd taken me to the club with him and his people. While there, a cat I used to go to the university with recognized me and spoke as I headed to the ladies room. To make a long story short, Shotta left me at the club without a ride home. I had to catch a ride with Charla, back home.

I was so heated, I couldn't think straight. I mean, fuck typa punk shit was that? Who left their woman at the club without a ride? So, I bade Charla goodbye and walked in the house intending to give the son-of-a-bitch a piece of my mind, but as soon as the door closed, shit got real spooky. Before, I could come up with a defense, his closed fist connected with my left eye. I'm not a punk bitch so after I got up off the floor, I fought him with all I had. My small fist didn't do too much damage so, in the end, I ended up with a swollen eye and a nosebleed.

"Jazmina." Charla snapped me back to the here and now. "I know that's my brother. Lord knows I love him, but baby girl, you need to do what's best for you. My grandma—moms—my whole family loves you, but no one will blame you if you leave his triflin' ass!" Inspecting my eye she stared at me as though, I was the saddest child in the orphanage. "I can't believe he did this to you. Your way too good for that man. You even left your dude back home for him—what else can he possibly want?" she fumed. "He shouldn't be hitting on you at all, but especially not while you're pregnant with his fucking child!"

Tears blurred my vision. The other day at the doctor's I got the surprise of my life. I had been pregnant for months! That means that it could either be Shotta's or Assata's. Life had been taking me so fast, I didn't even know when I first missed my menstrual. I cried all night. How could it be that I don't know who the father of my child was? Am I a hoe? Is this Allah's way of a sick joke? I didn't know, but if it was Shotta's I couldn't hurt Assata like that. So, I pushed him to the back of my mind, yet he lived at the front of my heart.

I loved that man so much! I wanted to go to him with all my soul, but that would only cause destruction! I couldn't do that to my baby, so I had to forget him. I had to, he'd never understand me having another man's child. He's not that typa man. So, forgetting him was my only option. Now I just had to convince my heart and soul to do the same.

***

~Pain~
4:15 a.m.

The after-hours was in full swing as niggas and bitches snuck off to get their fuck on. Me and Tomorrow tossed back shots of Henn Dog like it was water, we were lit. One of those lil' hoes was gonna take me to the room tonight, anyway. As a matter of fact, me and the lil' bitch, Tessa had been eye fuckin' all night. The lil' Meagan Good looking shawty had me on her game. Ever since she moved to the hood, I'd wanted to cut lil' baby. I heard she was rocking with the boy Twisted. I didn't know how true that was, but it didn't even matter. I ain't have no papers on the bitch and even though I respected the homie Twisted's get down, there was no loyalty between us.

"What's poppin', dawg—you just zoned out on me," Tomorrow interrupted my thoughts. The lil' nigga had drunk like he was a fish.

"Naw, bruh—I'm just thinkin' 'bout cuttin' something."

The look on fam's face told me he felt the same. "Why you don't pick one of these lil' hoes and smash out? You see all this ass up in here, P, ain't nan one gonna turn a breadwinner down. This shit is a molten pot of horny freaks. This the after-hours, that's what they came for, dawg. Why else will a bitch be out here at the after-hours with the vampires?" His young ass dropped a jewel on me.

I 'G' for lil' homie—he's a pup but possessed a big dawgs per-spective. The hood made old niggaz outta babies.

"Yeah, I'm digging that, lil' bruh. But the hoe I'm trying to bury my bone in is over there being sweated by the nigga Twisted." I acknowledged wit' a head nod in their direction.

Tessa was on the arm of Twisted and they were surrounded by shootas, yet her eyes kept checking for me, whenever her sneaky ass caught Twisted not hawking her. See that's why I didn't trust hoes. These lil' females are only loyal to the nigga that keeps their pussies wet and their bodies draped in designer clothes.

"Yea—that trick ass nigga got the hoe in a chokehold, bruh. You may as well choose one of these other lil' sluts 'round here, shid it's a few that's crushin' Tessa's punk ass." Tomorrow gave me an alternative.

I shook my head, as I pulled my phone off my hip. I texted a number I kept locked in, then told lil' bro I'd catch him in traffic, and I made my exit. I was gonna get that lil' bitch tonight—watch me work! As the door was closing I had to laugh at the last thing Tomorrow's stupid ass said, before I left.

"Damn, dawg—that hoe's pussy must be heavy on yo' mind if she got you going to the car to jack off! Come on, bleed—that bitch ain't even that bad!"

***

~Assata~

"Boy, quit lying," she exclaimed.

We ducked off in our own lil' corner. I made sure to pick a spot where I could see the goings and comings of the spot. There was way too many enemies to chill wit' my back to death. As soon as we left the club, I got my banga off the front tire wheel, where I stashed it for quick access when the sucka, Bear told me I couldn't bring it in. So, I was fully clothed now and the slightest implication of beef would be acknowledged with the whole clip.

"So, you mean to tell me, you've never been in love? Never believed in it? I don't believe that" she said in disbelief. "I can't believe that Assata, your poetry—your passion—it's—"

"It's just how I feel, love—shit, I've been through," I cut her off. "Love, naw—queen, I've never believed in it, but recently I thought that my perception was proven wrong. Yet—how wrong could I had been when I awoke after months in a coma to find that the woman I gave my heart to was absent. She packed her bags in the middle of a storm and ran off with my faith and lost hope of believing in the fantasy of love." Grey clouds roll over her eyes as she looked at me like a wounded animal. I laughed lightly to ease the mood. "It's Gucci, ma—I've learned that it's just how women are."

This ensued an offended look from her. I could see the confliction within her, so I changed the topic. "Freedom, is that the name your mama gave you or just the pseudonym you use to hide behind?"

Reluctantly, the frown eased off her face, but not before she lightly smiled. "You're smooth, God, but the earth has to understand God in order to rotate. We'll come back to that insult you just gave me, but—I'm a real woman, Assata. I have nothing to hide, so let's get that straight! Freedom, is my birth name my mother gave it to me because she was and still is a black liberationist. She loved powerful black women, especially Isabella Baumfree."

The look on my face screamed, *"Who the hell is Isabella Baumfree?"* she giggled and continued. "Isabella Baumfree became Sojourner Truth. She was an abolitionist and feminist born into slavery. She escaped in eighteen twenty-seven, and became a lead orator against slavery, as she fought for the rights of women. My mother idolized that woman, so she took the last four letters of her original name and named me Freedom! Now, you, mister *'it's just how women were—was'* is Assata your government, or do you have something to hide?" she smiled with an air of retribution.

I returned the smile. "Touche," I winked at her. "First off, I appreciate the history lesson, but I know all about Ms. Truth. I admit you lost me with the birth name, but we're never too old to learn. Secondly, Assata is, in fact, my birth name. It means— he or she who struggles." She cut in with a wink of her own.

She glanced at her watch, then jumped as if someone had doused her with a cold cup of water. "Oh, my God!" A pitied look etched onto her face. "I'm so sorry, King, but I have to cut this beautiful meeting short. I had no idea it was this late. I guess I got lost in your debonair company." She attempted at medicating any offense that may had been taken by her need to leave, but she had me confused.

I'm not one who took offense to a woman doing her. I ain't got tags on lady, anyway. I saluted her as I stood to take her back to her car. Following suit, she placed a hand against my chest to stop me. As I looked down at her I witnessed the storm roll back into her eyes. "Assata, have you not found yourself in my poetry?"

***

~Pain~

Marcella's phone vibrated, seeing the number, she smiled thinking he was calling about getting some money. Because Lord knows she needed it. She excused herself from her company and answered as soon as she walked into the ladies room, thankfully it was empty.

"What's up, shorty wanna be a thug?" she knew I hated that shit.

"What I tell you about that bullshit, Mar, I may be small but my dick ain't!" I cracked on the caramel complected bowlegged big booty, C-cup bitch.

"You know it's not, but so what—there's a million niggaz with big dicks," she retorted.

I'd run up in lil' baby a few times back when niggaz was wearing Platinum FUBU, around '99-01. She's a live catch but only for a nigga that had tough skin. The girl's track record placed her on the blacklist with live niggaz. She has fucked the whole Kreek and maybe them niggaz from the other side too. For some niggaz, that's Gucci, but I ain't having no hoe on my arm that every nigga I know, knows what that pussy like. A nigga needs something he can be selfish with and can't nobody be selfish with no freak. So, me and mama became good friends. She put me on pussy restriction, cause she couldn't control her pussy. Anyway, she turned me on to her homegirls, so shit was gravy.

"Dig, I'm tryin' to have a word with ya potna Tessa mayne make that happen for me," I proposed.

She did this little suckin' noise with her teeth, that she did when she was 'bout to get on her other shit, but I smashed that out the gate. "Damn, bitch, every time yo' dusty ass call me, I come thru but the one time I'm callin' you-you with the bullshit—fuck you, dawg." I hung up on her, then waited twenty seconds exactly before my horn rang again. "Yea, fuck you want, fam?"

"Damn, nigga, you always on that aggressive shit. Pain, I'm saying though—I just thought money was the topic, so you surprised me with the other shit," She whined in my ear.

I had to respect the girl for her mind frame, but my dick was smokin' right now, and I could give two fucks 'bout how her mind frame was.

"Look, Mar, I got some live bidness online for you, but we'll get to that later. Right now, I need you to get lil' mama to step outside so I can vibe with her real quick." I could hear the wheels spinning in her head, as her scandalous ass plotted on a way to pull it off.

"Give me a few seconds and she'll be out. That nigga Twisted all on her pussy. So, I'm with y'all to make shit look good, and miss me with that just to vibe with her spiel, nigga. You, not my nigga, pimpin'."

***

~**Armani**~

I won't lie, that dark and lovely specimen of a man, Assata had captured my mind. As I leaned over to whisper in Tessa's ear, I was driven to find out who dude was. The whole hood seemed to turn out for him, so he had to be from the Kreek, but how was that if our paths had never crossed?

"Tess, who is that dude over there with the girl, Free?"

Tess looked over in the direction, I was indicating and for some reason, a strange look crossed her face.

"Who, Assata? Girlll, that's a nigga you need to stay clear of!"

I looked at her with inquisition in my eyes. She looked like she wanted to drop the subject but knew I'd just get the fuck up and go ask someone else, so in reluctance, she explained.

"Mani, you know, you're my girl but Assata is spoken for—well—kinda," she said, exhaling. "You remember my girl, Jazz, we're always talking about?" I looked at her like yea, what the fuck about her? She rolled her eyes and continued. "Well, that's her dude. But right now, she's—umm—she's dealing with some heavy shit, right now. Let me put you onto something real quick though, this between me and you—understand?"

She stared at me waiting for confirmation like we we're making some type of high profile pact. I nodded my head in agreement. "I'm serious, Armani, this can't leave this table." My intense stare told her she was pissing me off with her procrastination.

"Look, Mar, is my girl and all but you gotta watch her. She's a serpent with a capital 'S'! She did some real foul shit too, Jazzy because Mar has had a thing for, Assata since we were little. Now that she thinks that, Jazzy is out of the picture, she has her eyes set on Satta. It would be in your best interest to watch her, and by all means stay away from that man over there," she dropped the bomb on me.

I was thinking, 'What the fuck?' I was still lost and not giving a fuck about what Tessa said regarding Mar. They were best friends and she was sitting there telling me all her girl's dirty little secrets. I was new to the circle and sure she liked me. But you don't spit on your girl's name like that, especially if you were in her face every day smiling like shit was all good. If I felt like that about one of them, I'd just pull 'em to the side and let 'em know the real. I was 'bout to say this to Tessa until Marcella stumbled out of the restroom, with what appeared to be tears staining her pretty face.

She power walked to the table. "Tessa, oh my God, can you please take me to the hospital? Something happened to my grandmother, I need to be there for her," she cried.

Tessa jumped up and wrapped her in a tight embrace—fake bitch! "Yes, you know, I got you, girl, you ready?"

Marcella nodded. Turning to a table over, Tess told Twisted what was up but it wasn't no need because all eyes were on Marcella. My heart went out to her as pain radiated from her body language.

"No pressure, lady, take care of your girl. I'll see you when you shake loose." He respected her space as they made their exit.

Mar turned to me, "Armani, can you come with us? I need my girls?"

I got up and grabbed my Balenciaga bag without hesitation. "Say less, girl." Together we left to support our girl's folks. At least that's what I thought.

***

~Assata~

"I really enjoyed your company, Assata, maybe we can do it again sometime soon," Free said, as we stood on her porch not knowin' how to cap the night off.

Well, I knew exactly how to end the night, but I didn't think that would be a good suggestion on the first date—if that's what you called it. Fuck all this teenage nervous shit, I stepped into her space, wrapped my arms around her waist, and pulled her into me. I placed my forehead against hers and let her see the beast hidden in my pupils.

"Listen, lady, I'm not trying to push and shove—no pressure on my end, but I'm digging you. Not saying I'm ready for relations cause, I'll just end up fuckin' something up cause—" I took her hand and placed it on the side of my chest where my heart was 'pose to be. "Cause, I don't have nothing here, life stole my innocence and left an animal inside me, Free, but even the beast needed the beauty to find that prince that lived inside of him." Without her consent, I placed my lips against hers then slipped my tongue between those juicy ass lips.

First, surprise caused her to tense up, but after a few seconds she wrapped her arms around my neck and obliged. I swear, I ain't the typa nigga that goes around smoochin' bitches, it was either this or get real barbaric and pop one of those juicy ass titties out and try my luck. So, I figured this would be safe and way more civilized. She broke the kiss with a soft moan and placed her hands against my chest.

Then she stepped back just a little to give our bodies a bit of space, before we did exactly what she spoke of in her poem, and combusted. She flashed those sexy ass dimples and for the first time, I noticed the braces. Maybe I had noticed them before, but was too entranced by the rest of her to give a fuck, now that I saw 'em it was ova with! It was just something about a woman with braces that turned me on.

"Assata—uhh—thank you for the—the umm. The beautiful way to end the night but I really need to get to bed. You know—work in the a.m."

I rubbed my hands over my waves. I had to mentally tame my nature. I wanted this lady—needed to bury this aggression inside her. But I knew she wasn't the typa woman a nigga could just run up in. She was a rare typa bitch period, without another word I turned to leave. She grabbed my wrist preventing me from leaving, so I turned back facing her.

She said some shit I'd never forget. "Black man, a woman is like a handful of diamonds. Let's say, out of the whole handful, only one is actually real? Let's say you cock your arm back as far as you can, and throw that handful of diamonds out into the world? Then you take on the journey of finding that one real one, let's say one by one you find everyone but the authentic one? Baby, just because it seems you'll never find it, doesn't mean it's not out there to be found. Peace, God, oh and by the way, I'll cry for that little ghetto boy."

***

~Tomorrow~
5:00 a.m.

As I stumbled outta the after-hours, I was on my ass. The majority of my niggaz had either went home to their wifey or crept off with one of the jump offs. Me and Dino had two lil' freaks that went to one of the universities, which one, I couldn't recall. But I do know, I was 'bout to run up in one or—maybe both of 'em, depending on the alcohol.

"Damn, folk, it's chilly as a mu'fucka," Dino exclaimed.

I was so busy watching the bitches booty cheeks as they walked in front of us, that I ain't even notice the hawk—until some heat lit up the night. The yella broad in front of Dino flew backward. The only indication that something was wrong, was the sound of that pipe sounding like a helicopter blade, as it spits fire at us—well that and the yella hoes face missing. I sobered up real quick. You can call me a hoe ass nigga or whatever, but I snatched the dark skin shawty into a choke hold, attempting to use her as a shield. I knew that wasn't gonna stop no major heat, but it served its purpose as lil' one's head snapped back like Mike Tyson had punched her in the face.

She got two heavy to hold, so I dropped her and up the Nina, letting loose blindly as I ran for cover. Diving across the hood of a grey Buick, the spray of bullets that zigzagged across it after me, told me that whoever was gunnin' for us was fa'sho wit it! Damn— fuck was Dino—God must be ready to beef cause as soon as the thought crossed my mind. I spotted Dino on one knee letting off with two pistols screaming some shit I couldn't hear over the thunderous gunfire. He had blood spilling from his lips and in live motion, I watched my niggaz head bust open, and his body jerk at the same time.

Heat filled my eyes as four blue-bandanna clad niggaz ran up on him. A big nigga stood over fam and emptied the whole clip. I heard the gun click as sirens interrupted the night. Three of the niggaz take off.

"Let's go, Cuz—the boys on the way," someone yelled.

Big dude pulled the bandanna from over his face and pointed the empty gun in my direction, then he smiled and disappeared into the night. Vengeance swam into my veins as I remembered the pussy ass nigga that stood in the line wit' the Rick Ross beard—the nigga that laughed like he knew the world's biggest secret!

Renta

Chapter Nine

Shit Done Got Real
~Ice-Berg~

Ever since I revealed my identity to my lil' homies Twisted and Lil Joe things have been bitter sweet. My lil' cuz Twisted was getting comfortable in his position of power, and truthfully it suited him, so me showing up didn't blow over to well, as he'd gotten used to the idea of me being dead and him taking the reins. But once I was able to prove, I was who I proclaimed to be, he had no other choice but to hail to the king. It was either that or die for something he'd one day get back. The nigga was family, but if I could kill my sister, a woman who came outta my mama's pussy. I would do the same to my uncle's son.

I sat at the head of the long oak placed in one of the dining rooms of my new seventy-five hundred square foot home, my mind carried me back to the day I first laid eyes on the opulence of Russia's mini-mansion. I vowed I'd have that shit, I knew I was destined to be a boss. The five bedroom, four bathrooms, and Akee wood floors was merely the appetizer to the main course, which was the shark tank I had built into my floor.

I had five baby sharks that inhabited it as the tank ran a curving trial throughout the house in the form of a river ending in the master bedroom. The glass enclosure made it look as though, you were walking on aqua water and my five pets. It was danger trapped within a place of beauty.

"Say bruh, you shoulda saw how that boy thinking cap exploded when we hit him with the whole sixteen, Cuz. I just wish I coulda got the sucka that dove over the car as well," D-Kuz raved as if he didn't get the wrong nigga.

My grey eyes flicked over to Twisted for less than a second. "Cuz, you didn't get ya man's! Now, not only will the niggaz be on alert, but now it's about to be a war! We don't even know for sure it was them niggaz that wet the block up, and to top it off, yo' stupid ass revealed yo' face to the nigga Tomorrow like he ain't a killa. That nigga may be young, but he's as vicious as the Chucky Doll."

I sniffed the imported cigar filled with Perique. My mouth watered at the thought of the strongly flavored black tobacco from Louisiana. "You missed ya man, fam. Now, Pain and Assata will be gunnin' for us."

Fear registered on his face, as I leaned to the left and allowed one of my henchmen to light my new addiction.

"But—but, I— I got—"

"Tha wrong mu'fucka!" I slammed my hand onto the table. "It's groovy tho, Hoova—you'll get 'em next time."

"Yea, you know, I won't fuck up like that no more, Cuz—that's on, OG—"

His words were cut short by the thin line of razor wire Twisted looped around his neck. The surprise was evident, as he tried to get his hands up under it, but that only made it clinch into his neck deeper. Hell burned in Twisted's eyes as he salivated for the kill. Through a fat cloud of smoke, I watched the fight for dominance between life or death, Twisted thirsted for death, but D-Kuz was dehydrating to live.

"Yea, Cuz, you will get 'em, but it will be in the next life where they'll join you. First though, purgatory. You'll take the same journey Dunte Alighieri took in his poem, *'The Divine Comedy'*," I hissed, as death took the lead on the will to live.

D-Kuz was a big dude so Twisted had to work a little, but as homie's eyes went white and the spasms ceased. I could tell all them push-ups family did in lock-up paid off. A thin sheen of sweat covered his face, as he had to force the wire out of the deep ravine that it sliced into dude's larynx. The eight men sitting there with me didn't seem to enjoy it at all.

"Gentlemen, when I say get ya mans—*You get your fuckin' manz!* If you whacked the whole house, you better be sure you get the people you came for!"

Twisted sat at the head of the table opposite of me, looking as if the kill had given him life. I smiled at fam, he was gonna make a good boss one day. I snapped my fingers, the room suddenly buzzed with the activity of my in-house staff, that filled the table up with specially prepared dishes.

"You cats enjoy your breakfast." I turned my eyes to look over at D-Kuz slumped over in his seat, his head was back, with the inside of his neck revealing.

I realized that life had fucked me up, damn Nutz, I warned you, Cuz.

***

~Pain~

"Oh—my—fucking—G—G—God!" Tessa screamed as I dug in that pussy.

I held her ass cheeks open and short stroked the pussy, as she played with her clit. The lil' bitch had just enough for me to hold on to as I did my thang, she threw it back at a pimp as I watched the pussy swallow me like a starved feline.

"Put—put your thumb in my ass, Daddy!" She was going stupid on the dick.

I put my thumb in my mouth, then pushed it against her exit wound, like butter it melted inside and locked around my knuckle gently, yet firm. I pulled my dick out halfway and drove balls deep—as hard and fast as I could.

"Ye-yeah—give it to me, Daddy! Oh, I'm—give—shit! Jesus—I'm 'bout—to—cum on this dick," she whined, as she tried to crawl away from the savagery I was putting on that fat mu'fucka between her legs.

She released sexy whines from her lips as my nuts tightened. My third leg throbbed as my eruption rushed through my body like a butted train with no breaks. I lifted my eyes from the sight of her shaking ass cheeks. I fell into a frenzy and looked over at Marcella as she stared at us. Her fingers were wet with her juices as she feverishly played with that monkey. I damn near saw stars as my soul exploded from my dick like it was cast out by Jesus himself. A loud moan caused me to look over at Mar as the last drop of my seed emptied into Tessa's essence.

Her eyes were somewhere in the back of her head and for the hundredth time, I asked myself why these hoes were acting like we couldn't all do us merely cause they were best friends? They had prolly done more than this before but now they were on the *'we got limits trip'*. Some females never ceased to amaze me. I wished we wouldn't have dropped Armani's thick ass off, but shorty wasn't with it. She seemed fucked up 'bout something but shit—it was what it was. I pulled out of Tessa and fell face first into the mattress on my last leg.

"Uh-hmm—nigga, you got me fucked up," Tessa laughed. "I know this pussy ain't put yo' lil' ass to sleep—not you— *'Mr. I'ma put that ass to bed'*," she teased.

Marcella grabbed her clothes and headed from the bathroom. "Bitch, if you're gonna be fuckin' this nigga and riskin' yo' life with Twisted's crazy ass, you better get used to it, cause Pain's sorry ass gets lazy when he got that brown liquor in his liver." That's all I heard before my lights faded to black—shit had just got real!

***

~Detective Hunter~

"Motherfucker, what the fuck, Hunt? Why didn't we call this in? They just murdered that man in cold blood and we just sat back and let it happen," Winslet hyperventilated.

I placed the binoculars in my lap and bit into the jelly roll, I'd purchased for the wait. Jelly dribbled onto my white button up, I used my hand to clean it up as best as I could. I looked over at Winslet, the expression on her face was a mixture of disgust and horror.

"Winslet, have you forgotten, I'm on disciplinary leave for the botched arrest of James Swanson," I asked heatedly. "We sat here and watched them commit murder because for one that's one less murderer that we have to deal with. Two our mission is on a much larger scale than what we just witnessed, and last but not least, the undercover work you're about to do for me won't blow over too well, if you would've jumped out like you're a female version of

Alex Cross." The confused look on her face prepared me for the war of words about to ensue.

"*Undercover work?* What undercover work?" she exploded.

"You're about to infiltrate Assata Jackson's circle. He's the key to finding the scumbag, David Swanson. We have to bring these guys to their knees. Our dear city depends on—me being reinstated, Winslet. I need you to back me on this partner. I can't pull it off without you." Before I could even finish pleading my case, she shook her head.

"No—I'm not having anything to do with this, Hunter. This is absurd! I will not place my job, nor my life on the line for your crazed obsession with a ghost. We both saw that house—the blood stains. The shell casings—the man is dead, Hunt—dead. Now if you want to get your job back, I suggest you go to your superiors and plead your case. You have a license to your own practice, fight for it. Don't keep shoveling shit on top of the fresh batch you've already wiped your ass from. We've been working together for a long time, Hunter, I've always respected you as an upright officer of the law, don't make my belief a past particle."

A wicked smile creased my lips, "Oh, you'll do it—in fact, you'll do it and like it," I growled. "If not, the whole force between here and Fort Worth will know your dirty little secrets.

***

~Armani~
Two days later

"Mami—Mami—Mami, Aunty Kris is here. Mami—Mami—wake up!" My five -year old daughter jumped up and down on my sleigh bed, on the verge of making me pop her lil' ass.

"Bitch, you still sleep? It's two in the afternoon! What time you get off last night? I know them niggas wasn't throwing that many dollars," My sister Kristasia laughed, as her black ass opened my drapes to let some light into my room.

I groaned in frustration as an instant headache made me squeeze my already closed eyes tighter. "Bitch, why you gotta be so loud, Kris?" I pouted like a lil' girl, then threw back the comforter, and stumbled out of bed. My ass cheeks jiggled with each step and since I'd slept in nothin' but a t-shirt and thong, it wasn't no controlling it. "Arugh, you get on my nerves, Kris!" I slammed the door to the bathroom and shook my head at my sister's laughter.

The night had been long indeed. I did overtime at the office building I worked at, in downtown Dallas. At 6:30 p.m., I rushed into class ten minutes late. If that wasn't enough, I made it home just in time to take a quick shower and get to the club before them thirsty hoes I worked with sucked all the money up. By the time, I made it home, it was two o'clock in the morning and I had to be at my primary job at five! Shit, I had to call in! I washed my hands and splashed cold water on my face to wake up.

As I looked up into the mirror, my Nubian skin radiated, but my eyes contradict my beauty. I was so sleep deprived, I knew, I'd have an old face before the age of thirty-one if I didn't slow my ass down. I popped an Advil and stepped back into my room to find my bed made, and my sister in my closet flipping through my clothes. "What the fuck! Kristasia, did I forget to tell you, you get on my nerves?"

She burst out in her goofy ass laughter as she exited the closet, right as I laid across my bed. She threw a skin-tight pink Marchesa gown, and a pink and gold pair of Zanotti, shoes elevated with pistols for a heel on the bed also.

I looked at her confused. "Girl, you know you can't fit my clothes. All that ass you got, you'll bust my shit. If you do, that ass is coming off some of that money you and that nigga got put up for that wedding!"

She merely rolled her eyes. "Mani—why the hell would I need to squeeze all this ass in one of your dresses when I have a closet filled with clothes I haven't even worn yet? No, sweetheart, this is for all this ass to squeeze into," she said, as she slapped me on my bare ass cheeks reminding me I was still in my thong and t-shirt.

I scrunched my nose up, she must had shit confused! "Uhh, I'm not going anywhere, Kris. I have a ton of homework to do and I got so much shit to do here that I've been putting off. I—"

"Bihh, miss me with the extras. We're going to the block party in the Kreek. You better be ready by three. We ain't kicked it together since I started my business." I had to laugh, as she gave me her best puppy dog look. I loved my girl, she knew, I couldn't tell her no.

***

~Assata~

The block was on and popping as I pulled up in the Kreek in this wine red painted monster. The 2018 Navi was squatting on twenty-eight-inch chrome, big heads that was blinding as I pulled to a stop in front of my Aunt Pearls house. The high and lows flooded the interior of the truck as J. Cole's *'Three Wishes'* beat so hard from the push of the subs in the back. It was hot as a bitch, so I had a forest green bandanna tied around the fresh, high, bald-fade I'd just got this morning. I was shirtless a usual, after enduring all the pain for this ink on my skin, I'd better show it off.

I was dressed in tan Gucci shorts that cuffed at the bottom revealing the forest green and red Gucci pattern, that also accentuated the forest green Gucci shoes with the tan Gucci logo. You already know my ice game was sick! Kush smoke snaked from my lips, and as I observed my corner through rose-tinted Versace lenses. One thing became powerfully evident, more than it had ever been. My people had become complacent with dire circumstances, the ghetto!

I glanced down at the Uzi 22LR in my lap, and ran my hand over the twenty-round magazine, as I wondered how did we as a people become so barbaric to the point, that in order to enjoy a sunny day in our own neighborhood, we had to have submachine guns at the ready? Somehow, the war stopped being with the mu'fuckas tryin' to keep us in the hood and started with the mu'fuckas that's 'pose to be fighting the same fight. Jarred from my thoughts, the passenger door opened, I tightened my grip on the Uzi, with a beastly look on my face.

"Damn, Damu, you safe—this our hood," Tomorrow laughed sliding in and closing the door.

"When that ever stop bullets from flyin' lil' bruh? It's in our own hood that our lives became a question," I schooled him, as I passed him the crippy that had me high as Neil Armstrong. I laughed, as he tried to big chest that bidness and damn near coughed up his lungs.

"Fuck this, bleed?" He asked between coughs.

I rocked with lil' bro, he was a troopa! "That's that new shit everybody talmbout, fam. That bidness needs to come with a warning sign, huh?" I laughed, as he handed it back like it was the plague.

"You ain't never lied, big homie, but bleed this the traps been jumping and you ain't picked up none of your dust. You got niggaz sittin' on ya bread like they don't steal no more."

I glanced out the tinted windshield, I had to admit that since I came outta that coma and found my world upside down, my dope money had been the last thing on my mind.

"Yea—go figure, fam. Boys do steal and I'm not saying they won't test me, but I am saying most of 'em ain't got a GED let alone a high school diploma. Testing me will only earn them a 'D' on their report card, the 'D' on death," I said, as I opened the door and slid out of this gorgeous designed machinery.

I had the Uzi in hand and the blunt in the other. I wanted boys to see how long the clip was. They already knew I'd use every round, on my mama!

***

~Armani~

By the time we got to the block, it was going down! I got out of my pink and black Buick Regal Sports-back. Me and Kris instantly became the center of attention. I had to switch my attire from the ridiculous assemble that Kris had picked out. I wasn't about to be on my feet all day in those heels and these block parties always came with the bullshit, so I refrained from wearing the dress as well. Instead, I opted for something more leisured and comfortable. A simple pink skin-tight Couture tee cut off right at the bottom of my titties, allowing just enough of them to hang from the bottom, so niggaz would be staring at all day in hopes that they spill all the way out.

The diamond in my belly button glistened in the sun, as it dangled from a thin chain. The pink Couture boy shorts that hugged every curve, were pulled up enough so that the print of my monkey winked as I walked, but the sexiest thing about these French cut shorts was the word Couture written across the back. As they slid between my cheeks. I could only imagine how many niggaz stared in an attempt at deciphering what it said. Last but not least, the pink white-on-white Air Forces I wore, with no socks complimented my attire.

Kris was just as hoochie as I was in a white see-through military jumpsuit, with nothing under it but stickers in the shape of stars over her nipples and a blood red thong. The Brian Atwood heels she had on was fierce as she strutted beside me.

"Girl, Art, is gonna put his foot in your ass if he sees you out here showing off his goods," I said as we walked down the block just sight-seeing.

"Bihh, please, that nigga know, I ain't trying to hear none of that," she sassed. "Besides, he knows this pussy all his. He better not try to get active out here. Say, ain't that Mar and Tessa nem over there?" She pointed in the direction of Bonnie's house.

I rolled my eyes and got heated all over again. I hadn't fucked with them since they pulled that act at the after-hours. Armani even had Tessa fooled. When we stepped outside, out of sight of Twisted and his crew.

The conniving bitch wiped her face. "Shit, fucking water ruined my make up!"

Bewildered, me and Tessa looked at her like she had two heads. She went on to explain that the nigga Pain wanted to see Tessa, and in order to get her from up under Twisted's phycho ass, she had to do something. The look Tessa gave me screamed. *'See I told you!'* I thought she was about to spaz on the sneaky bitch for playing foul, but when Pain pulled up beside us in a black-on-black Lexus RC 350 sitting on black six's. The bitch fixed her face and looked at the nigga like she wanted to suck his dick, smiling all hard and shit.

I was fucked up that they prevented me from introducing myself to that black ass nigga, Assata.

"Assata, what's up Bitch?" Kris screamed beside me causing my heart to beat outside of my chest. How does she know him? My confusion was shadowed by my lust, as I spotted him standing with Tomorrow and Pain next to a beautiful burgundy Navigator on some of the biggest rims I'd ever seen. The thing that stole my attention away from the beauty around him was the monstrous gun in his hand.

***

~Assata~

My bro Pain had us in tears as he told us how he passed out on some pussy that he'd waited on for as long as I could remember.

"NyQuil! I'm telling you, bruh, that girl got that tucked in pussy."

Me and Tomorrow glanced at each, then turned our quizzical eyes back to him, but it was Tomorrow that asked the thousand-dollar question.

"Fuck is tucked in pussy, fam?"

Pain looked at us as if we had been living on Mars. "Bruh, it's self-explanatory, *'tucked in'*—after you come outta that wet-wet, somebody gonna have to tuck you in, on blood!"

I opened the door to the truck and laid the tool on the ostrich interior.

"Assata, what's up biiitch?" A loud female's voice made me smile.

I turned to see my homegirl who's like a sister to me coming straight for me. This bitch was thick in all the right places. She had long, jet-black hair, with a ridas ambition. She's a boss niggaz prayer. We had never crossed that invisible line where there was no turning back and we never would. She was my peoples and I respected her too much to shoot at what was between her legs, but it was a plus cause all her homegirls were game for a live nigga.

"What the b-i, bihh," I said, as I pulled her into my embrace.

"Nigga, why you ain't call to check on me? You know, I've been worried about you ever since I heard what happened. I came up there, but I doubt you knew that. They told me only family was allowed. Yo' gal, Jazzy, said she would tell you, but I bet her stuck up ass ain't tell you shit!"

My face instantly balled up. "That ain't my gal, fam—and naw, I didn't know you came. But, I love you for the love, my nigga." I tapped my chest with my fist as an indication of feeling that shit in my heart.

"Oh, excuse moi," she said sarcastically. "I heard she was your gal, at least that's what the hood says."

"Damn, Kristasia, you don't see nobody else, but Satta or something?" Pain barged his jughead ass in my mix. She turned her gaze to him and rolled her eyes. "Sup, Pain—you okay?"

"Shid, I would be if you let me see what's up with that tuck in," he retorted.

Me and Tomorrow burst out laughing. The confused expression painted on her face only made it more comical. She stared daggers at bro, even though, she didn't have the slightest idea what he was talkin' 'bout—she knew him! She gave him the finger, then acknowledged Tomorrow before turning her attention back to me.

"So, what's up for the night? I know your black ass got something live to get into."

Showing her what expensive teeth looked like, I shoot my regular curveball. "Shid, hopefully, one of yo' potnas! Quit playing, what's up with lil' baby you used to kick it with?"

She thought for a second. "Who—oh—Tonya? Boy please— that bitch was not good enough for you, but—" I saw an amused look ease into her features. "I think, I got somebody you will like to meet. She's my sister, but she's different she's just your type," she said, as she grabbed my hand and led me away.

"My type, what's my type, Kris, a one-night stand?" Without saying another word, she dragged me through a crowd of folks. I felt naked for some reason. Then it hit me—I forgot to grab that burna. Fuck, pussy always made a nigga forget what he was 'pose to be doing. Where he was supposed to be and, in my case, that I got enemies.

Chapter Ten

Pieces of The Puzzle

"Mama, you have a package at the door. They want you to sign for it, they won't let me," Mena yelled to her mom.

Ma Duke came quickly to the door as if she had been awaiting the package. She stood curious to know what it could be as the took the package to be signed. She gazed at the mail man in question and handed him back the signed document. With no name on the package, you saw her mind wondering as her face wrinkled. Ma Duke grabbed the package then closed the door.

Mena rushed back to her room as frustration surged through her veins. Her mind carried her back to the argument that her and Lil' Joe had before he dropped her off at home. She'd been having a bad feeling all day. It wasn't anything specific, it was just one of those women things that couldn't be explained. She felt it in her limbs and to top it off, her brother Qua had been missing for days. To some, that may not be anything to set off alarms, but for her brother that was unusual.

His phone kept going to voicemail and his baby's mom as well. Today she planned on driving out to Lewisville to check on them, yet she felt something bad was gonna happen. She couldn't quite put her finger on it, but she just knew. Her nerves got the best of her, she took her iPhone off the dresser and plopped down on her bed, knocking some of the many stuffed animals she'd collected over the years onto the floor. She held the number one down as the word *'Baby'* popped onto the screen.

Turning onto her back and staring up at the ceiling, the ringback tone played the song *'Juice'* by *'Yo Gotti'*—on the second ring he picked up with the music blasting.

"Sup, fam—don't be in my ear with all that crybaby shit. I told you I'll be there to get you after I get back from the Cliff." He got straight to it before she could even tell him the reason she was calling. Now that she was sure he was peace, a big smile formed on her lips as her free hand twirled a lock of her hair around her finger.

"Boy, miss me with that big boy spiel. You know, you're missing this wet-wet—don't be Cubic Zirconia."

"Fuck that mean, Mena?"

"Fake, nigga—Cubic Zirconia is a fake gem—don't be fake," she said with humor in her voice.

"Yea, whatever, bitch you know I'm missing that. But let me focus so them boys don't sneak up on me. I'll get at you when shit nice, boo."

"Alright, baby, make sure you be safe, Lil Joe, I don't feel right. I told you not to go, but whatever. Just make it back to me, okay?"

"Lady stop all that stressin'—I'm at you in traffic," he said and disconnected the call.

"Arrgh, I hate when he does that shit! Always hanging up the phone without saying, *'I love you'*," she fumed.

As she scrolled through her call log, she tried her brother again, as soon as the voicemail clicked on, shrilled screams of her mother, forced her off the bed into a full sprint to the living room. What she found discombobulated her at first. Her Ma Duke laid balled up in the fetal position as she retreated in one herself. The only words that Mena could decipher were the ones that closed her heart and opened up a furnace of hate.

"My poor—poor baby—not my baby—nooo, Lord—not my Qua!"

She cried a heartbroken melody that only those who loved her could dance to.

Mena was confused as she rushed over and dropped to the floor beside her mama, she shook her and cried. "Mama—ma—what's wrong—talk to me!"

Her only response was the same repeated words. "Nooo, Lord Jesus—not my babbby—not, Qua, God—Nooo!"

Mena's eyes watered without consent. Something terrible had happened to her brother, but what? She released her moms, attempting to stand, but her world turned upside down and it appeared as if she was walking on the ceiling—or maybe the house had shrunk—nothing made sense, except one thing. Her Ma Dukes hands were bloodied with a stomach-turning stench emitting from them. There in her hands, clutched closely to her bosom was half of Qua's face.

***

~Assata~

She pulled me pass the porch where the O.G. Hub was workin' the grill, then we stopped in front of a group of thots on my Aunt Pearl's porch.

"Heeyyy, Assata," They all said in unison.

Well, all except one, a chocolate skinned female, with a body that would make a preacher fornicate, lil' baby acted as if the God wasn't standing before her.

"Mani, I want you to meet somebody—this is my boy, Assata. Satta, this is my little sister, Armani," Kris introduced.

Ms. Lady scanned her eyes over me in a quick assessment. Shid—I ain't knockin' it, my shit scanned over her curves. I knew she saw through the lenses of my shades and could recognize the hunger of the beast residing behind the playrisms of my nature. I reached over and took her hand into mine, without an invite or consent. She wanted to fight it but the soft, yet firm grip I had demanded her undivided attention. I wouldn't accept nothing less.

Ever the bold nigga, I stepped into mama's space. "Dig, queen, you can front all you want, but God sees it all. Your nonchalance is cute, but don't let it cause us to miss out on what maybe something that can last forever. Within the first five minutes of a nigga, a woman knows if she will fuck him. So, that means if you shave two and a half minutes off that five, that leaves two and a half minutes to know if she is attracted. So, what's up ma?"

Her slightly slanted eyes bored into mine as an amused expression eased onto her face. "How long you been practicing that line?"

I laughed. "Shid, maybe my whole life or maybe they were just manifested from me being willing to say or do anything to spark your interest. Either or, do you fault me for being willing to do it all to win you ova. At least the God should get an 'A' for effort!"

The fight was lost. The smile on her chocolate face told me that much, but what was more evident was the clouds that rolled in Marcella's eyes—fuck.

***

~Detective Winslet~

Maneuvering through the thick crowd, she spotted her target. Three of them actually. Bennie Weatly a.k.a Goose, Dunte Jackson a.k.a Pain, and Tomorrow Lawson. All three stood next to a white Benz truck. Goose was in the driver's seat with the door open. His long dreads were held back from his face by a navy-blue bandanna. His eyes were observant and it was a guarantee that he had something inside that truck ten times more dangerous than his stare. I placed myself in plain view of the crew as I tried not to look too out of place, yet conspicuous. Taking out my phone, I texted the other piece to my puzzle, but as I waited the impatience in my stance spoke volumes. Yet, that was just to the naked eye.

Truthfully, I was disgusted with my attire. I had on a one-piece short suit. The hem of it was cut so high, I expected my ass cheeks to spill out at any minute. I stood five- foot ten, six-one in the Valentino heels. I looked like a tall prostitute. My usual ponytail was gone, and my hot-combed hair hung loosely around my face, it was bleached white with streaks of black giving it life. I had the front of the one-piece zipped down to the center of my chest, to allow the firmness of my breasts to wink at whoever cared to look. To complete my ensemble, I made sure to spray an extra spray of Prada La Femme onto my breasts. The gold glitter lotion that moisturized my body had me looking like a paper sack brown goddess.

"Sup, babe, what's yo' name?" A chubby, afro wearing ape crowded my space. I attempted to ignore him and pasted a look of irritation on my face. "Come on, sweet cheeks, don't be like that. I'm just tryin' to get those digits," his corny behind tried to spit game.

I almost laughed in his face, but instead, I elaborately twisted my neck in a snaking motion trying my best impression of one of those ghetto chics. To the naked eye I was giving him a piece of my mind, but to him, I said, "Tony, you have to at least try to be smooth. You got to have better lines than that! Digits—they stopped saying that back in the early nineties." Tony was one of the best undercovers in the unit. To take down these boys I needed all the help I could get.

"Winslet, I'm already sticking my neck out for you, don't add insult to the humiliation of an upstanding cop!" He smirked in a way that seemed as if he found my theatrics amusing. I frowned and rolled my eyes in faux irritation.

"I owe you one, but put your game face on, my knight in shining armor is headed our way," I said, smiling internally that our plan worked.

"Sup, Ms. Lady, this sucka bothering you?" Goose asked, with his hand close to the bulge of his waist.

Lord, please don't let blood spill.

***

~Over on Hic Street~
Hours Later

The trap was jumpin' as *'Jeezy'* played from the system in the living room, *'If Them Birds Could Talk'*, had the atmosphere set for the hustle. As he stood over the counter and held the top of the blender in place, he watched the lactose and heroine mix blend. Twisted nodded his head as

'Jeezy' spoke the Gospel. Lil' Joe sat at the table with a blunt in his mouth, as he watched the money machine flip through a stack of bills, separating eighty-grand that was already stacked on the table before him, neatly piled into banded stacks. The vibration of his phone jarred him from his task, yet without taking losing focus, he pulled it off of him and took a quick glance, then tossed it on top of the eighty bands. He exhaled a cloud of smoke and shook his head at Mena's constant calling. She knew he hated to be disturbed while tending to his B-I, but the bitch had called ten times in the last thirty minutes.

"Fam, this bitch, Mena, getting on my nerves. She on this superstitious vibe—dumb bitch trying to ruin my vibe, Cuz. On Hoova I'ma smack her when I get done." He turned off the blender, then Twisted walked over and took the blunt out of his mouth.

"Cuz, shawty means well. You can't be fucked up about her giving a fuck about you. You coulda got one of these blood suckas that don't give a fuck 'bout you, nah mean?"

"Yea, fam, but she knows how I am about bidness, feel me?

"Yea, I feel you, bruh but what if she hittin' you 'bout something important? Ain't nobody gonna be blowin' up yo' horn like that just cause they care," Lil' Joe laughed.

"Yea, you ain't putting that dick in yours right, that's why they ain't on your jack like that!"

"Nigga, you got the Twist wrong if you don't think I handle mines. I got that stalka meat!" Lil' Joe looked at him curiously. "You know—that meat that will have 'em on stakeouts in front of ya spot," Twisted clarified, as he did a lil' jig to demonstrate his meaning. They shared a laugh.

"Naw, for real though—what's good with bro-in-law, Qua? The nigga been MIA on that thirty he owes us."

"Shid—I—"

The sound of the front window breaking ceased all conversation as both savages went for their heatas.

"Fuck, cuz," Twisted said, as he gripped the Mac 10 with the fifty-round drum on it.

The bitch was pretty with a twelve in cooling system on it. He rushed into the living room, war-ready wit' Lil' Joe at his back with an AR. Twisted surveyed the shattered window. Lil' Joe came around him and when his eyes landed on what captured Twisted intrigue. His lunch came hurling up from his stomach. Twisted turned his eyes to his potna in crime.

"Nigga, all the work we put in and you still get queasy at the first sight of a little blood?" Twisted shook his head, then turned back to the ruined floor. Half of Qua's face and what seemed to be his heart perfumed the room with a foul odor.

"I wonder where the other side of homie's face is, Cuz. I'm fucked up 'bout that thirty bands. I'd like to pick his brain to find out where it's at," he said, as he laughed at Lil Joe still spitting up the contents of his stomach.

***

~Goose~

"Thank you—thank you—um, your name is again?" She smiled a bashful smile.

"It's no need to thank me, lady, the name is Goose by the way. I noticed the distress in your body language. I had to see 'bout you. I usually don't get into other people's mix like that, but yo' sexy ass needs to be protected by superman every day!" I got on my bullshit and she blushed.

She stuck out her hand, "Pleasure to meet you, Goose. My name is Kamika."

I took her hand, interlocked my fingers with hers and pulled her to my side. I guided her towards the truck. "Who you come with, Kamika?" She rolled her eyes dramatically, seeming as if my question bothered her. She diverted her eyes to stare into the distance, it seemed as though she had something heavy on her mind.

"Just some bozo I call my boyfriend. He got mad at what I'm wearing, and as soon as my feet touched the ground, he pulled off and left me here. I'm so pissed—like really! I don't even know anyone here. I'm new to the city and this son-of-a-bitch pulls a stunt like this. I'm so through!"

I'm glad she said that, cause I'd hate to have to add more beef to an already full plate. Yet, I'm a killa, it ain't shit to me—Weatly Kourts stand up!

***

~A face in the Dark~

I knew this bitch from somewhere. I never forget a face and this bitch was looking real familiar! As I kept my distance from the crew, I had to fight to stay semi-incognito. Even though I adorned these baggy clothes and hat, some assets just couldn't be hidden. Especially, my most prominent feature, so you know the vultures were out. I lost sight of Assata when he was whisked away by that hoochie, that was out here damn near naked. I won't lie though the bitch knew how to make naked look good! I had a plate of bar-b-que in hand, as I took a seat on the hood of my car, still watching the crew through the oversized designer glasses. As I bit into a beer link, I couldn't help but observe the dude with the dreads that I'd learned was Assata's older brother.

He looked dangerous and knowing Assata if they're anything alike, I knew he was a ladies man. A sudden shock caused me to pause in midbite, my plate tumbled to the street, and my mouth hung agape—naw—couldn't be! It seemed as if she stared straight at me. Yet, that's not what fucked me up and set flame to an already chaotic situation. Even though, she'd dyed her hair, trying to pass as sexy—well, she's always been sexy, but circumstances robbed her of her flare long ago. The point was—I knew the bitch, she's a cop!

***

~Armani~

"You asked for five minutes of my time away from my girls. So, here's your claim to fame, don't waste it because I'm not average and I don't need no nigga!"

He smirked and looked at the activities of the block party, Assata acted as if my statement was never made. "It's crazy ain't it, ma? How we can burn for the opportunity—take the ghetto for instance—we yearn to escape oppression, but when the opportunity to seize that desire presents itself. We don't know what to do with it—so what we do? I'll tell you—we find pleasure in the idea of what it would be like to possess it and become comfortable within a promise that one day we will." His eyes turned to me slowly, through the designer glasses I felt how intense his stare was.

"Ma, I saw you the other night at the after-hours. How you was checking for me. I saw when you leaned into Tessa, no doubt askin' 'bout me. So, yeah, I asked for five minutes, but it's been ten and you ain't walked away yet. Physically, you get my attention, but baby girl, physical attraction only lasts so long, we all grow old." He lifted his hand to the part of my exposed breasts.

I slapped his hand away and he chuckled. "That shit right there, the way you carrying it, ma. A nigga will only respect what you show him. The way a woman dresses speaks a lot about that woman."

"So, what you saying, Assata? I'm a hoe or something, because—"

"Miss me with that," he interrupted. "Don't put words in my mouth, fam. I just jeweled you, earth, but what I am saying is, don't find pleasure in the idea of what it would be like—we have the opportunity to make it a reality."

Chapter Eleven

Plans, Blood, Betrayal
~A month later~
Nizhny Novgorod, Russia

Russia sat on the terrace of his ninety-five-hundred square foot home, staring out at the Volga River. The table before him was set for Kings, well—in this case, Russian drug lords. There were cultural dishes adorning the table, such as Frittata an open-faced omelet with cheese, mixed into the eggs rather than as a filling. Tonnarelli, Orecchiette, Trofie, and Mezzemaniche were merely a few of the cuisines on the menu. He sipped his white Negroni, as he waited for the arrival of the last member of the Black Mamba Mafia. A branch of the Russian underworld, the five present members spoke in their native tongue, as he absently rubbed his hand over the newest addition to his war wounds.

It was a three-inch scar running from the corner of his mouth, inching towards his chin. He'd acquired it during his haste to escape the brutality in Ice-Beg's room that night. He'd underestimated the young killa and lost two of his best men for the blunder. He'd almost lost his life to a fucking nigger! Every time he thought about it, the scar began to itch.

"Vor, you seem to tink hard, hmmm? Please share—" a short dark-skinned member trespassed into his thoughts.

His eyes burned into Russia's as he gorged on everything he could bet his hands on, Russia's eyes were pitiless. "I'm thinking that if you and the tiger ain't successful in the states. I'm gonna have you both castrated!"

"Guud—I'll be luuking forward to it, but until then, why don't you tell us how the son-of-a-bitch escaped you!"

***

~Assata~

A lot of niggas took life altering chances for things that will never justify the means. They found themselves buried under them white folk's prisons with the typa number that out of the seven billion people here on earth, only five or six will ever grow ole enough to see, or wind up sharp as a thumb tack with their people standin' over them sayin' their last goodbyes. All because being broke is the worst reality in the world. We go head first into shit without a limitation, and that's how niggaz find themselves doing eighty-five percent in the feds, cause they tried to make trappin' a career, rather than a means to an end.

Everybody wanted that one lick that would set them straight for life. That was exactly what I'd been plotting for the last thirty days. As I sat here with my back against my mama's headstone, I stared out at the last dying rays of sunshine. That time of the day when the Heavens were several different colors at once? More pink than blue—slightly purple—a touch of red, beautiful!

"What's good, mama? I know, I ain't been by to fuck with chu in a minute but things been crazy, Queen. Shit, honestly, I don't know where to begin. Since I'm not too sure 'bout Heaven and Hell, I don't know if you've been watching your boy. But, either or—I'm still above ground, mama. Still that same lil' nigga you left behind. It's just that now—that lil' boy is trapped in the body of a beast. Can I tell you a secret, mama? Something in me died when that nigga took you from me." Soft winds blew, as I used my fingers to unearth a handful of soil—it may be mental, but just as I pulled that little bit of dirt off of the six-feet that hid her from the pain of a gangsta, I felt just a lil' bit closer to her. I rubbed the dirt back and forth in my hands and continued to watch the sky bruise.

"I've lost a lot, ma—done a lot of shit, I wish I could rewind, but I guess life don't work like that. Yo' kids good though—we ain't close as we used to be. I guess sometimes life draws up its own conclusion. It's life, ole lady—heard you got some grandkids out there somewhere. I ain't met 'em and proly never will, but at least someone will carry the name, huh," I laughed at my own lack of emotion.

The wind seemed to blow harder and I noticed it was now kissed with a slight chill. I busted open the Garcia Vega, I'd brought for this special occasion. I emptied the tobacco onto the grass. A sun-dried leaf slapped me dead in the face as the wind kicked up a notch.

I began laughing. "Mannn, Moose, where else I'ma dump it? It's a plant too, chill," I laughed a little bit harder at the thought of my moms being heated 'bout me fuckin' up her patch of earth.

I filled the cigar leaf with this Kush they call, *'Blue God'*. I twisted and put flame to it to ensure it was all the way dry before I spared it. I took a deep pull from the gut, the potency instantly made me regret not respecting it. It felt like my soul was on fire, as I choked and tried to regurgitate the smoke. Tears were in my eyes—I got back to my T-Jones.

"Me and ole'-man's kids still thick as thieves. Pain ain't changed, and Goose on some religious shit, but them my ridas, mama. Naw, I ain't even met you no daughter-in-law. Shid, ma, I can't even find the right woman, that I can respect enough to put my seed in. These females out here weren't created to be queens mama. But, I think I've found a rida—I'll let you know how it turns out. Beyond that, Queen, the real reason I came here today is cause I need a favor. I've been planning something in my head for a while, I'm ready to put it in effect. How it's gonna turn out—that's in God's hand—or maybe the Devil's. I don't know, but what I need from you, is if you can see me—watch over me—talk to God if He's up there. Any of these things, I need it, mama. It's not a promise, I'll walk outta this with my life, and I ain't goin' to nobody's jail—never again! So, if you don't hold me down, I'ma be on my way to see you—soon. Tell God or whoever running shit up there, this is my last ride. If I succeed, Ima do shit different. If I fail, shiid, I'm comin' with a Draco and a hunnid on the drum. I'ma be mad as a bitch!"

***

~Detective Winslet~

It's been two months since the day I met Goose, and things have been real intense. I hadn't seen much, but the money I'd helped count had to have come from somewhere. Truthfully, I should have been bowed out of this insanity and went to the Board of Investigations about Hunter, but the threat he held over my head, was one I never want uncovered. I'd successfully infiltrated the circle of Bloods, and unearthed some interesting information. Just sittin' around the traps and listening to the young boys, I'd learned that there was a small war brewing.

There was some new guy speaking and supplying Hic and Oak Street. He's said to have no regard for human life. It's hard to believe that Goose or Pain are the monstrous guys they're said to be. Goose is attentive and smart, he's God-fearing and to top it all off, he's not gang-related. Pain seems kinda sneaky, always watching and quiet.

The dude Assata was never around, but his protégé, Tomorrow, seemed to be the wildest. He was the only one I'd seen deal drugs. The other day he got drunk and cried—blubbered out the shooting that transpired at an after-hours spot out on Teasley Lane. He cried and admitted to nutting up in an attempt at saving his own life, but couldn't save his homeboy, Dino's. I wondered how he'd react if he knew I was there.

"What's on your mind, partner, you seem preoccupied? Listen, Winslet, I know, I kinda forced this on you, and I owe you one. I know these guys are a dangerous bunch, but I promise you when things get too deep, I'll pull you out. You know I mean well— right?" Hunter stared out of the window as we exit the city limits.

I nodded my head in acknowledgment. The problem wasn't how dangerous they are, it was now about how dangerous I am now that my heart was in the equation.

***

~Jazzy~

These past few weeks, things had been beautiful between us. Though Assata was a constant thought, I had to place him in the back of my mind. Now, that I thought about it, maybe things turned out how they should have. I mean, Shotta was a good dude, he just had a temper. He grew up watching his father beat his mother, so he acquired a sad trait. Yet, he loved me—he has to. How else can you explain traveling thousands of miles across the states to bring me back to him?

At least that's the rationality he gave me, and it seemed quite logical. I never asked for this shit. I couldn't get Assata and Lovey killed! I didn't know how they felt. However, if there was a chance to go back to my man, I would. But, there's consequences to actions and who's to say Assata would accept me back? It's too late now anyway, I'd gotten engaged. As I stared at the three-carat solitaire, a bitter smile quirked at the corner of my lips. Charla and mama loved it—I loved it—but my heart was way in Texas. Keeping that thought, I walked into the clinic with determination in every step.

***

~Pain~

'Lil' Boosie' blasted from the boisterous speakers as Lil' Joe and Mena sat at the light on Bonny Brea. The ganja smoke was so thick that it was a wonder he could see the road. Mena had her phone in her hand texting as the track changed to, *'Oh Lord'*, one of her favorite *'Boosie'* singles. As they waited for the light to change, an elderly lady pushed an old grocery cart filled to the brim with her life possessions across the street in front of them. Due to the hunch in her back, she moved slowly as a snail. A long dingy pastel sundress flowed in the wind as she pushed along. No one noticed the backward wig on her head, but Lil' Joe.

He burst out laughing at the sight of the vagabond having the nerve to have a little dog in the cart, with a small evidently broken television. Mena rolled her eyes at his silly ass as he slapped the steering wheel in humor. His jewels glistened through the cloud of smoke, and one could tell he was getting it in. The light turned green and the old lady was still trying to lug the heavy cart across the street. Horns could be heard everywhere, but it was useless because the wheel on the cart seemed to be broken, and the old lady seemed adamant about moving it. In frustration, Lil Joe stepped out of the car with a frown on his face,

"Damn, you, old hag. I don't know why the fuck you tryin' to move this busted ass shit anyway," he growled, as he grabbed the front of the basket and yanked it out of her grasp.

To his surprise, not only did it move easily, it was also light. The little dog yelped as Lil' Joe turned his eyes to the old lady, by the time he realized the fix was in, it was too late. Granny came from under her dress with a Mac 11, equipped with a suppressor attached to it. Three short busts opened on him, flipping him. Blood erupted from the intimate wounds from the Mac, as Lil' Joe fought to hold on to life while choking on his own blood. His eyes were to the Heavens as specks of red blood blended with the freckles on his face. The old lady stood over him in broad day and stared down, then attempted to empty the remaining inhabitants of the extend into him. Lots of screams could be heard from the car as granny took off in the direction, she'd come.

Mena screamed and screamed, as she called 9-1-1, yet fear held her in place as *'Lil' Boosie'* shook the interior of the Delta 88'. *'Oh Lord/I ain't—gonna do no mo' wrong/ohh oh Lord—'* he rapped.

***

~Twisted~
Hours later

"Wait—hold up, cuz— Fuck you mean, Joe got hit?" I shouted into the phone.

"Baby, he was hit twenty-one times. He was found over there in Concrete City off Bonny Brea." Tessa wept into my ear-piece. "He was barely breathing when the ambulance got to him. I'm up here with Mena as we speak."

I was silent as a cemetery, as the devil forced himself into my veins. I couldn't cry, as I pictured my nigga laid up on some cold slab of steel.

"Twisted—Twisted," Tessa panicked in my ear.

"I know this nigga ain't hang up on me—I know not," she yelled.

"I'm here, ma," I whispered.

"I'm sorry this happened, baby. I know how close you and Lil' Joe was, but please don't do nothing stupid."

Even though I just boo'd her up, me and Tessa had been close since middle school. She'd been fuckin' wit' a nigga through it all, TYC, boot-camp, and three years in the big house. She's kept it 'G' with me. Even though, she's given her pussy to other niggaz. I knew, I always had her heart.

"Look, Tess—I'll get wit' you when I finish my issue. As a matter fact, I'll meet you up there, which hospital you say he's at?"

"We're at Regional, but baby the laws are deep. Why don't you wait till—" I hung up in mid-spiel?

Berg walked in at the end of the conversation. He was wiping his hands on a paper towel. "Who was that—fuck you lookin' like that?"

"Lil' Joe dead, fam. The ambulance picked him up on the Brea," I growled.

He looked at me like I had two heads. "Fam, dead people don't take a ride on an ambulance!"

***

~Pain~

As I stripped outta the hot ass wig and dress. I laughed at how lame niggaz could be. Hoe's couldn't be trusted, and Lil' Joe was a testament to that shit. The whole while he was fuckin' the bitch Mena, he never took the time to observe the hoe. The thing about Mena was that it was more mental than physical. When Mena found out 'bout her brother, she automatically turned to her nigga, Lil'

Joe, for solace. The nigga was so caught up in these heartless streets, he ignored her heart and guess who listened to it.

Yep! The same heartless streets. She called Tessa as she was doming me off, I heard the entire convo. From there, it was nothin' to spread a little dirt out there, knowing it would get back to her. The streets told her that Lil' Joe and Twisted rocked the nigga to bed cause he owed them some cake. Everybody knew he hustled for them boys, but what they didn't know was that he kept his bread at his mama's house, stuffed in the teddy bears his sister had all over her bed.

The dumb bitch told Tessa, thinkin' she was her girl and Tessa told me during pillow talk and a mouthful of dick. Long story short, it was nothin' to pull up on her during her moment of emotion and confusion. I offered her not only a friend but also a cold plate of revenge. She led his stupid ass to Concrete City and as I laid in wait, she texted me, and let me know their whereabouts—the rest was history!

"Damn, dawg—Kasha 'nem gonna be fucked up 'bout this shit. Lil' Joe was a good nigga, bleed—that's our, fam. I ain't gonna lie, that shit gonna sit on me for a minute," Satta said.

I looked at him as if he had got the plague, yea, Joe was our fam, but he was a beast! A beast that killed for the other side. Only a fool would feel some typa way for whacking a loose lion—twisting the cap off a Big Red. I told my brother exactly that!

Chapter Twelve

Surprise
~Assata~

After a long meeting with my hounds, and a dope-fiend named, 'Get There'. I tried to wind down, what better way to do so than by spending some time with the lady, Free? Her job whatever it was, kept her tied like shoelaces, so it was almost like trying to walk into a penitentiary with civilian clothes on to get her away for a few minutes.

"Call Freedom," I spoke into my Bluetooth. *'Calling Freedom,'* it replied. The phone rang 'bout three times before it was answered by the voice of a lioness.

"Hello?" she sang.

I ain't on no weak shit, I swear, but an instant smile formed onto my lips. "The bidness was, Goddess?" I asked.

A long whoosh of breath sounded as if she'd just collapsed into her chair. "Work—work—and more work!"

"Well, how about a break—can you do brunch—or maybe dinner?" I proposed hopefully. I swear if she puts me off again it's—

"Dinner will be fine. I'll be able to finish up at the office and take a nap before I'm whisked away by my thug in shining armor."

"Good answer."

"Huh, what you mean?" She giggled, but I thought she already understood my double meaning.

"What's understood needs no explanation—what time can you get away, ma."

"Ahhh—bossy much," she laughed merrily. "I like—I like—so let me see, I leave my métier job at five and I—"

"I'll be there to get you at eight-thirty, Ms. Lady—and Free?"

"Yes, Assata, what is it?" Free replied.

"Wear your hair down for me."

"That's peace, God, but will I be overstepping my boundaries to ask where we're going and what's the attire?" she asked.

"You've read the Bible before, Free?" I questioned.

"Of course—but what does that—"

"Everything! If you can come as you are to church, what makes any other place any different?"

"Umm— maybe because they may say that, but you'd never see anyone actually coming as they are. The church is a molten pot for fashion."

I laughed at the authenticity of her revelation.

"Surprise me, Free," I exclaimed.

"That I will do."

***

~Twisted~

When I reached the waiting area, the first thing I notice was Tessa rocking Mena back and forth in a sister embrace.

"I love him so much, Tess—I feel like—like, that shoulda been me that took those bullets—it all happened so fast. The old lady—the gun—she-she shot him! Over and over and over again! A fuckin' old lady, Tess," she wept.

Tessa consoled her the best she could. "Baby girl, this ain't your fault. If you woulda been the one to take those bullets, it woulda tore that man up. Then it woulda been meaningless because he still woulda been hurt. I know you're hurting baby, but it's gonna be okay, Joe's a strong man—he'll pull through." Tessa hugged her tighter as she inconspicuously wiped her own tears away.

Twisted watched the scene before him with an aching heart. As the whole, Hic and Oak Street poured into the room. A beautiful red-skinned woman with a face kissed by freckles appeared, surrounded by a gang of blue bandanna clad men and women. Her eyes were bloodshot, but alert. I rushed to embrace her, with water in my eyes. I could only hold her and share in the heartbroken melody that played between two mu'fuckas brought together under a seal of loyalty for one thing—revenge! She wrapped her arms around my neck, placed her lips inches from my ear, and spoke in a sotto voice.

"Twisted, I raised you boys from lil' locs. We all knew the consequences of the life we live. My baby is a gangsta, he wouldn't want us to be on all this emotional shit, when we can be using our time on something more productive, like finding the sons-of-bitches who has him in there fighting for his life. I want you to find 'em, baby. Find 'em and make their whole family pay in blood and tears for what they've done to my son," Ms. Pearl proclaimed in anger.

She took my face in her hands, her bloodshot eyes revealed a mother's pain, but also the danger that she tried so hard to bury. As our eyes communicate what our lips shouldn't, an Asian doctor walked over to us with alarm in his eyes. The waiting area was filled with gangstas and every one of us had the taste of blood in our mouths, so his fear was warranted. Denton's finest was ever present, and as Pearl faced the doctor, she whispered to one of her three daughters to clear some of the niggaz out.

"Are you the family of Joseph Williams?" the doctor asked.

"Yes, we are, doctor—I'm his mother and the others are brothers and sisters. How's my child, doc?"

A skeptical stare was plastered on his face, as he glanced in the officer's direction and stuttered as he asked— "Can we step into the back Ms.—Ms.—"

"Pearl—Ms. Pearl—and no, we can't step anywhere doctor. Why don't you just give it to us straight, so we can skip all the extras."

One of Denton's finest walked up with his hand on the butt of his weapon. "Is there a problem, Doc?"

My face balled up instantly. "Say, Cuz—" I growled.

Pearl put her hand up. "Never mind this Uncle Tom ass nigga, Twisted!" Her eyes locked onto the officers. "If you woulda been that quick to do your job. My son wouldn't be laid up in this hospital fighting for his life. You mu'fucka always come around after the fire, but you shoulda came around when you saw the smoke!" Spit flew from her mouth, as she was now inches away from the officer's face with no fear. Pearl rolled her eyes at the officer and addressed the doctor. "Now, Doc—how is my fuckin' son?"

Fear etched the doctor's features, he looked to the heated cop then back to Pearl. "I'm sorry— he didn't make it."

"Nooo," Kasha, Joe's sister screamed, as she crumbled to the floor. Fam attempted to calm her, but she was inconsolable.

Mena came and stood by me. "He didn't make it, did he?" Tears were already in her eyes and her body language read my answer before I could even speak. I shook my head in confirmation, she turned and ran out of the room. As I stared at the destruction around me, I wondered why real niggaz had to go? Berg leaned against the wall seeming to be in deep contemplation. I made my way over to him and his eyes lifted to mine.

"What's crackin' dig, I ain't gonna sit here and act like I feel yo' pain cause I don't know how to feel that shit no mo. I done lost so much that my feelings fucked up. I can say that yo' tears are mine and when my tears fall, revenge is the only remedy for me," Berg stated in anguish.

I looked at my big cousin. "Something ain't right, fam—fuck was homie doin' in Concrete City?"

***

~Asatta~

I valeted the G-5 at the curb—Betty Wright knocked at mid-levels as I observed the scenery. It was a clear night, the moon looked as if someone tied a rope around it and pulled it closer to her Victorian themed home. The terracotta roof, shined under its illumination, giving off a wet glow. The stars looked like small diamonds on a velvet cloth, it made me want to take my horn out, snap a few pictures, and send them to Jazz—she loved the stars. Then it hit me, and my chest turned cold as I was reminded of the betrayal, the fuckery! My horn vibrated on my hip, snappin' me out of my regret. 'Chocolate' flashed across the screen.

"What you know about it, mama?" I answered.

I heard the smile in Armani's voice. "Nothin', what you doing, bae?"

I glanced at the house and reclined my seat to get comfortable for the wait, and to vibe wit' lil' baby. Over the past few weeks, me and lady had been rocking kinda tough. I fucks with her hard body, but I'd noticed something was off 'bout baby. Naw, not no ill snake shit, but bipolar—nigga. I'll bleach yo' clothes, bust yo' windows—but I love you with every breath I got typa shit.

"Assata, you hear me?" she yelled.

"My fault—I'm tending to some business—what's good wit' you, ma?"

"You always tending to business—don't forget you added a little more to your plate. A businessman can't start businesses all over town and forget to tend all of them. Each one adds something to your success. So, you invest your attention equally!"

I chuckled lightly as I listened to her philosophical humor. "Let me find out I got you open, Chocolate?" She did this little sexy ass laugh as *'Playas 'Cheers to You'* came on.

"Chocolate, huh? I like that, yeah Satta, you got me open, boy. Open like a Super Wal-Mart, but I will close if I ain't yo' flavor. I know you've been hurt by people you loved, you've told me that much, but give me my own story to create. I'm nothing like those girls—not even a little bit. Dick don't move me and it ain't shit for me to be loyal."

I reclined my seat a little further back, as I listened to Chocolate's thoughts. "Listen, I know your heart still beats for that girl—umm, what's her name?" She questioned as if I didn't know the streets had already told her.

"Jazzy," I humored her. I knew damn well she ain't forget it.

"Yeah—her—I'm cool with that because I know, I'll make you forget about her. You need to, she's showing you her caliber." Chocolate paused and with a soft voice she said, "Just don't hurt me, King."

As I laid in wait, listening to Chocolate's spiel, the door to the house opened and Heaven walked out.

"Dig, lady—we'll catch up in traffic, business is on the way. I need my undivided attention, so I don't make any mistakes."

"Um-hum—it's cool, daddy, just make sure you think about what I said. Even Wal-Mart can close if it's located in a neglected area."

"Peace, lady—if any door closes and gets locked. What you think they make master keys fa?"

***

~Goose~

I snapped the pin back into the SKS after oiling it, my mind was filled with uncertainties. Many things could go wrong. This shit Assata had planned was the ultimate last lick but intermingled with the possibility of being the ultimate fed's case or burial. It was in stone though, the squad knew their position. I trusted my lil' nigga and the heart to heart him, Pain, and I had last night at Lovey's sealed our agreement, that this would be our transition away from the game as a whole.

Shid, it was time for a change, I'm forty-three years old, and God has been talking to me for quite some time. The doorbell interrupted my train of thought. As I placed the SK under the bed, I heard Lovey at the door talking to someone. As I came around the corner she yelled, "Ben, you have a package at the door!"

"I'm right here, Lovey—stop all that yelling woman," I teased.

"Chile, you know, your ears are just as bad as mine and you're just in your forties," she giggled.

I laughed at her truths as I show my I.D. and signed for my package, some typa envelope. The aroma of Lovey's cooking made my stomach growl, so I went to where my nose led me—the kitchen. It was empty, except for the pots simmering on the stove. I sneaked over to the biggest one, removed the top, and the heat from her famous Cajun Gumbo splashed in my face. The big spoon sat on the counter. I grabbed it and dipped it into the pot, finding a few shrimps and sliced sausages. I closed my eyes in preparation of the explosive taste, my taste buds were already on fire. Steam beat the spoon to my lips and just as my mouth opened, a snapping sound could be heard before the sting.

"Ouch," I screamed, knowing what the bidness was before I even set my eyes on Lovey pulling the towel back for another pop.

The spoon was already on the floor. I ducked outta there as fast as I could, but not before she got another good pop on my arm.

"And don't you come back in here until I'm done, ya hear?" she laughed.

We've been doing this same ritual since I was a lil' nigga running wild and my big mama used to send me down here to get me out the Courts. Once I made it back to Satta's old room, I closed the door, plopping down on the bed and opened the envelope. What the fuck? The contents spilled onto the floor, as my blood boiled and something dark snaked into my veins. In Islam, it was called, Iblis—Christianity, Satan.

***

~Assata~

The candlelight flickered, casting soft shadows to dance over our faces.

"Are you two ready, to order?" the waitress smiled.

I looked at the menu. "Yes, I'm ordering for me and my lady." My direct eye contact told Free I had her.

"I'll have the Chateaubriand and mashed potatoes with brown gravy, and Moussaka and wild rice for the lady."

"Got it—anything particular to drink?" the waitress inquired.

"Yea—bring us a bottle of Chateauneuf du Pape and a bucket of ice—that will be it," I requested.

"Excellent! Coming right up, but until your meals are prepared, enjoy our complimentary amuse bouche. She pointed to the bite-sized slices of lamb. The surprise was painted all over Free's face. She placed her hand to her chest in mock astonishment.

"I'm floored— not trying to sound uncultured or as if I've never been away from home. But, I'm the typa girl that believe in asking questions when I'm lost. So—umm—what did you just order us?"

I nodded my head in understanding, I respected her realism. I leaned closer to her as if I was preparing to tell her the world's greatest secret.

"Plainly, I ordered myself a double, thick-center cut of beef tenderloin, stuffed with seasonings." I used my fork to grab a piece of the finely cut lamb and placed it in her mouth." For you, it's a Greek dish with layers of ground lamb and eggplant topped with cheese." Using the pre-set napkins on the table, I wiped the corners of Free's mouth. "I tried it last time I was here, just thought you would enjoy something different. Now, enough about our dinner, I'd rather vibe about something more intriguing."

"Like?" she asked with a smile.

"Where did the Queen, Freedom, come from? I mean, you popped outta nowhere. To top it off, the accent gives you away. What is it, East Coast?"

Her eyes twinkled. "You're full of surprises, Mr. Lamar. Yes, I'm from New York—Queens to be exact," she stated boldly.

"Why come way down here to the dirty—I mean, I ain't complaining. I'm just saying—you coulda went anywhere, but as fate would have it, you're here with me."

She looked at me bemused. "I thought we didn't believe in fate?"

"We don't—the word just fit the conversation."

She busted out laughing, "And a sense of humor—a girl could spend forever with a brotha like you. But to answer your question— fate did not bring me here. My occupation sent me here to help open another branch. After that, I'm going back home." Free took another bite of the lamb as fulfillment filled her face.

Surprise plastered my face. "Going back? But, you just said a girl could spend forever with a brotha like me. I guess forever ain't that long.

"Yes, Assata, it is but it's more to me than poetry. I can't up and pack my bags and just leave behind my family and friends back home. Besides—forever is more than the notion of time. It also consists of what we make it. The lengths we go to in order to add chapters to a story, can either be a long or created in series."

"Peace, Earth—that's deep waters I can swim in all day. But, let me ask you something."

"Shoot," she said.

"Am I your paramour or am I really this lucky to find you without God? How long have you been, Earth?" She did this little giggle that I'd grown to find delicious.

"Well, if you put it that way—it's complicated. My father is a God, but my mother was born N.O.I. My father introduced me to the Asiatic Black Man, my mother had me doing Salat. My father hated it but loved her, so he respected the fact that after she prayed to Allah, she praised her God—Him. God—do I have one? No!"

"So, you're confused?"

"Not at all, I just respect the pantheism."

"Pantheism?" she lost me with that one.

She smiled and jeweled me. "The belief in and worship of all Gods. I feel that the world was created by, Allah! The only logical explanation of existence." She saw the rebuttal before I could verbalize it. She put her hands up in the peace sign. "Peace, God—I've read Darwins 'The Descent of Man', and his 'On the Origin of Species'. I've studied True Islam's 'The Book of God'— 'The Quran', all the way down to the Bible. I can't tell you how we got here, but I'll take my chances on Allah versus an explosion."

Before I could speak, I remind myself that everyone has a right to opinion. So, I would be out of line to excoriate her for hers.

"I respect your lane, ma. I don't know how we got here either. But, I don't know the spook in the sky. Yes, I think people have the wrong perception of their studies. I know we as a people misread shit and create our own philosophy," I stared at her.

She must have taken my statement as a jab at her cause she frowned her pretty face. "I don't have—"

"Hold up, Queen," I interrupted before she allowed her anger to sink any deeper. "I wasn't speaking of you! What I'm saying is that we can create our own perspective based off of another person's facts. I'm God-body and the way I interpret the Bible and the Quran may differ from a Christian or Muslim. Take, for instance, Genesis— it speaks of God creating the Earth—vibe with me. It says, in the beginning, God created the Heavens and Earth. The story of Adam and Eve when she was taken from his rib.

"Earth, Genesis 1:2-4, the Earth was without form and void, and darkness was the face of the deep. Think of a woman before a man sticks his dick in her—her stomach is flat, right? Now—think of her stomach during pregnancy—her hips expand, her ass gets fatter, can you see it now?" I educated her.

"Yes, I see your philosophy, but darkness—explain that?"

I smiled wickedly. "While the child is in the stomach, it's dark in her womb. The child can't see—now when He separated the Heavens from the waters. It was the process of a woman's water breaking, the child slipping from her womb, and letting there be light," I said comically as our food arrived.

She laughed with me, but I could see the wheels spinning in her head.

***

~Jazzy~

As I sat with my legs spread wide open in this harness, I felt cold—lost—confused! The doctor turned to me with an empathetic smile. "You don't have to do this, Jazmina."

"Let's just get this over with. I can't take the chance of the gamble," I said, as tears cloud my vision.

His nurse looked at me in understanding, or maybe pity—either or, she said nothing. As he prepared the anesthesia, I shook my head at the doctor. "No, Doctor Lewis, I won't be needing that." A confused look was shared between them.

"Jazmina, I can't allow—"

"This is my fucking body! If you don't want to do the procedure, bring someone that will!" My emotions spilled out of me like lava from a volcano.

"You're right, Jazmina, it's your choice. Just lie back and—"

As he went into his rant about the pressure I'd feel on my abdomen and blah—blah—blah—I laid my head back as my child cried through my eyes. Something cold slid into my garden as a poem by some cat named *'Lamar Ridge'* echoed in my head.

'Love Can Sometimes be Blind'

"What made you do it, was it too much to bare?

I thought you loved me—wanted me

But now, I know you didn't care

Late nights I felt it—your pain—your pleasures—your hurt

I could feel when you shed a tear

I even heard the words as you spoke to God as you prayed for deliverance from your greatest fear

I'm part of you, that's why you always sick

I loved you with all of my small heart, that's why when you did anything wrong to your body, I'd give you a gentle kick

I knew when you and daddy had sex

I'm the reason your pleasure was so great—I'm also the reason your moods swung, the times you didn't want to talk—didn't want to be touched—didn't want to text. I even knew the time you and the other man met

But mama—I wouldn't have told daddy your secrets, we all have faults

So, mama—please stop thinking these bad things—I can read your thoughts

Today you told Daddy you were going to Granny's house confirmed my greatest fear

I guess it's because that talk you had with the doctor, you didn't know I could hear

On the way to the clinic, you silently wept

Vowed to never tell Daddy about me, so your secret will be solemnly kept

"Mommy, I love you," I screamed, as you sat on the table and savagely shook

I felt the pain as you fell asleep and the doctor yanked me out with his hook

"Mama, why?" I cry, as I lay on the floor as an embryo and begin to close my eyes
Right, as I take my last breath, I realize that in the events of my demise, love can sometimes be blind."

***

~Assata~

Again, I stood on Free's porch under the radiance of the stars and moon, the silence was thick. The silk sleeveless Tulle Oscar Delarenta mini she had on looked transparent under the pale light. Her nipples saluted ya boy, as I tried to etch each and every detail of her face into my memory, as it framed by the matching silk scarf that only allowed a peek of her hair to be displayed.

"Hard-headed," I whispered.

She looked at me confused. "I told you to wear your hair down, but you're just as classy." In the same movements, I made the first time. I wrapped my arms around her waist and pulled her close, "I thugs with you, Free, for the first time in life, a nigga wishes there was more than twenty-four hours in a day." I kissed her lips prepared to make my exit.

"L.A." She grabbed my hands and placed them on the back of her thighs—bare skin! Her hands guided mine up under her dress, my dick rocked up as they slid over her curves and silky skin—all over her ass cheeks.

"L.A means no in Swahili. La, Satta—don't leave—since you remember so much. You'll remember, you told me to surprise you," she whispered in my ear before turning to give me her tongue.

Surprised was putting it lightly—as I tongued lady. I was still trying to figure out where her panties went. Her dress was up to her waist and she was as naked under that mu'fucka as Eve was before she ate the fruit!

Chapter Thirteen

All Work—No Play—Well?
~One Day Later~

The family fell into the dilapidated building like roaches in the dark. Red and burgundy flags were tied around faces, necks, and wrists. Piru, Blood, and some Weatley Court gangsta's were on deck. Nobody knew the reason why they were summoned to the spot, but when a ten-sixty was called, niggaz had betta show up. After the last of the squad poured in, the doors shut and goons stationed themselves around the room—piped up. Everything from SKs, M4s, and .40s were locked and loaded. As they stood in the center of the madness Assata, Goose, and Pain stared out at the killas in assessment.

Goose, not being from these parts, wondered how they were gonna react to what was about to transpire. He knew just because a nigga could shoot a banana didn't make him a gorilla. Assata aimed his burna in the air and fired off three shots into the roof of the warehouse. Dawgs and civilians alike clutched their heat, yet the shots had its desired effects.

"Dig, you niggaz, listen up. This ain't no mu'fuckin' party! Every one of you boyz know what's poppin' in a few days, and ain't no bitching up now. We ain't leaving nobody behind. Nan nigga we come with get left unless he's dead! Death is the only option for fuck ups. Anyone of y'all got that pussy of just scared to die—any weak links—get tha fuck out, Bleed! Now, if you in—" He allowed anticipation to make love to the room. "We'll be filthy rich, if we fail—" He looked around at the fifty-six men present. "We holding court in the streets, but—failure is not an option. I've planned this shit for a minute and trust is all we need. Follow instructions as they are given and by this time next week, you boyz will be somewhere counting your share of paradise. But first, we gotta get that bag!" He turned his eyes to Goose.

Goose stepped forward. "Before we smash out, I need you, fellas, to sit tight for a second. I got a show y'all may enjoy." He turned to Kamika and wrapped one arm around her waist. She stiffened at the feel of the barrel of the pistol, he poked in her back.

***

~Detective Winslet~

I was the only female present amongst a room filled with lions and crocodiles. Pretty peculiar, but I tried not to look as jittery, as I felt. Something just didn't feel right though, but now I had a lot to report. There was something big going down in a few days, and we were about to see what it is. That was my thoughts before I felt the bad side of Goose's gun dig into my back. I stiffened with a sharp breath as he leaned into my ear.

"Bitch, I suggest you stand still and don't give the slightest indication you're not enjoying the show. Or you'll be found somewhere full, spoon-fed the whole clip," he whispered harshly.

A door opened at the side of the room, Tomorrow and Pain dragged in an unconscious, naked man with some type of cloth over his head. I watched as Assata sat a chair in the middle of the room and they went about tying the man to it. A sick feeling filled my stomach once they secured him to it. Pain pulled the cloth away, and acid rushed up my throat, but with every ounce of strength I could muster, I forced it back down.

The man with the dusted lines that approached me at the block party, now sat strapped to the chair, beaten within an inch of his life. There was so much blood—so much. Oh my God! What had I gotten us into? Pain walked over to us with what looked to be an Israeli AK. Goose stepped from behind me with a gold tooth smile etched on his face.

"Enjoy the show, shorty."

I glanced at Pain, the look in his bottomless eyes told me, he knew—he knew, I was a cop, but more importantly, that I'd committed treason!

***

~**Assata**~

I watched big bro take off his shirt, his dreads hung wildly. I was curious to know what he was 'bout to do with this law boy. He fucked me up when he showed me the stack of pictures of the pig and Kamika. There was pictures of Kamika in a black Dodge Charger with the cock sucker, Hunter that had been sniffling 'round the hood. Her at some typa Academy Graduation. Her being a fuckin' cop, period! After bro saw the big boy in one of the pictures, he recalled seeing him at the block party. He said, he was sweating shawty, but I bet it was all staged.

The bitch played my dude, now I was 'bout to— fuck! Big bro just pulled out a pretty ass long scalpel with a gold handle. Lost, I looked over at Pain. He flashed me all thirty-two gold teeth and used two fingers to point from his eyes too big bruh as if to say watch. Tomorrow walked over to the boy with a tin bucket of water in his hands. As he pulled his arms back for the dash, you could hear the ice cubes clinking together inside of it. Using a hard arch, water and ice punched dude into consciousness.

As though, he was drowning, he struggled in the chair speaking gibberish. The only coherent words were four that I'd heard a lot in life.

"Please—don't—kill—me!"

Goose gave him an evil sneer, as he rubbed his hand back and forth over the sharp blade. Me and bro have ridden dirty a million times in the past. I had never seen him with no knife. He was a killa fa sho, but had he spilled over into the waters of a lunatic? He turned and made eye contact with us before.

"The other day I was maxin' at my people's crib, and some of the spookiest shit happened! I got a package without a return address," Goose said allowing his eyes to scan the crowd. He made eye contact with as many people as he could before he resumed his speil. "That may not sound like no big shit, huh? Well, this when shit gets ugly, fam—I'm not from here. Nobody outside of the squad knows me or most of y'all."

I watched as bro ran the sharp blade over his open palm. A thin red line opened up. The sight of blood surprised me because he hadn't used any pressure to the gesture. That was indication that the blade was dangerously sharp. Me and Goose's eyes met in a deadly clash, and even though, I still didn't understand his angle, I knew his intent was death.

"Nobody knows my government outside of my brothers. I know neither of them gossips like bitches." He nodded with an evil smirk on his face. "As I opened the pack, I'm thinkin' this ain't gonna be good news. Low and behold, picture after picture of not only me and every nigga of the block, but also this fat fucker," He said, as he slapped the fat part of the blade across homies face, blood squirted instantly. Goose grabbed a handful of the fat dude's afro and forced him to look at him. "It took me a minute, but once the pieces snapped into place, it fucked me up! This the same nigga I been seeing 'round the block coppin' work from us. The same nigga I stepped to for hawkin' a bitch. This nigga is in several of these pictures. This dick sucka is coming out a precinct in what I found out to be in Fort Worth. Long story short, the sucka is an undercover snake that's been put onto us somehow." He turned his attention back to dude and shit got crazy.

"No—no, you're wrong—you're—oh, Saint Joseph—help me! Somebody—plea—please," he cried, yet Satan had no sympathy for tears and with a meticulous control Goose cut through homies sternum down through his stomach.

The blade was so sharp flesh was still in place, but in slow, live motion. Blood oozed from the wound and just at the bottom of the slit near where the duodenum was located, his insides snaked onto his external. Goose laid down the blade, Tomorrow handed my brother what looked like a syringe. We watch as he took the cap off and pushed the injector just a bit so that an unknown liquid shot from it. Goose smiled like a child who'd discovered Willy Wonka's Chocolate Factory. Fat boy was in a daze, as he watched his interior slowly, but surely easing from the confines of his body.

"This shit right here—" Goose held up the needle like he was a salesperson, promoting a new invention. "I found this shit on the black market. It's 'pose to calm you—slow your blood flow to give you precious moments to spare. Its origins date back to World War II. It was given to soldiers that had been maimed to give them just a little bit more time to live until help came." As he injected the serum, all you heard was fat boy releasing a soft cry that sounded like his soul escaped in a whoosh of breath.

Then he relaxed noticeably, yet still, amongst the living—he was somewhere far off inside a euphoric nightmare. The shit that happened next was something outta a scary movie. One of the homies brought in what looked to be—dog food! Goose took the bag from dude, then kneeled before the fat boy and before our eyes, fam opened dude up, careful to push his split intestines back inside of him. He began to infuse dude with the dog food. By now, a few cats had tossed their lunch.

"Aww, man—dude fucked up mentally, dawg," One cat moaned in between regurgitating his breakfast.

A quick look at Pain told me he was thinking the same shit I was. Big bro missing a few screws, but this boy right there was a weak link, and it was better to eliminate the potential of a problem rather than have to deal with it later on down the road when we're too deep in the mix to press rewind.

"He gotta go," Pain whispered to one of the homies.

I watched as he took Pain's place by the law bitch. Pain and another homie escorted, Mr. Weak Stomach outside under the pretense of getting some fresh air. Seconds later, three gunshots sung him to sleep and from that point on if niggaz felt some typa way, they held their tongue and their vomit.

I turned my attention back to Goose just in time to see two white Pitbulls brought into the room. These bitches were beautiful, but their growls and snarling teeth revealed the hunger within them.

Goose smiled. "Catrina—Heaven, sit," he demanded.

Both dogs obeyed while licking their chops—never taking their eyes off of big boy. Their noses were in the air as if they could smell their meal.

Bro turned his eyes to Kamika. "I bet y'all wondering why I brought my bitch here tonight, huh? Well, this is why, she's been next to me—next to y'all—and as far as I know, she is down by law," he snickered at the inside joke. "Yet, just like everybody else in this bitch, she has to walk through fire to prove that shit!"

I turned my eyes to lady—her eyes were filled with fear and confusion! Yet, the one thing that couldn't be denied was—she knew, we knew. She knew it was do or die at this point.

***

~Winslet~

"Oh my God! He's going to kill me, I just know it!" I thought as my eyes blurred, but for the sake of my life. I blinked away what would surely be the death of me.

"Come here, baby," he called to me.

My feet were tons of cement, or maybe pounds of it because as much as I tried to will them to move, they just wouldn't comply! In frustration, I looked to Goose to tell him exactly that. The look he gave me triggered my body, suddenly I stood before him as if I was having an out of body experience. He palmed my face and looked deep into my eyes. His hand limped across his face as blood dripped off of his hands—staining my face. An officer's blood! He pulled his gun off his waist, glared at me, and allowed evil to slip from his lips.

"You got two choices—you can either put him to sleep or join him in eternal rest," he said, so low I could barely hear him.

He noticed the reluctance, then aggressively grabbed my wrist and forced the gun in my hand. I entertained the thought of using it on him, but a quick glance around me ensured, that act would be suicide. In a harsh whisper, he forced me to commit cold-blooded murder.

"You can either put a bullet in his head or deal with every nigga in this room, taking turns fucking and sodomizing you before I put one in your head! Nobody knows who you are, but they will if you don't get active. Now, put him out his misery," Goose demanded.

I glanced behind me at the present members of the organization—then to Tony. We had been through a lot together. I was the reason he was here—in a warehouse in the country on his deathbed—death-chair. What—the—fuck—ever. Yet, and still, he was dead either way, by my hand or not. I swallowed the lump in my throat and stepped to my shit. I stepped back a few steps and aimed the cannon at my longtime friend. His eyes were unfocused—dazed. He stared at me, but recognition didn't set in until tears blurred my vision, and my hand started to shake. I mustered every hurt—every betrayal—and when Hunter's face replaced Tony's.

"Ka—Kamika—Winslet—d—don't—please!" My heart cracked down the middle because it was Hunter's face, but Tony's voice. A solitary tear tumbled from my left eye as resolve snuck into my being and right as he attempted to plead again, the pistol jumped in my hands. Once—twice—over—and over and over—click—click—click, until it was empty.

"Psst—Psst—sic him, girls," Goose said.

Two white blurs raced past me, and snarling turned to moans of pleasure as they tore into his stomach. The sound that could be distinguished above the beastly feast was—click—click—click—click.

***

~IceBerg~

"Oh, Papi-Chulo—oh yass," she moaned, as she reached her peak.

Belle rolled off me and laid within our essence, attempting to catch her breath.

"Chu are the baass," she screamed.

I laid there satiated but tried to put all the pieces to the puzzle together. My manz, Pablo told me a big shipment of *'Boy'* was on its way to the spot as we spoke. Pablo was Belle's relative that headed the El Sai out of Cali. He was the new plug for the fam now that Belle's pops had got whacked by the boy, Russia. Speaking of homie, his silence had been paramount, that's what fucked with me. Although, he didn't know what I looked like, or where I squatted at, I knew men like him were relentless.

"Wha is it, David—chu seem distant, and after you've partaken of tis sweet poosy, me no understand hum?" Belle rolled onto her stomach and propped her face in her hands, she stared at me quizzically.

"It's nothing, mama, shit just been moving at the speed of light and this boy, Russia, is too silent. To top that off, these Piru niggaz wildin' and makin' shit hot 'round the way." I exhaled a breath of frustration.

I thought 'bout steppin' to Assata and revealing myself. I knew real street niggaz didn't respect new faces, and before shit went up in smoke, me and homie had an understanding.

"Chu worry 'bout noting! Russia, si—him mos be dealth with vedy soon. Time is of te essence, and the Holy Death waits for no man. The Pidu—" Belle stated.

"Piru," I corrected her.

"Si—whatever—they noting! Chu have mi cousin and his army at chu desposal. Chu chos focus on Russia and tis poosy and chu will be vedy rich man," she said, as she reached over and grabbed a handful of my nature.

***

~Lovey~

A huge lion with a thick mane walked into the clearing, eyes aflame and aggression in its stance. There in the far corner of the meadow, a huge tiger sat poised on his sharp claws, with anticipation electrifying in its eyes. The sky darkened, grey clouds covered as the two predators stared each other down. The king of the jungle versus the carnivore of Asian folklore. A streak of lightning splashed across Heaven's floors, and as if that wasn't a signal to battle, the two beasts clashed in a vicious meeting of contempt.

Their Claws slashed, their teeth sunk into flesh. The tiger slashed across the lion's thick mane, taking a patch from it. Yet, the lion was ferocious in its attack, a loud roar escaped its jaws as it sank razor-like teeth into the throat of its formidable foe, only to take a deep slash across the face. Back and forth, the battle exchanged power between the two until a lightning fast tumble ensued with the tiger ending up on top of the king of the jungle. Something like victory swam in his eyes, the tiger roared in defiance, sharp teeth dribbled saliva as the ancient cat growled. Rain began to tumble from the dark sky and just as a powder blue tint bullied its way into the darkness, an earth shattered roar could be heard, as the tiger opened its powerful jaws and clamped down on the throat of the king.

Then— "Lord!" Lovey popped straight up out of her sleep. Her skin was aglow as perspiration and anxiety oozed from her pores. She slid from the bed and kneeled beside it with her hands in the prayer position. "Lord, I've been your humble servant my whole life. I've not always been as righteous, but God, I've left my unclean life behind years ago. You've lead me through the shadow of death and laid me down in green pastures. I don't ask for much, but I need you to protect my babies. I'm no saint Father, but I do my best. My only request is that if you must, take me before you take them, my heart is too fragile to be standing over their caskets. Please, God— take me before you take them is my sacrifice. In Jesus name, Amen."

Clairvoyance snaked through her veins as she felt another presence somewhere near, but suddenly it was gone, as quick as it appeared. Goose had overheard her talking while on his way to the bathroom. He stopped to make sure she was okay, and found his heart broken, as he listened to his Queen ask God to take her life in place of her babies.

Part III
Get Ya Manz

Last night, I played chess against my soul. As we sat down for the game, I studied the board intently. I decided to move the pawn that would allow my Queen to move as she pleased. I observed as my soul duplicated my move. In an attempt at creating a diversion, I decided to move my knight in a position to be taken. This simple move would merely be a sacrifice for my strategy, but to my frustration—my soul mirrored my move once again.

This instantly continued until finally, my soul exclaimed, "Checkmate!" I stared at the board in awe.

"Soul—why did you copy my every move? How did you checkmate me, when your every move was a reflection of my own?" My soul smiled wearily.

"Assata—your first mistake was going against me, "your soul!" A man and his soul are one! When a man goes to war with his soul, he becomes lost. You were so busy trying to use your Queen that you never took the time to protect her, she is you. Observation is key. You and I should never be opponents—whenever we become two, we become enemies. You, your Queen, and I are like the divine trinity, except—rather than the Father, Son, and Holy Spirit—we're Mind, Body, and Soul! That's the ordination of man—what makes him, God—Cypher!"

Chapter Fourteen

Get Ya Manz—Get That Bag
~Two Weeks Later-7 a.m.~

The morning was brisk. The early morning commuters tried to beat the traffic that the day was sure to bring. On the corner of Fry Street, a young man in a Brooks Brothers suit, stood with a Rough and Tumble Suede Bottega, Veneta Sachel in one hand and a steaming Starbucks cup in the other. He watched the traffic, as his eyes rotated back and forth between his Breitling wristwatch and the doors to the Wells Fargo. Impatience stirred within him, as he waited. He could use the ATM, but the withdrawal he needed to make was too big, so there he stood—waiting.

"Five more minutes," he huffed.

He lifted his eyes at the sound of oncoming traffic and watched as two U-Hauls pulled up to the curb, blocking his view of the bank.

"Damn," he hissed in frustration.

He needed to get the money out of his account before he had to clock in on the job. He tapped his foot against the pavement, as he observed an armored truck pulled in front of the U-Haul. A few moments later, the passenger exited the vehicle. He observed his surroundings with keen eyes as he made his way to the rear of the truck, with his hands tight around the pump action Mossberg. He opened the rear doors, and three fully armed uniforms jumped down, with weapons in hand as they took up their stations.

The passenger and one of them entered the bank. The young man on the corner stood agitated—swearing at the time. He could have been made his withdrawal and been on his way to his white-collared occupation. He knew better than attempting to approach the bank while the armored truck made their pick up, so he sat tight and awaited their departure. Twenty minutes later, he watched as the truck was filled with bags of money and secured before it pulled off. He made his way towards the bank wondering why the hell would two U-Hauls be parked in front of a bank. Security must have had the same thoughts because as he stepped behind the second U-

Haul, he heard the argument between the drivers in the first truck and the security men.

As he passed, he nodded good morning to the driver of the second U-Haul. He continued to pass until he reached the back of the truck, then he dropped to one knee, and opened his Satchel. He pulled out a rubber mask of Obama's face, put it on to a snugged fit, before pulling out a modified Tech 9 equipped with an eight-inch cooling system. He gazed around before turning to the back of the U-Haul and unlocking it. He counted down the seconds in his head. The door rolled up and forty-four men in identical attire spilled onto the concrete.

The only differences were the faces of the president masks and caliber of weapons. After hearing the commotion, one of the security personnel turned to investigate. He bent the corner of the truck and walked into one of the most mind-boggling scenes he had ever set eyes on. Every president that had ever been in office stared back at him.

Obama swung the Tech on him. "Don't be no hero, homeboy," the masked man said.

He gave a signal and forty-three presidents bummed rushed the bank. The second officer was caught off guard as he reached for his weapon, but the sight of Donald Trump aiming a .50 caliber Desert Eagle, froze him in motion. Keeping the monstrous gun trained on him, he unlatched the second U-Haul, and out poured twelve vice presidents, yet rather than following the first group, they milled about on the sidewalk. Suddenly, it was hard for the guard to get a grip on reality, as he stood stunned with his hands in the air. Trump relieved him of his weapon before Lyndon B. Johnson put the steel to the back of his head.

"Stand still, homie, let's not turn a robbery into a capital murda," he hissed, as Trump opened his satchel and pulled out a contraption with different color wires attached to a timer. He held it out to the officer. "Hold this."

The officer he stared at him bewildered and sweating profusely. "Hold it? Why—why would I do that?" asked the officer.

"Maybe because your life depends on it," Johnson whispered in his ear, as he pushed the barrel harder against his head.

Not wanting to push his luck, the guard accepted the bomb. Trump instructed him how to hold it by placing his hands on either side of it. He pushed his thumbs down on two different detonators.

"There—keep your hands just like that! This beauty is what we call pressure bombs. If you change your grip on it, even the slightest, the pressure change communicates to the detonator, and in seconds you go *'boom'*! So, stay still, and be good."

***

~Detective Winslet~
9:15 a.m.

"That's it—he made you do what? I can't believe this wacko! That's it, I am pulling you out of this operation! It's getting too dangerous," Hunter heatedly said.

I'd just told him about the warehouse. I had to, my life had become so different since I had been on this case. For one, unbeknownst to him, the past week I'd been numb to everything. Goose and I had a heart to heart—we fought—we kissed—we fought again—and finally, I compromised the entire investigation. We made love—rough—passionate—emotional love! The bomb he dropped on me was, and still was exploding within the walls of my mind. I'm surprised that my nerves didn't have me shaking, yet I damn sure wouldn't be surprised if I started to.

"Winslet—you hear what I just said?" Hunter stared at me sternly, yet before I could answer him, the radio squawked.

"All available officers report to Fry and West. The silent alarm at the Wells Fargo has been tripped! I repeat—all available officers, code red, Fry, and West!"

Hunter and I looked to each other astonished. He flicked the squad lights on the grill of the supped up Dodge Charger, as he did an illegal u-turn, and put the pedal to the floor. He must had forgotten, he was not supposed to be on duty, but I assumed that was the last thing on his mind, as he bent a sharp corner at a devastating speed that almost flipped us. We were only six blocks away from the bank, so it didn't take us long to bend the corner to Fry Street. We pulled to a stop about twenty feet away from the crime scene, and what we saw blew our minds!

It was crazy—confusing—brilliant! John Nance Garner, Richard M. Nixon, Gerald R. Ford—Vice Presidents dressed in suits congregate outside the bank. They walked back and forth in front of the entrance to create a strange effect. The assault rifles they brandish warned anyone that wanted to play hero that the stand-off will last for days. Hunter called it in, notifying the dispatcher that we were on the scene. The flashing lights must have caught the perps' attention because they all stopped their pacing and looked straight at us.

Nixon said something to his cohorts and in formation, they turned and disappeared into the bank, leaving behind a lone security guard holding something in his hands. He looked petrified. Hunter pushed his door open with force and without letting me know his intentions, attempted to pursue the fleeing group of men.

"Hunter," I screamed his name.

His back was to me as he unholstered his pistol. Without turning to face me, he spoke over his shoulder. "Dammit, Winslet, it's a bank robbery in progress!"

"Listen, before we go in guns blazing. I just want to tell you I'm sorry!"

"Sorry," he asked, finally turning his head to look at me.

His eyes exploded in surprise before the lick of the flame escaped the barrel of the 9mm that Goose gave me just for this occasion. Hunter's head snapped back—still contorted with that look of surprise. Yet, now he had the mark of Buddha to his temple. In slow motion, he fell forward, and as soon as he did I got to work. First, I text Goose the code to let him know the deed was done and to go through with the next phase of the plan.

My nerves were wild, but I wasn't worried about anything coming back to me. For one, Hunter wasn't even supposed to be on duty, let alone responding to the alert. Secondly, well, a girl can't reveal all of her secrets. I snatched the radio off the seat and screamed, "Shots fired—shots fired! Nine-nine-nine! Nine-nine-nine! Nine-nine-nine," as I yelled the code for officer down.

***

Keith Urban played softly within the armored truck, as the driver pushed a questionable ninety miles per hour on a lone blacktop in route to their destination.

"You have more of that long cup Copenhagen, Joey?" he asked the passenger, as his crave for the smokeless tobacco ate at his nerves.

Joey sang along with the country song as he reached in his back pocket and pulled out a fresh can of mint snuff. He passed it to, Bob, the driver, as a roaring engine caught his attention. His eyes absently traveled to the huge side view mirror attached to the truck. His eyes stretched wide in excitement as a lone rider in a red leather streaked past them with the front wheel of a black and red, KTM 1290 Super Duke, in the air.

"He has to be pushing a hundred or more on that thing, doing a wheelie! He's a fucking psycho," he exclaimed.

Bob spit in his cup and didn't acknowledge the wildman. He viewed his own mirror to make sure the tail was still with them, spotting the deputy, he was about to turn his attention back to the road, until something out of place caught his eye. A caravan of bikes, and what looked to be one of those Rubicon Jeep Wranglers was coming up fast. The fear that eased its way into his nervous system was unwarranted. This was the very first time he'd seen this type of enjoyment on this road.

Yet, it was no surprise because of its infrequent traffic. As they get closer he noticed it was the fucking Hell's Angels and something didn't sit right with him.

"Joey, something is up, call it in and—"

Bob's words get caught up in his throat as a red crotch-rocket zoomed alongside them, at the same time, the CB sparked to life.

"Boys, I think we have a problem we—" oblivious to what the deputy had said, they watched as the driver of the motorcycle handled the powerful beast expertly. It was the passenger that aimed a strange device at the side of the truck that had their attention. The devices discharged what looked to be a metal prong, it lodged itself to the truck, and an instant shockwave erupted from it. The country song cut off, and the radio scrambled. Joey snatched the radio off the dash and attempted to call it in.

"National One to base; we're under attack—I repeat—we're under attack!" He started at the CB as if it was offensive and tried again—and again, but he might as well had been talking to himself.

All satellite communication was blocked. The device that the riders attached to the side of the truck was a communications scrambler. It was a tool the CIA used to deflect national radio transmissions.

"The fucking radio is scrambled, Bob—its blocked! Oh God, this is bad—oh God—"

As if God found it funny, automatic gunfire erupted behind them. They glanced in the rearview and watched in horror as the deputy's car fishtailed out of control, as motorcycles on both sides fire into it. As if they'd done this type of thing a million times, the riders created a wide octagon around the swerving car before speeding ahead as it swerved violently into the wide expanse of land, flipping as it rolled into a trench.

"Joey," A voice came from the cab of the truck.

"Bob, what the hell's going on?"

"It's a fucking robbery you dip shit!" Joey screamed as he jacked a shell into the Mossberg pump.

At the same time, five bikes zoomed in front of them forming a triangular barrier. In the rearview, Bob watched as the same formation was made. By now, he was pushing the truck at a dangerous hundred miles per hour. Unexpectedly, gunfire ensued from the back, it was no doubt the three trained men in the back that vowed their lives to protect the U.S currency.

"Step on it, Bob—these motherfuckers are going to kill us!" Thomas screamed from the rear.

The jeep sped by, but not before a small black object was thrown on the back door of the truck. As it sped past, a masked gunman fired a burst of heat at the window. It merely scratched the bulletproof glass, yet—he smiled as if he knew the world's best-kept secret, and twenty seconds later, it was revealed. The motorcade opened up to reveal a line of spikes thrown over the road. They were surrounded on both sides, and the only way to avoid the trap laid ahead was by sideswiping their pursuers.

Bob was a devoted Christian, and his heart wouldn't allow him to do it, but about five feet away from the spiked trap, Joey reached over and yanked the wheel to the right.

"You fucking imbecile," he screamed, as the truck veered violently off the road, but not before the front left tire was punctured. The truck flipped into the air instantly killing three bikers but turning the tides into the crook's favor.

***

Inside the bank, President Obama watched as his cohorts gained control of the room. He observed everything, even the little white man that just pushed the button to the silent alarm hidden under the desk. Everything was going as planned, he thought before a beautiful woman was brought from the back room. He'd seen her before—in fact, he'd been seeing her consistently since the day she gave herself to him. The man that found her in her hiding place mishandled her, and that set aflame to Obama's temper.

He rushed over and hit President Reagan in the face with the butt of his gun, damn near knocking his mask off. He crumbled to the floor in heap of pain. Obama turned his eyes to the beautiful woman, confusion—sympathy—craziness played in his stare. Their eyes met in collision of communication. Fear and inquisition in hers—indecisiveness, and apology in his. Obama grabbed her by her arm, he led her to a chair and without words, forced her to sit. She never took her eyes off of him, yet not testing his patience either.

"One minute-thirty seconds we're out of here," Obama screamed.

He glanced to the second security guard sweating his life out, as he tried not to take any pressure off the bomb. It was identical to the one his partner was holding outside the bank. The beautiful woman still had her eyes on Obama, but her mind was everywhere. Why weren't they taking the money? Why was it so many of them? *Why weren't they taking the money?* It was as if they barged in with bombs and machine guns only to walk back and forth.

"White House—White House—time, fellas—time," Obama screamed into a handheld radio.

It was as if a dream forced its way into reality as vice presidents stormed the small establishment.

"Let's move—move," someone yelled, just as quick as they came, they disappeared.

Somehow, they knew about the back door that only employees knew about. It led to a back alley and onto the next street over.

Only two presidents were left—Hoover and Roosevelt. "Y'all did good, but sadly, we can't leave behind any witnesses," Roosevelt said.

Fear was plausible in the atmosphere—all eyes turned to the machine gun-toting president.

"Bu-but, we haven't seen your faces—we can't identify you," a hysterical woman cried. "Ple—please," she begged.

There was no room for mistakes. Aiming the assault rifle at the group of people, he let loose a volley of fire, bodies jerked and red splashed everywhere!

***

Laid in a tangled mess, the inhabitants of the armored truck moaned as they tried to disentangle themselves. Smoke rose from the engine, but the worst damage was done on the interior. Bob, the driver was killed on impact. Since he was riding without his seatbelt, the impact of the crash threw his body against the armored windshield. His vertex smashed into the walls of glass, it shattered his vertebrae and neck in less than three seconds. Joey was still breathing—barely! He stood ten feet away, as twelve bikers awaited their leader's signal. They didn't have to wait long, he pulled out his phone and punched in a unique sequence of numbers.

A moment later, a barely audible beeping noise could be heard as the red light on the small device, attached to the back of the truck blew the doors off. A head signal was all that was needed for the hungry wolves to descend on the paradise that was no doubt awaiting them in the truck. The rider in red leather was the first to reach it. He was hungry and inattentive, as he rushed in and that's when hell broke loose. A high-powered shotgun exploded in what seemed like slow motion, the red-clad rider flew backward, dead on arrival! It took a few seconds before the thirst for blood registered to the remaining eleven.

Once it did, hell had no fury for the melody of a gangsta's anger. Street sweepers spoke that pipe talk until they were empty. They were more cautious, but knowing they were pressed for time, they went for what they knew. As expected, everything in the truck was DOA—just like the different presidents on the front of the different denominations of bills floating in the air.

"We got less than twenty minutes to clear this bitch out before we're surrounded by them alphabets. Let's work, fam," Goose screamed from behind his grey helmet.

"Almost there, God—let me make it out of this and I'm hanging up my guns—I swear!"

***

Captain Flemington stood in the middle of the bank and scratched his head, he just couldn't figure it out. Why would someone go through all this just to escape through the back door? He had to smile at how they found the two security guards. They had the bomb squad on the scene and all—and for what? For two fucking alarm clocks made to look like explosive devices. When the piece of shit detonated, everyone hit the ground, only to be stunned by mere explosive vibration. To make the situation even more comical, they found the tellers and bank manager leaking red—red paint that is. The sons-of-bitches held the bank up with paintball guns and alarm clocks—classical!

"Captain—cap—it's a set-up—it's a fucking faux! They're going for the truck," The new lead detective screamed, just as the Fed boys showed up.

"It's a fucking diversion!"

***

"Let's go fam—it's time—it's time, Goose screamed, heading for his bike.

The jeep was miles down the road watching for the first sight of the boys in blue. Everyone rushed for their bikes and just as the getaway seemed clean, and in their grasp, a lone gunshot screamed from behind the truck. Goose turned just in time, to witness a helmet wearing biker drop the bags of money and pause in an upright position before he crumbled to his knees. His heart broke as he watched the biker pull his helmet off his head. As bullets flew in the direction of the opposition. Lil' Jackie rushed over to the lil' nigga that the hood raised. Lil' Jackie dropped to his knees and took his head into his lap, while Tomorrow stared at him with blood exuding from his lips. He coughed as a spray of blood shot up into the air.

"Th—they—got—me—Ja—Jack!" Lil' Jackie's eyes mist over.

"Hold up, lil' homie—we gonna get you out of here—just—hold on, fam."

"Te—tell Sa—Satta, I—I—tell—I—"

One last deep breath and Tomorrow's soul escaped from his body. Goose rushed over to them and stood behind Lil' Jackie. Instant pain rushed through his heart, but self-preservation was in his veins, all the while, Lil' Jackie shook Tomorrow—bending at the waist, he did CPR—shook him again.

"Get up nigga—get up!"

"Say, fam, we got to go—now, Lil' Jack! You know the rules fam, we can't do shit for homie. Not even a funeral if we cased up," Goose said as he glanced from the road back to Jackie.

Naw, Goo—we can't just leave him like this—we can't, fam!" Lil Jackie's voice cracked.

The radio sparked to life,

"Twelve on the radar fam—we gotta burn. Clear out—them people on our heels!"

Goose eyes turned back as Lil' Jackie continued to reanimate, fam. Putting the burna to his dome, he tried one last time—

"Fam let's burn," Goose exclaimed.

The roar of motorcycles disturbed the peace as Lil' Jackie shook his head no—

"Help me get him up, bruh—he can make it," he said without turning his head.

Goose nodded in affirmation. "Tell lil' homie we'll mourn him til' we join y'all."

Boom—boom—boom— Three shots rocked Lil' Jackie as Goose dashed to his bike and the squad rode off into the sun.

Renta

Chapter Fifteen

Paradise
~Twisted~
A Week Later

My cell phone rang and disturbed my beast rest. I reached over the naked bitch I been caked up with the for the past five nights and snatched my shit off the nightstand.

"What's the bidno, big homie?"

"Nigga, fuck you been, you ain't 'bout this money no more or what? I know that shit that happened to Lil' Joe got ya' head gone, but niggaz die every day. We gonna get them boys who did, bruh in, but first, let's get to this mula. We can't go to war broke, fam," the voice on the other end proclaimed.

"Maaann—sho you right—I just been going through it. You know, Joe, was my hip, homie—that did some sick shit to me," Twisted professed.

A pause could be heard on the other end of the line.

"Dig, Twist, I raised you two boys from lil' locs to YG's. I'm just as heated as you but crying ain't gonna bring fam back. We gotta ball fa Lil' Joe—he wouldn't want it no other way! Get up out that funk, lil homie, and meet me at the spot, so I can show you how to celebrate the dead. On Hoova we gonna sign it in blue for bruh—but we can't avenge him if our head uptight and our bread ain't right."

His words marinated into the thick fog I allowed myself to be sucked into. I glanced over at lil' mama that was asleep next to me. She was bad with a capital 'B', she'd always wanted to give me the kitty, I just respected the house cause she belonged to a dear nigga.

"I'll be there in an hour, homie," Twisted stated.

"One," he replied then disconnected.

As I slapped shorty on her bare ass cheeks, I laughed at how only one eye rolled open. Mena stared back at me as if I'd interrupted the best sleep she's ever had.

"Time to go, boo—I got moves to make," I told her, as I rolled out the bed.

The stench of sex and something fouler aroused my senses—frustration ate at me.

"Bitch, I said get the fuck up—it's time to roll."

She had the audacity to stare at me with that one eye like I was nothing more than a pest. I snatched the tool off the table, aimed, and squeeze two shots into her frame. The girl was tough—she didn't make a sound. The bullets puncture her flesh with a popping sound, rigor mortis was already taking its toll. Mena's been dead for five days. It took me a little bit, but I put a few of the pieces of the puzzle together. It was no reason Joe was 'pose to be in Concrete City.

The '*why was he there*' played into my mind for days before it dawned on me that there was only one mu'fucka that could answer that question, Mena! I hit her up under the pretense of taking her away from the madness for a little bit, she went for it. The slut probably thought I'd finally come to my senses. Yet, my mind was on the fact, that if a bitch was really grieving as deeply as she seemed at the hospital. Why would she be so quick to jump on the next niggaz pimp stick? Let alone someone that would bring thoughts of her deceased man?

I got her out here at my duck off in the country and from there I started my investigation. I had to shoot the silly broad in both of her knees before she divulged the shock of my life! Joe was crossed by his own, fam! I smoked lil' mama. One to the dome—two to the heart. That was the first night—the other four, I sodomized and fucked her to death! I see why them morticians be humping the dead—ain't no pussy tighter than rigor mortis pussy!

***

~Agent Harrison~

I'd been grilling Detective Winslet for six hours straight! She was either the best liar there was or she was telling the truth and my instincts were sending false alarms.

"You say when you and Detective Hunter got to the bank, there was an exchange of gunfire between him and the accused? I stood with those ballistics techs for hours. The direction of the bullet that pierced the window is consistent with the flesh wound, but the killing shot had to come from a different angle. I—"

"What exactly are you trying to say, agent, that I killed my own partner? Make sense of why I would in the middle of a bank heist?"

"Faux bank heist," he interrupted.

"Yes, what the fuck ever. The point is—why would I kill a man that taught me all I now? First of all, maybe he had something to do with the set-up. How else would you explain a suspended detective in active duty? You're—"

"Maybe, both of you were part of it, and you decided to become rapacious at the last minute—maybe—"

"That's enough, Agent Harrison, you are violating my clients Fifth Amendment. She has nothing else to say. Now, if you're not charging her with any crime, I demand she be released immediately!" A sharp dressed Jewish man bombarded my investigation.

I was about to give this asshole a piece of my mind when the director of the bureau walked in.

"Do we have just cause to hold her?" he questioned.

I paused with a frustrated look on my face. She was guilty of something, I could feel it.

"No Sir, but—"

"No, buts, Agent—cut her loose to her attorney and meet me in my office."

He turned to walk away, but not before informing Winslet she would be hearing from us.

***

~Assata~

I ended the call frustrated. It was my tenth time calling Freedom to no avail. I wondered for the hundredth time if I shoulda whacked her. It ain't like she can identify me, but, she knew it was me in the

Obama mask. I felt it, it had been a long week—after we divided up the loot, everybody was left with a nice chunk. The dope-fiends we hired, they just wanted payment in work, so it worked out in everybody's favor. The only thing I'd forever regret was the death of my lil' manz, Tomorrow. Lil dawg was meant for something way grander than the nap he took.

My eyes watered with just the thought of the loss, gangstas cry too. It's too late for regrets, though. I gotta push on to the next phase of my life. I'm through wit' the game—it's ova! I made a vow, I planned to stand on it, and my new hustle was fa sho money. I will also spend up an imports and exports distribution for my homies, so they can broaden their horizons. I knew what would be transported, but any creature that's molded from the wild habitat would always be wild, even if the beast is tamed on the inside. It's like a killer becoming a lawyer, just because he changed his suit doesn't take away the fact, he's got blood on his hands.

I tossed the phone on the passenger seat, pulled up in the apartment complex with my head on the swivel. This was my first time coming to her spot. I didn't know these boys over here, so I was strapped like a seatbelt. I retrieved my horn, highlighted her mathematics, and await her sweetness to fill my ear.

"Heyyy, baby! Where you at?"

"Come outside, ma—"

"Huh—oh—you're here?" I heard the clicks in my ear.

Twenty minutes later, she peeked her head outside her apartment. She used her pointer finger, beckoning me to Heaven. I slid out of my SS, with the tool on display, just in case niggaz was lurkin'. I fucks with lady, but ain't no tellin' what typa bidness a female got planned for a cat, who moved blindly to her wickedness. Soon as I got up on sweet lady, she opened the door in a short t-shirt, and a pink thong, her nipples protruded like she'd been thinking 'bout my lips wrapping around them. I glanced down at her bare feet—small—pedicured—white tips. My lower muscles rose to the occasion.

"You gonna stand there and stare at what's already yours? Or come in before all these thirsty ass niggaz see what I've kept secret for you?" she smiled seductively.

She grabbed my hand and led me in with a soft kiss. The décor was immaculate in earth tones. Forest greens and tree bark brown. The hardwood floors shined as if they'd been freshly waxed—shit nice.

"Would you like something to drink—water—soda? Maybe something a little stiffer?" She asked on her way to the kitchen.

I grabbed her by the wrist and pulled her back to me.

"If I wanted to drink, I'd stayed at my own spot. I got something taboo in mind."

"Taboo—what might you have in mind handsome?" she questioned.

I flash her my diamond smile before lifting the shirt over her head and rolling her chocolate nipples between my thumb and forefingers.

"What 'bout some real freaky shit on the first date?" I suggested.

***

~Jazzy~

The breeze blew softly off the Pacific, as I strolled down the shore. Foamy waves rolled over my feet, as I gazed out at the horizon, so much played within the walls of my mind. My future, my past, but more importantly, Assata. I missed him so much. It was two weeks to my wedding day and I didn't feel like a woman about to say, 'I do' to the man of my dreams. I felt as if I was a prisoner about to pledge forever to a man who loves me fatally, but I would never love him with my heart. A girl could always convince her mind to love a man, but her heart couldn't be deceived. While a man found love through his dick-head and vision.

A woman found it through her heart and soul. The lesser bitch found it through a man fucking her right. Assata held my heart. I'd thought about going to him on multiple occasions, but what would be the use in running to only have it bathe in blood? Tessa kept me informed on all the happenings back home and it broke my spirit to know Assata had someone new. It killed me to know I'd hurt him so deeply, and if he only knew, I'd spend the rest of my life making up for it. As I bent down to pick up a grey and white seashell, I studied its beauty. For a moment, I fell in love with a fairytale as I imagined tossing it as far as I could into the ocean and somehow Assata found it, knowing it was sent from me.

***

~Assata~

I bent lady over the couch and used my thickness to slide between her cheeks. She moaned deep—hungrily, as I growled primally like a savage! My dick throbbed—as soon as the head submerged, and she screamed my name. I drove in fast and hard, gripping her waist; I looked down to see her juices saturating me. Then out of nowhere—my mind started to play tricks on me. Jazzy—she was missing me—willing me to her—fuck?

***

~Jazzy~

I sat down in the sand and looked at how the fading sun seemed to dip into the water, as my heart cried for him. I wondered if he felt me. I pulled my knees to my chest, trying to find where the orange and yellow sky ended, and where the ocean began. There was nothing more peaceful than the view of the sun setting over the ocean. It was what dreams were made of. The typa thing a girl shared with the man she loved. The wind was soft, as it carried the scent of the water to me. I allowed my spirit to venture across the ocean, over rough terrain, somewhere in Dallas, Fort. Worth, to a special someone I'd give my last breath for. I whispered to the wind, I love you, Assata. You'll never know how much cause even I couldn't explain it.

***

~Assata~

I plunged deeper into her essence faster and faster. She was sweating, trying to be a big girl, as she took the dick. I tried to be a big boy and take the pussy as she threw it back. I grabbed her neck gently, pulling back as far as I could without coming completely out. I drove as deep as I could—as fast as I could on the down stroke. Her body quivered—my nature roared—she cried—and I growled.

***

~Jazzy~

"Mama Ellen, help me. You know where my heart lies—that love is explosive. I'm with a man I love in order to protect the man I'm in love with. Yet, I'd rather love Assata to our deaths than to live with the man, I'll end up hating and regretting for not being with the man I love for in the first place. Maybe it makes no sense to some—but—but to you, I know it does. What can I do, Granny? Tell me. Are you even listening to me? Should I marry this man even though my heart is absent? Should I go to Assata? Please, hear me, help me."

Tears welled up in my eyes as confusion ignited within me like gas fumed after a match had been struck.

"So much has happened, Granny—I hear, Assata, is with a new woman. My heart breaks. There are so many people dying around him. I don't know when he'll be next, but I do know I want to be with him regardless of what life has in store."

The waves rolled over my feet in a foamy bath as a lone crab stumbled forward. It paused and played with the seashell, I tossed aside. Just as I thought it was about to move on, it turned towards the ocean and parked itself on the sand next to me, as if it knew I could use a friend.

***

~Assata~

I honestly didn't know how the peach scented candles got lit, but the erotic atmosphere was aglow with the dancing flames. Chocolate laid with her head on my chest, with her left leg over my thigh as her hand traced up and down my stomach.

"Assata, don't you ever get tired of the streets? The possibilities? I mean, I' not trying to change you, it's just a question," she murmured.

For some reason, the first thing that came to my mind was the girl Six. The conversation we had at her spot so many moons ago. I never understood how females could meet a street nigga in the streets, yet somehow wind up wanting him to stop being what attracted her in the first place. Now, that I thought about it, the question never deserved this much of my energy because it was evident. When they first meet a nigga, it's all physical. They didn't give a fuck about 'em. They were just attracted to the bread and the thug appeal, but when that dick gets good and emotions are born—they began to give a fuck.

"Feel me, Chocolate—the streets loaned me the tactics of survival. They demand my loyalty as payment. Yea, I get fed up with the life, but so does the square when things ain't going his way—it's life, ma."

She lifted her head up and kissed my lips. "Assata, all you have to do is recognize, that even if your yearn exceeds your deserve. The truth in what love can develop castrates all ties to the teardrops of a lonely gangsta. What makes you chose the life you live? Do you hate life so much, you'll continue killing our black generation, or worse—get yourself killed?"

My silence was thick, as I studied this woman that spoke with so much conviction.

"Look, baby, it's time to grow up. Yeah, I respect your gangsta, but the streets don't love nobody. You're loyal to something that can't be loyal to you. Haven't you ever thought about a family—getting married? Baby boy, there is so much more to life that you haven't seen yet. There's such a beautiful and articulate woman that's willing to cater to you—wait on you hand and foot. All you gotta do is open your eyes. Don't no woman wanna lay awake at night wondering if her man will make it home safe. You feel me, Satta?"

I pulled her down for another kiss I had to give it to her right-eously. "Yea—I can dig that, but vibe with me, queen—all my life I've journeyed through the struggle trying to find the beauty in it. I can't lie to you and say I've never thought about turning my back on the streets. But, the truth is—even if I square up, the streets is me! It's just who I am—I'm a dope-fiends son, ma. Yea, it's not all I know, feel me?"

"Yea—I do, but see Assata—the reason I'm so shook about giving you all of me is because I've endured what comes with dealing with a man of your caliber. First, it's the thrill of being the good girl with the bad guy. Then comes the empty promises of sweeping me off my feet and taking me away from all the drama of the streets. I have dreams, though, Assata. I'm more than the average street girl. I'm a Queen that—"

As placed my finger against her lips, I crushed that spiel. Every female I've met has either said she's been raped or she's nothing like the next or last female. Sometimes that shit didn't have to be said, show me. I flipped Chocolate over and rolled on top of her. I kissed each eyelid—her forehead—her nose—and last, her lips. The passion screamed in her eyes—so much resided in mine. Real shit, I was scared to release my heart. Shawty was tuggin' on it, but I'm holding on to it for dear life.

***

~Jazzy~

I closed the door behind me, our dog, Blue damn near trampled me. His tongue was hanging outta his mouth, as he sniffed and rubbed up against me. I could tell he was happy to see me.

I smiled. "Sup, baby—you enjoy the beach?" Shotta said as he walked from the back room.

He stepped into my space and pulled me close to his hard body. Upon contact, his nature-raised—every inch. My mind and body wasn't in accord, yet I wrapped my arms around his neck, lifted my face, and gave the sexiest look I could muster. I reached down, massaged his girth—I want him—no! I want Assata! He started peeling my clothes off layer after layer. Then he began to kiss my body—every portion. First my nipples—then my stomach—hips—inner thighs—calves—knees—ankles—feet—legs and thighs—thighs—paradise!

Chapter Sixteen

Gangsta's Party
~Face in the Dark~
Three days later

"Oh, shit," I whispered, as I watched the four Russians in the black Mercedes 600.

Even though the tint on the car was pitch black, I knew that the four shadows in the luxury vehicle were armed with the type of firepower that would allow a war to ensue for days if they were not killed first. As bad as I wanted to make that possibility a reality, I just couldn't reveal my identity to these men. I'd had dealings with each of them on different occasions, and one of them had been between my creamy thighs for the past four months. I watched as they watched the object of both of our interest.

Assata and his brothers stood outside of the house that I assumed they thought no one was privy of, having a conversation that seemed heartfelt, seriocomic. I watched as the three men laughed and Pain sparked what was more than likely a blunt of something exotic. Their hands were turned in the opposite direction in which me and the gunmen were positioned, and just as I was 'bout to get comfortable for the wait, a red beam landed on the back of Assata's head. It was like watching a horror movie in slow motion—like Phil Collins must have felt as he watched that man drowned when he had the opportunity to save him but didn't.

My breath froze in the same instant that Assata paused, then put his phone to his ear, in what must have been spiritual intervention, his phone dropped. He bent down to pick it up as a deadly whisper hissed through the air as the silenced bullet streaked over his head. A strange looked crossed Pains face as he took a studious look around. His instincts must have been working overtime because his stare landed directly on the 600. Right as he tapped Goose to get his attention, the Mercedes eased away from the curb. A trained eye would have noticed the tint passenger window rolling up as it picked up speed and zoomed into the twilight. Damn, God had plans for this man. He's dodged more bullets that Craig and Smokey on the movie Friday!

***

~Pain~

"Fam—did you hear that?" I asked Goose, as my senses kicked into gear. "Maybe this good Kush got me trippin' or—"

"Naw, what you talkin' 'bout, lil bro?" Goose questioned.

"That buzzing sound that just zoomed through here?"

"Mann, that bidness y'all smoking got yo' head gone—that wasn't nothing but a mosquito. You and this nigga trippin'," he said, as he looked down at Assata kneeled down looking at his phone as if it was an artifact that was gonna prove some type of history.

"He's so high he can't even stand back up! Look at him, see—that's why I don't smoke, bruh. That shit would have me doing some real spooky shit," he said, between fits of laughter.

Looking down at bro, I must admit that this some fiya green, but—one thang I know, two thangs fa sho, if that was a mosquito, it was the fastest, hottest mosquito that eva flew past my face. Secondly, the look on Assata's face ain't the look of no high mu'fucka! In fact, he looked as sober as a reformed drug addict at a sobriety meeting.

"Sup, bruh—why the fuck you lookin' like that? What's wrong wit' you?" I asked, my eyes still roamed as two problems occurred at the same time. I tapped Goose to show him the black Benz that had already pulled away from the curb, and in the same instance, Assata rocked our galaxy.

"Fam, we need to get to Denton Community—Lovey just had a heart attack."

***

Lovey stared out of the window of her hospital room. The sun still hid just beyond the surface as birds created pale shadows in the sky. Silently she thanked God for bringing her through the mild heart attack. The news the doctor gave her was devastating, and the first thing that penetrated her mind was the prayer of God taking her before He took her babies. She was at peace with it if that was His plan. She was even more gracious that He'd given her another day to see the sun kiss the Heavens. While lost in her thoughts of the future, the door to her room flew opened and her boys spilled in like a violent storm. Assata was the first to make it to her, yet he merely stood above her with an intense look in his eyes.

"Boy, you's a sight for sore eyes, give your Lovey a hug and stop standing there looking like you've lost your manners!"

Assata leaned down and wrapped his arms around her—tight and vice-like.

"Boy—you about to squeeze the life out of me," Lovey wheezed affectionately.

He still held on tight. The visions he had while stuck in his co-matose state played behind his lids, thoughts of losing her took his breath away—made him sick.

"You bet not eva—eva—eva scare me like that again, young lady, you hear me woman?" he grumbled, as he broke the embrace.

Pain pushed him out of the way and wrapped her up in his love. "Get out the way, fam— you ain't the only one that needs this typa love," he kidded Assata. "But, like he said, Queen, don't eva do us like that again! You made me throw away a gram of Kush!"

Lovey fixed him with a quizzical stare as she tried to figure out what the hell Kush was. The room exploded in laughter as Goose elbowed his brother out the way.

"Never mind him, sweetness, how are you?" Goose gazed down into her pretty browns, anyone with eyes could see the turmoil that resided just beyond the loving smile.

"Aww hush—all of you," she smiled, as mist converged in her eyes. "Y'all sho' know how to make a lady feel special, I'm blessed." She attempted to downplay the storm that was sure to spill from her eyes once she revealed the devastating news to these three men that loved her more than life.

Goose, ever the observer, saw the storm before it spilled from her. "Tell us what happened, mama, what's going on?"

It's as if his voice—his request—it all cracked her façade, and the truth that she wanted to hide from them exploded in her morale. They deserve the truth! She taught them to never keep secrets from one another, especially from her. Knowing this, she would never be able to forgive herself if she was to be viewed as a hypocrite in their eyes. She made eye contact with each man individually, her gaze finally settled onto Assata. He was the baby of the three, yet the one the devil toyed with the most.

She reached for the remote connected to the bed and adjusted herself into a sitting position. Once she was comfortable, she scooted over just enough and patted the empty spot without breaking her stare.

"Come, sit right here chile, I need to feel your energy." She cracked that smile, that always gave solace to the wilderness that resided within each one of them.

Assata didn't fall for it, yet still complied out of respect. Pain sat at the foot of the bed, and Goose kept his post standing. He could feel the darkness that was rolling from a corner of the world that he nor his brothers had ever ventured. His eyes turned to slits as a cold chill snaked itself around his heart and held on tight. They could count on one hand without using all five fingers how many times they'd witnessed Lovey cry. Even when her other half, her late husband, was gunned down in 1965, two days after the Watts Riot. This had to be some deep shit!

She took Assata's face in her hands, they all understood that Assata was her baby. She took on the duty of mothering him after his moms died in 2002—the day after Valentine's Day.

"Assata—you've been angry at God your entire life. Chile— you remember when you and ya' mama was in Oak Cliff, and she was about to spank ya narrow behind for accidentally setting her couch on fire? You ran and locked yourself in the room and called me. Till this day, I still don't' know how a five-year-old chile remembered all them numbers, but you did—umhm—you sho' did. I remember you cried, and when I asked you why, you said—Lovey, mama trying to whoop me cause I was tryin' to get Gods attention. I asked you what you meant, and you said—I was praying, but Him wasn't listening so I thought if I used mama's lighter he could see where I was at. But, Him let mama's couch light up—now she wanna whoop me, but Lovey, I promise it was an accident. I just wanted God to listen!" The room ignited in laughter.

Even Assata smirked at the trip down memory lane, but his smile didn't quite reach his eyes. As he searched hers, he couldn't seem to shake the ice that seemed to be solidifying around his heart. Anticipation sliced the throat of his patience, and the words slipped from his lips—

"Lovey, what the fuck is going on—we—"

'Smack—' There was no surprise—no anger—just deep waters as he rubbed the spot that Lovey just slapped.

"You watch ya mouth, ya hear? You ain't too big for me to turn ya behind red. You ain't out there with them heathens—you respect ya, Lovey, hear me," she chastised.

"I'm—I'm sorry, Queen, I—it's just—"

"Sorry is a title for lazy—trifling negro. I know I ain't raised my boys to be either," she cut him off. "Now, I know you feel something amiss, baby—all of you can, but that's what I'm telling you. You must cage that animal within you, chile, it has no place here. Chile, I reminded you of that memory because I know that same little boy that called me that day still resides in you. He's gonna try to get God's attention again! This time, the fire he may cause will be too great to extinguish—" she paused, as she looked over at Goose. "This time, Goose is the one to lose his grip with patience."

"Lovey, you're spooking me—just tell us what's going on, so we can know what to do to help."

Lovey shook her head slightly as she turned eyes baptized in pain onto him. "There—there's nothin' you can do, chile. I'm dying y'all, my heart is old, and has gone bad on me."

***

~Ice-Berg~

Two Days Later

The black tar heroin, I got was raw—fresh off the boat. I sat in the kitchen and watched as Twisted taught Tessa how to mix the quinine, lactose, dextrose, and bonita in a perfect mixture in the blender before cappin' it up. I stared at the twenty bricks on the floor, it reminded me of the day me and my lil bro, Nutz sat in that warehouse, the day our paths took different directions. This ain't how I envisioned shit. This was my brother's dream—his death sentence. Thoughts of my fam touched me somewhere deep. My mind began to get the best of me until Tessa asked a question that even I wrestled with.

"Baby, has anyone heard from Mena? It was not like her to not get at me, and ever since they admitted her moms to that psych ward, I'd been worried about her."

My eyes found Twisted, he never broke his concentration on his work. "Naw, bae, I ain't heard shit from lil' mama ever since she ran up out the emergency room when they told us about Lil' Joe."

To the naked eye, nothing seemed astray, but to a person that's known him his entire life, the fabrication was evident.

"Say, bruh, you good? I'm 'bout to murk out," I interrupted his flow.

He turned his red-rimmed eyes to me, I could tell he was sampling the product, or maybe the mask wasn't thick enough to prevent the power of the morphine that danced against it.

"Fam, you know, I got this bidness—and if things get to cookin', my lil' friend will help me simmer it down." He nodded to the M4 on the counter.

I nodded towards the living room. "Rock with me real quick, it won't take long."

As he turned off the blender Twisted pulled the mask off his face and a long string of snot hung from his nose. He used the back of his hand to wipe it away. I shook my head as I turned to leave the room. Shit crazy mayne, my niggaz head not right. We entered the living room, and the first thing that caught my attention was the boarded-up window my lil' homies noggin' came crashing through.

It was just one of the many indications that shit had gotten too thick, and it was time for a sit down with the boy Assata. But, first— I had to get things correct with lil' buddy, right here cause he was gonna end up taking down the entire clique if he didn't tighten up. I turned to face him, it was apparent that he was as high as Jesus— I shook my head in disappointment.

"Damn, homie, when you start fuckin' with the boogeyman?"

His eyes drooped as a wicked smile parted his lips. "Ah, bruh, its nothin' serious. I just bumped a little bit to take the edge off, feel me?"

"Naw, I don't feel that dope-fiend shit, fam! We 'posed to be getting to the money, not indulging ya nose, look at you. Twist— you can't show up nowhere looking like Pookie off New Jack City! If the homies see you off yo' note, the cubs gonna want yo' seat, bruh, you're 'posed to be setting the—"

"Nigga, fuck outta here. Them niggaz know not to move crooked round me, I'm certified! Fam, let me do me, I got this— damn," Twisted cut me off.

I stared at him—yea, lil' bro' was nefarious 'round the city, but what he didn't seem to understand was that these young boys were just as vicious and ambitious as he was. I've learned the hard way that you gotta let a man earn his own scars. Experience will be his best teacher.

"Look, Twisted, I'm not in yo' mix, my dude, but when the shit you do interferes with my mula. It becomes a problem, we both know how I deal with problems." I stared him down.

"You say all that 'G' shit to say what, family?" he seethed.

His eyes were twitching and murder was snaking from his body language. We faced off like two cowboys, but what he seemed not to recall was that his heat was in the kitchen. I relaxed my stance. Even though I had the ups on fam, he's my family. I didn't need his blood on my hands.

"At ease soldier—ain't no smoke ova here, but—I'm sayin' kinfolk—you so off ya stick that you at work on the day you mourn. How you gonna let the squad see you like—like this?" I used my hands to punctuate my point. Confusion was his best friend as he stared at me perplexed.

"Fuck you talmbout, Berg, ain't nobody gonna see me like this, I ain't leaving the spot, we got work to do."

I smiled at him sadly. "So, you mean to tell me you forgot we layin' Lil Joe to rest today? You gonna miss ya manz funeral?"

***

~Armani~

"You did what? Uh-uh, bitch—you lyyyiin'! Please tell—" my sister, Kris overreacted.

She was always extra, but, she was my best friend. There was no other person more down for me than her. We've been through it all.

"Damn, bitch, lower your tone before they kick us out of here," I whispered theatrically.

I hated to be embarrassed! Marcella giggled as if the shit was funny, but the food here was oh-to-good to have these silly broads get us tossed out. I sat up in my seat, my eyes absently turned to slits as I used my fork to cut into my slice of Tiramisu. I closed my eyes completely as to savor the exotic taste, it was as good as an orgasm—infused with rum and layered with mascarpone cheese, topped off with grated chocolate, this delicacy was delicious.

"Mani, damn bitch, that cake can't be that good. I've been calling you for twenty years—damn." Kris interrupted my vibe.

"Naw—that ain't the cake that has her out of space like that, it's that *dick-a-thought*," Marcella added her two cents.

Kris looked at her with an arched eyebrow. Marcella released an exaggerated roll of the eyes. "Yes, bitch—the *dick-a-thought*— is when the dick is so good it becomes a thought! Every stroke— the girth—that—dick so good, that when he's not around, you just daydream about it. *Dick-a-thought*." She fanned herself like she'd just gamed us on some real top-notch shit.

Kris had the nerve to high five her like she was gonna add the phrase to her repertoire of things to say. I laughed at their silly butts. Dick didn't stay on my mind like that. Assata's sex game was the bomb.com, yet that's not what moved a real woman as myself.

"Are you gonna give us the details or not?" Marcella demanded as she popped a black cherry in her mouth.

Despite the things Tessa has said about Mar I embraced her. I even went as far as telling her and my sister about how Assata did the strangest things to my body. A woman should never tell her bedroom secrets, but my sister was my sister, and I wanted to mark my territory with Mar. Even though I gave her a chance, I hadn't forgotten how devious she could be, nor have I discarded Tessa's advice about her wanting Assata.

"No, details, but—let's just say that only a big girl can wrestle with that lion!"

"Heeyy—Armani got her a ruff-neck," Kristasia sang as she did a little jig in her seat.

I rolled my eyes at her and focused my attention on Marcella. As she used her straw to stir the cream in her strawberry daiquiri, she smiled this *'you go girl'* smile, but her eyes told a totally different story. To one that didn't know any better, they'd overlook it, but to a bitch like me, I saw it—envy—jealousy. I notated it and store it in the back of my mind.

"So, what you gonna do about, Jazzy?"

I arched my eyebrows and tried to figure her angle. "I don't get it, what does she have to do with me?"

"Shit, girl, she loves that boy. I talk to her every day, and he's all she talks about. She's 'pose to come back to town next month, that's why I can't believe, Assata did that—niggaz ain't shit, I swear," she hissed.

"Soon as a girl goes to tend to her sick grandma, he's stickin' his little dick in the next bihh!"

Shots fired! The look I gave my sister. We're both hip to the fact that Jazzy left Assata for another man. We're also hip to the fact that Jaz does not talk to Mar because Tessa finally let the cat out the bag about how Mar feels for him. Maybe Tessa was onto something when she tried to warn me about this girl. If only I'd known just how right she'd turn out to be, maybe I wouldn't regret so much later down the road when her warning turned into reality. I would had been better off cutting the head off the snake than embracing it. Snakes can't be tamed, it don't matter if you've defanged them. It's only natural for them to bite!

***

~Ice-Berg~

The church was packed to capacity. It seemed as if the whole metroplex showed up to pay their respects to one of the city's most ambitious sons. It's crazy how people could turn even the most devastating events into a fashion show. Minks and Gators—designers such as Valentino, Officine Generale—Dior Homme, and many others could be seen on display. It was so many jewels that it looked as if someone looked at a picture of ancient Egypt and attempted to breathe revivalism into the atmosphere.

I sat up front with Pearl as Reverend James sweated at the pulpit. He'd been up there lying out the front of his teeth about how good a man Lil' Joe was, and how he was in a better place. I laughed, this nigga ain't even know, fam! Lil' Joe was a killa! No need to act like we ain't all here to mourn a gangsta. This was why I hated funerals, too much fake shit. I glanced at the Audemar on my wrist, frustration was evident on my face. Fuck this boy at?

Twist was 'pose to be here thirty minutes ago. I knew it didn't take this long to put that work up and lock the trap down. Pearl musta read my body language because she patted me on my knee in a soothing manner.

"And God says, for the body shall perish, but the soul, the soul will—" James said before the doors of the church blew open with force.

All eyes turned to see who, or what could be so bold as to disturb the eternal rest of lil' homie. A few of the homies stood to investigate, but it was not warranted as a lone figure stepped in Crip walking his way down the aisle, stacking and chunking up the set as if Dub-C taught him that shit personally. Fam made a spectacle. He was dressed in a navy-blue Dickie's unit, blue bandanna tied around his head, wrist, and neck, but—it was the portrait of him and Lil' Joe one the back of his shirt that made his outfit worth more than every Mink and designer outfit in attendance.

It was a picture of him and Lil' Joe standing in the middle of Hic Street, clutching AR-15's. Above the picture, it said, *'Crip in Peace till I Get There'*. No one moved to put an end to his antics. In fact, Pearl smiled so big I wondered if this shit was preordained. I turned my eyes back to my little cousin, even I had to acknowledge the gangsta. Even though, his attire had to be the cheapest one in the building, financially—sentimentally it was worth a mill ticket. As he made it to the casket, he began taking the bandannas off one by one and laid them over its surface.

"Now hold on one minute, young man, this-this isn't'—" the preacher began before the reaper cut him off—

"If you enjoy standing ova that casket rather than being in it, you need to find you a seat preacher. Right now, I'm grooving with my nigga. You don't want to invite the devil in." Twist said, as he walked up and snatched the microphone out of his hands.

He gazed at the crowd, he sneered before he fucked the whole congregation up. "Fuck all y'all! My nigga ain't know none of y'all! You niggaz ain't stood in them trenches with us when we was pitchin' fifty packs by the food sto'! You niggaz came here to stunt fa these nothin' ass hoes but see—y'all ain't gonna squat at my brothers last stop and come up on some of the same pussy he laid in before. He checked out. So, this what the bidness is, and it's fair considering my first impulse."

He reached under his shirt, Twisted pulled out a grey and black .40 with a small drum attached to it. He sighed and deep intakes of breath could be heard as mu'fuckas anticipated his next move. Everybody knew the boy was nasty with his work, so his next words were heeded with haste.

"All you mu'fuckas get the fuck out," he roared, as spit flew from his mouth.

A stampede ensued as people jumped over each other in order to make it out with their lives. Minutes later, the church was as empty as a deserted island, except for a few gangstas, Pearl, her daughters, the preacher and yours truly. He turned his eyes to Reverend James and grit his teeth, as he pointed the tool at him.

"Fuck I just say, dude? Get ya fake ass out, nigga! God ain't give a fuck 'bout him while he was living, so we ain't trying to hear him now. This a gangsta's party, only gangsta's invited!"

Pearl fanned herself. "Hallelujah," she stated, raising her other hand to give praise.

Chapter Seventeen

It's Really Me Fam
~Pain~
Days Later

Heading out of the house, I ran straight into Tessa. Little lady was lookin' real bossy in a Marchesa short set, with a pair of stiletto Jordan's on. Her hair was pulled back tight into a bun, and her sex appeal screamed for a boss to take her somewhere and fuck her till she was sleeping with her thumb in her mouth.

"Whoa, lil' mama." I grabbed her by her arms to prevent her from fallin' on her ass.

Once she was steady, I leaned down and smooched her on those succulent ass lips. "What's good, mama?"

Her pretty ass looked at me with a blush and laughed like a school girl. "Where you going so fast—huh, Papi?"

"I'm 'bout to mash to the spot to see how that bag lookin'. I'ma bark at you after I'm through getting my hands dirty," I revealed.

The look crossed her face, but as quickly as it came, it went. She smothered it with a fake smile, but I ain't for the fakin', so I checked it asap.

"What's the bidness with that face you made?" I questioned.

She tried to downplay it. "Boy stop, just make some time for me when you get loose," Tessa flirted.

I looked at lil' one with one of them, *'yea right'*, looks and smashed all that weak shit she spat. A female was only as gamed up as the nigga that's molding her, and I'm a true sculptor so I saw the cracks in the shallow façade she was putting on.

"Sup, mayne, you fuckin' wit' me or what? I ain't gonna be there long anyway. You may as well slide with me," I said, as I hit the automatic start on the blood red Jag XF Sport-brake I'd just copped.

"What, nigga, don't play. I know you ain't going to nobody's trap dressed like that," she retorted, indicating the Prada unit I adorned.

Bingo! That's what crawled up shawty's ass, she thinks I'm 'bout to cut the next bitch.

I laughed lightly. "Ooh, I get it. That's why you blowing all that smoke out ya nose. You think I'm checking for the next hoe?" I stared at her with a crooked smile. "You caught feelings for a nigga, ma—you jealous?"

"Bruh, you got the wrong one talking about catching feelings, and shit! Jealous, boy look at me!" Tessa spun around, that little petite ass jiggled as she did a 360 on me.

"I'm a bad bitch, and you know it! Miss me with all the extras."

I stepped into lil' one's space, "Tess, you ain't gotta front wit' ya boy. I know you on my game like that, that's gravy cause I'm fuckin' wit' your flavor as well," I said, kissing her forehead, followed by a trail of wet kisses down her neck.

"Umm, Pain, you, betta—bet—quit boy, you know that's my spot," she moaned, then untangled herself from my embrace.

I learned at an early age that it's two things that will humble a tough hoe. One, showing her, you don't need her, and two, preyin' on her weaknesses. Shawty finally decided to discard the games.

"Pain, what is this? I'm fa real, can we even put a title on us? I mean, I'm fuckin' with you cause you make me feel like no other nigga has—my body—my mind—they crave you, but you insist that I keep fuckin' with Twisted so you can get ya ups on him and his crew. What happens when he senses that shit? When can it just be us? Are we just friends with benefits—lovers—what?" Tessa showed me her vulnerability.

Our eyes searched each other, as I allowed my mind to wrap around the possibilities. I'm feeling lil' mama in a major way, but—can I trust her?

"Look, this how I see shit if you're ready to take it there, that exclusive shit? I'm with it, but I demand loyalty, ma. No in between, I'll kill you for treason!" I gave it to her as solid, as it was once given to me. "There's a lot that comes with fuckin' with a nigga like me, ma. So, before you jump into the water with a shark, you need to be sure that's what you want." I gave her the ball to bounce in her court.

I know Tessa has been giving her pussy to numerous niggaz. She's set niggaz up for her duole and even shared herself with other bitches. Yet—her heart ain't ever been held by a real nigga that sees her beyond jumping up and down in her pussy. I can tell from the way she walks—talks.

"Pain, I'm tired of playing games. Yea, I'm feeling you. Yea, I wanna be yo' girl, but what price do I gotta pay in order to hold that title? I'm not scared of being hurt, but that doesn't mean that I'm in a rush to experience that typa emotion," She said, with something deep in her eyes.

"Look, ma—in every relationship, pain lurk within the shadows. If you can't accept what comes with love, what's the use of trying to possess it? Love and pain mix in the same pyrex, you can't have one without the other. If you've never grown from the pain of the one that you love. How can you profess this sacred emotion, and know fa sure it's sincere?"

Tessa sighed, "So, what your saying is I should take the risk of investing my heart in you, knowing that you may hurt me in the future?"

"Naw, ma—what I'm sayin' is if you accept a person with their flaws and can still find it within your heart to love them. Then you take the risk of being hurt anyway. All in all, I'm asking you to take this chance with a real nigga, knowing that I'd neva intentionally hurt you."

Tessa stared at me—her eyes search for an indication of game. Seeing none, she did the only thang left to do, snatch the keys out my hands. "I'm driving this pretty bitch. You just sit back like a boss and show me where to go."

***

~Assata~

The needle glided over my skin as my ese potna, Hector inked my neck. He was freakin' a big ass lion head, and I was trying to be 'G'd up under the pressure of the gun, but whoever said tattoos didn't hurt was a lying son-of-a-bitch! Focusing my attention on the sound of the money machine clicking, and the activities around me—I tried to blink it out.

"I'm almost done vato—just be a 'G' till I'm through." He smiled down at me.

Something soft entered the room and her aroma was sweet—cherry blossom—sexy! "Ahh," I growled as the gun cut off.

"All done ese, tell me whatchu tink?" Hector said.

Holding up the hand-held mirror, I stared wide-eyed at his work. Homie gifted. "That shit nice, daddy—fa real!" Marcella said next to me—too close for my comfort.

I got up from the couch, I dug in the pockets of my Louis V's and pulled out a knot. I peeled four bills from the stack and attempted to hand them to bruh, but he pushed my hand away.

"Nada, amigo, tu know we too good for compensation. Don't insult me, ese," he frowned.

I laughed and dapped him up. He was right, me and homie been rocking since middle school. When shit between the browns and blacks wasn't so accepted. Yet, me and ole Hector put that shit to the side cause we recognized potential. Now fifteen years later—we still counting commas together. My phone jumped on my hip, taking it off and looking at it, the number was unfamiliar. I didn't know what made me look up, but I came into eye contact with Mar. For some reason, the bitch just made me feel? I didn't know really, but I did know that in an attempt at breaking eye contact, I answered my phone.

"Yea—Yea?"

The voice on the other end was silent, yet I could hear the breathing.

"Man, fuck who playin' on—"

"This Assata?" The familiar voice froze my blood. I'd recognize it anywhere!

He laughed. "I see yo' paranoid ass is still observant. I take it you already know who this is, so we can skip the formalities. Dig, I need to vibe with you, homie—it's important."

I'm really speechless. The whole world been lookin' for this nigga, and here he was on my shit.

"Where—when?" I hissed.

"Shid, now! We can meet up at that old spot your boys got out in the country. You know—the spot y'all did ole boy at. Hour plus, homie."

"Hold the fuck up—you talking real reckless on my shit, fam," I spazzed, but it was useless cause he was gone.

Ice-Berg hung up, but—how the fuck he know 'bout tha spot?

***

~Freedom~

The spotlight was against my skin. The microphone felt powerful in my hands. The crowd was silent—anticipating—awaiting my voice to place into words the thoughts that most couldn't verbalize. The room was smokey—electric! To me, it was a deserted island lost within a moment of déjà vu. I'd been here before, yet—it felt so empty—so foreign!

"Come on girl, preach that Earth talk," A queen encouraged me from somewhere beyond the light.

A wounded smile kissed my lips as I acknowledged her wit' a nod of my head. My hair was wild tonight, the same as emotions—the condition Assata left them in.

"Peace Gods and Earth. Tonight, I stand before you all as I am—a volcano of emotions. Due to circumstances beyond my control, it hurts me to say, but tonight will be my last night gracing the stage."

Hushed whispers ensued, and some midnight black brother said, "Come on sista, don't do us like that. Hell, you're the reason I come to this hellhole!"

The host blue said, "Hey now, don't get ya ass kicked!"

The crowd roared at his jest—I smiled in spite of it being the last thing I feel like doing.

"It's okay y'all, cause tonight I plan to leave y'all with something to remember me by. This piece I'm 'bout to give y'all is my mind, body, and soul all wrapped into a tropical storm that's raging around this room in search of the only God that can be tamed it. Since he's not present, y'all just let it wash over 'yall in the rawest form. It's me personified, Free! I call it, *'Standing in a Tropical Storm'*. I wrapped my hands around the mic before caressing it in my signature way—sexually—intimately, my lips parted, and an invisible storm was created in the form of words.

"Loving you is like spending two and a half days wandering the Sahara Desert, twelve hours away from becoming dehydrated

Only to stumble upon a paradise in the form of a gangsta, a partial cup of water that isn't enough to quench my thirst, yet just enough to make me rehydrated

So, I hungrily sip from your cup as if it is the cup of eternal life

Only to realize that love is blind like a sightless woman that prays for eternal sight

I give you me—naked as Eve was before she came into the knowledge

Yet, you give me your hypothesis—a taste of your love—and your dick, as if I'm a crazy woman, and it's the new word for psychiatrists

Yet, I'm Earth—the third planet from the Sun, Revolution period of three sixty-five point twenty-six days at a mean distance of approximately one forty-nine point, six million kilometers, and it takes me twenty-three hours and fifty-six point, zero seven minutes to rotate around you

Meaning—perfection within our distance—if we become any closer, there'd be fire within our kisses—I know I'm not beyond your comprehension, yet Sun I need you to listen.

I've witness Heaven cries from the number of seven eyes—

Lost so much in my life that I began to question God—Allah!

Yet, I know that nothin' will make me more unbalanced than saying goodbye, having to live with the fact that we didn't even try

But, how is this real if you're living a lie

Telling me God comes from under the mud, when I was taught he resides in the sky?

Y'all, I don't want to love him anymore, yet my heart is an alcoholic for his taste

Knowing that even if I moved on with another, I'd end up replacing his face with his face

That would be treason—a fake bitch—a love misplaced.

So, I'll wait—

Not wanting to love him, but needing to in order to breath

Standing in a tropical storm searching for an escape, but knowing I'll never leave."

***

~Goose~

Me and Kamika pulled up beside Assata's SS. Soon as I killed the ignition, she handed me a Ninna Ross, amm1, that looked vaguely familiar, but I couldn't place it just yet. My mind was stuck on the twist in the game that Assata just hipped me to. The cat Ice-Berg that I'd saw all over tv had resurfaced. Here—at our spot! Since I first touched down in this hellhole, I'd had my investigation in full swing! I heard of the ongoing beef between him and Assata, so quite understandably I suspected him for the shooting that landed my baby brother in a coma! Yet, I also suspect the girl, Jazzy. Even though, Assata disagreed, something didn't sit right with me.

I remembered her telling me about the dude Gusto but now he's dead! Who shot him? It's as if someone was cleaning house and as long as they was still breathing, Assata wasn't safe. I knew his mind had been preoccupied trying to figure it out, but my eyes and ears were to the asphalt! Back to the here and now—fuck this sucka been hiding? How he knew about this spot? The law boy that we slumped? There's too many questions that only he had the answers to. So, with that in mind, me and lil' one exited the truck at the same time.

Assata pushed the banana clip into the Draco AK .47. Two more carloads of our shootas swerve in beside us, everybody was war ready! Once everybody was on deck, we all turned to Assata, it was his call. His eyes studied the abandoned building as if it was his first time seeing it, but the sound of tires moving fast over gravel snatched all of our attention. A fleet of five SUV's pulled to a stop in a 'V' formation. The lead truck was a black Infiniti Qx80 that squatted on black big heads.

The front doors swung open and two well-dressed Mexicans stepped out brandishing assault rifles equipped with drums so big it looked like a workout just holding them. We watched as they stepped to the back of the truck and open both doors. A bald dark-skinned cat stepped out. He was clap doctor clean in an all-white Giorgio Armani two-piece, accentuated by a pair of gold Gators. He was accompanied by a Mexican dressed head to toe in colorful Versace. I knew because the silk button up that depicted the big Medusa head on the front was in my closet at home.

As the four men stepped towards us, the remaining trucks spilled out a mixture of black and brown gun-toting men that caused me and Assata to make eye contact. He ain't tell me we was meeting the Mafia! The closer they got, the more crazy shit became. All of the ese's have big ass tattoos on their face. The most recognizable was the MS-13 stamp. I'm familiar with El Salva Trucha. There was a few in the Tone that came down from Cali. They're not Mexicans, they're Salvadorian. Beasts! Barbarians! Midway they stopped and assessed us as we repaid the same assessment. I turned my eyes to Assata; he looked a bit confused, as his eyes searched the crowd. I didn't know what was up, but I did know that this was the wrong time to become indecisive! Naw—straight up!

***

~Assata~

Fuck he at, is this a setup? This nigga playin' a dangerous game, and to think I started to respect his pussy ass after the Russian lick.

I saw my brother getting antsy besides me. His grip tightened on the bullshit nine in his hands. I told fam that we were coming to see a gangsta, out of every gun we got on deck, this boy brings a fuckin' nine! No need to trip though—the short booty choppa I'm clutchin' gave me reassurance that if shit got ugly, I would be able to cover me, bruh, and his bitch! I stepped forward and spoke my peace.

"What's the bidness, where Berg at?" I waited, but my only response was blank stares and a deadly silence. So, shid—I did what any gangsta would do, I aimed the tool and drew the line in the sand. "Since you boys jumpin' out on some mafia shit like it ain't real ova here. What's poppin', bleed? Y'all trying to get on some real cowboy shit or what? I ain't askin' no mo'—fuck Berg at," I hissed loud enough for the world to hear me.

Every cat that knew me, knew I was 'bout to get on that dumb shit. I guess that's why all the click-clacking of weapons on both sides of the line could be heard, but most importantly, the reason the bald-headed cat stepped out with a smile on his face. That's cool, he would be the first to go where niggaz like us go after our time had expired, I aimed in his direction.

***

~Ice-Berg~

The atmosphere was lit with tension—murda—testosterone! I put a hand in the air so that my shootas saw, I held it in the air silently letting them know we good. Weapons lowered on my side, but the opposition wasn't respecting nothin' but Assata's word. I smiled, as I stepped towards the young lion.

"If you know what's good for you gangsta, you'd stop where you're at," he said, when I'm 'bout nine feet away—almost face to face.

The diamonds rocked him as I allowed them to gleam in the sun. He knew I was the only one with sapphires and gold in my mouth. That was his first indication that it was some strange shit in the mix, but once I spoke, his face contorted into a look of wonderment—curiosity—disbelief! Yet, he lowered the burna and tilts his head slightly with a million questions in his eyes. Then he said, "Fam, this some real freaky bidness."

***

~Assata~

I've seen some real spooky shit in my day, but this? This bidness right here was what them urban books authors be writing 'bout. Now, either this boy had got the exact grill as Ice-Berg or he whacked the boy and pried them shits of his teeth, but what he couldn't have done was stolen homie's raspy ass voice. I'd recognize it anywhere!

"Sup, homie—you look like you saw a ghost," he laughed at his own joke.

"Look, Assata, I know this is a lot to swallow, bruh, but let's step in there. I'll give it to you from the hip."

He nodded towards the building.

While he assessed the man, Goose leaned over and whispered. "Yo—why are you looking like you seen a ghost? We 'bout to make these tools talk or what bruh—you got me off my square."

"Fam, that's not Berg—I mean—it is Berg—but, it ain't his face— Maaann, just let me think, bruh." I turned my attention back to Berg.

If he wasn't who he betta be, a lot of us was not gonna make it home to our families, and I was goin' to spend as much time as I possibly could with Lovey before she closed her eyes. On gang!

***

~Face in the Dark~

I placed my binoculars down beside me, I was as lost as the tv series. Who the fuck were these people, Assata was meeting with here in the country? The bald guy was the boss—his aura was thick—demanding! Yet, the Mexican had the walk of a drug lord. Could it be that Assata was plotting to get deeper into the drug business? Why does the bald guy walk spark familiarity? Hmmm? Something was off about this whole situation, but no matter what these boys had goin' on. They were going to need every gun they could find because the tiger touched down in the city today. I must keep Assata alive in order to help me break the chains of the new master.

Then—only after, am I at free will to kill him myself! Kill him and fuck him? Fuck him, then kill him—whichever occurred first.

***

~Ice-Berg~

"Yeah, homie, it's really me," I repeated, for the third time in the thirty minutes we'd been in this hot ass building.

After I explained the entirety of what transpired after we went our separate ways from the Russia lick. Assata and who I'd learned to be his older brother stared at me in awe—fascination! The cute lil' broad who I assumed to be Goose's lady friend stared at me with what I assumed to be starstruck admiration, but, it was something-something strange about her stare. I couldn't quite put my finger on it, but if I was right, I'd be fuckin' her somewhere down the road. I had a feeling Goose recognized the chemistry as well, but he said nothin'. I liked him, he was a playa personified.

"Look, homie, all this bloodshed is costin' me a fortune, I—"

"All this bloodshed coulda been avoided if you wouldn't have been on all this mysterious kingpin bidness, dawg, now some solid homies are underground all because you allow yo' arrogance to blindfold you to the bigger picture, nigga!" Assata seethed.

Heat instantly flooded my veins, but before I could check playboy for interruptin' me, my phone sang Belle's ringtone. Fire was in my eyes as I stared him down and yanked my horn off my hip.

"Yea, what's up, ma, I'm busy!"

My face turned a darker shade of black from what she just told me. I hung up and looked to homie—we gotta problem!

Chapter Eighteen

'Let's Make A Deal'
~Assata~
Next Day

"We have a problem! We have a problem! We have a problem," he ranted.

"Fuck you mean, we got a problem?"

"Damn—damn—damn! How the fuck they know? Do they know? Fuck—say, we gotta do something—quick," Ice-Berg said as he paced the littered floor in a frenzy.

"Say, fam," I said, as I stepped in his path, blocking his stride.

"Fuck is wrong with you, who has a problem!?"

His eyes were unfocused—distant. He looked as if he was searched for answers to questions beyond him. A rat scurried across the floor, and without warning, this nut case snatched up the Draco I'd laid on a makeshift bench, and damn near whacked the harmless rodent. All eyes turned to him like he'd lost his head, even his own men had curious looks on their faces.

As if he just realized he was the center of attention, he looked to me. "The Russians are here, they touched down today!"

I looked at him like, so fuckin' what! But, he dropped a bomb on me and everybody in the room.

"Fam, they know it was us!" Looking as if he'd whacked me, rather than risked me givin' him up, he said, "They comin' for me, and you, bruh. They won't know what I look like, but you won't be hard to find fam."

My mind spun out of control. Coming for me? Fuck they know, I had something to do with the lick? Fuck they know 'bout me, period? I guess we musta had the same thoughts cause his eyes bore into me.

"Somebody talkin', homie, but who?"

"Assata! Assata," someone's persistence penetrated my reverie.

I turned my head in her direction, confused. "Sup, lady, fuck you yelling in my ear?" I stared at her from hooded eyes.

The Kush got me lovely, yet, I guess not lovely enough to steal my mind from the storm headed my way. Armani took her eyes off the road for a brief moment to study me.

"Whoa—where did you go, baby? You went to a dark place, huh?" she said, as she reached over and took my hand to hers.

I reclined in my seat and turned my gaze out the window. "I'm always in a dark place, ma. The story of my life, ya dig."

Slightly squeezing my hand, she offered me one of the most powerful things a woman can offer a man, her ear.

"You want to talk about it? You know you can tell me anything, right?"

My silence was thick as I observed the condition of my city, as we exited loop 288 and headed for the hospital to see Lovey.

"Right," she persisted.

I finally turned my eyes to her. "You sure 'bout that? Anything, what if I told you, I'ma killa and there was so much blood on my hands I could donate some to a blood bank? What if I told you its' not safe to be with me because my enemies want me dead, and they'll kill everybody I give a fuck about in order to get to me? Better, yet—what if told you, you're wasting your time loving me cause I can never love you back?" I breathe the fire that would purify her truths all the way down to its rawest form.

She released my hand, as she returned her attention to the road. "Look, Assata, I'm not one of those lil' girls you're used to. Naw, I ain't from the same background as you, but you best believe I ain't green. I won't pretend that the shit you told me doesn't scare me to death, but you know what, I've been scared before, so fuckin' what! You don't know me as you will in time, but, know this—when I got in the car with you, I buckled my seatbelt. All this tryin' to run me away mess you be on, miss me with it! Now get your foot out your mouth and put that gun that you have on waist under the seat. We're here, you're already smelling like that stuff you be smoking," she made a goofy face as if she smelled something foul.

"I don't want to have to end my day at the county trying to bond you out for being too gangsta," she said, as she exited the car.

I cracked a smile in spite of myself. Lady was tuggin' on my heart! Real shit, she's yanking on that bitch.

***

~Pain~

The day had been long as fuck, but progressive. After I checked the traps to make sure shit was Gucci, Tessa surprised me with some real freaky shit.

"Baby, you ever had a ménage a trois?" I looked at her quizzically.

"Naw, why, you trying to give me my first one?"

She snickered like a real slut, "I've been known to suck a pussy or two—or three!"

I put the blueberry swisher to my lips and inhaled its essence, her revelation didn't surprise me, a nigga could always tell if he had a freak on his hands, no matter how hard she attempted to hide it. Hoeism was like a perfume to a seasoned playa, he could sense it out the gate! Long story short, that's how me and Tessa ended up in the backseat of my Jag with some ese bitch driving us someplace unknown.

"Say, shawty, where you going?" I asked through a mouthful of smoke.

Lookin' out the window nothin' was familiar. We must have been on the outskirts of the city cause we were surrounded by a bunch of trees and sprawling pastures. Tessa nuzzled the side of my neck as her hand disappeared into my pants.

"Baby, calm down, let us have our way with you. What, you think, we're going to kidnap you, and hold you hostage or something?" She cooed as her fingers wrapped around my flaccidness. She kissed my neck and whispered, "Even, if we were, would that be so bad, daddy?"

As little mama maneuvered the truck expertly, our eyes met in the rearview mirror, with catlike eyes she ran her tongue seductively over her lips.

"Save me some, chula," she said to Tess.

She must have been feenin' for the dick cause her skin was aglow with perspiration. Maybe the hoe was sick or something, I asked anyway.

"What you sweatin' for, mama, you sick or something?"

"Naw, Papi, mi chust con wait to taste tat dick! Mi popped a molly too," she replied, as Tessa's head bobbed up and down with lightning speed.

Her head game deserved straight 'A's! Bitches like this were dangerous because they'll suck a lesser niggaz pockets dry—literally! Layin' my head against the leather, I felt the change of the terrain as lil' mama turned down a dirt road. I was 'bout to protest, but Tessa's lips were like the jaws of life. All I could think was fuck it—I'll wash it tomorrow. If I woulda been on note, I woulda noticed senorita's eyes focusing on the parked car on the side of the road. But, it didn't take long cause a funny feeling caused my eyes to crack open, and that was the first thing I saw.

"Saayy, mann, where the fuck we going," I spazzed, pushin' Tessa off me.

I reached for my tool at the same time lil' one passed by the white Lexus. I saw that the driver's side door was wide open, and someone was slumped over the steering wheel. The dumb hoe stumped down on the brakes, causing us all to jerk forward.

"Hold on y'all, let's see if they need help," she murmured.

I instantly exploded. "Bitch fuck that nigga, he ain't our concern. Drive this mu'fucka and get us outta here before we wind up cased up for a murda we ain't commit!"

My words musta fell on deaf ears cause this ditsy broad was already out of the truck. Me and Tessa watched as she spoke to whomever it was.

She looked back and said some of the craziest shit I ever heard. "Y'all, this man needs some help."

I frowned as I let the window down all the way.

"Say, you gonna either get your lame ass back in this truck or end up driving that Lex back to the city. We ain't no damn good Samaritans, I'm a drug dealer!"

"Baby go help the man, you wouldn't want nobody leaving you out here in the middle of nowhere fa dead. What if that was me? Would you want somebody to pass me by when they had the chance to save me?" Tessa responded.

My first impulse was to put her ass out with her podna, but she was right. I wouldn't want nobody to leave me for dead. Her—shid, I could get another female, but I couldn't get another me!

"Mann, fuck," I growled, as I opened the door.

I watched as ole girl tried her best to pull homeboy from the car.

"Baby give me the fuckin' gun and go help her, you don't need that shit, right now," Tessa reprimanded.

I shoulda followed my first instinct and smashed off, but like any other nigga in a rush to get his dick wet. I handed ova the tool and made my way over to help.

"Give me a hand, Papi—he's hurt bad," senorita said out of breath.

By now, she's drippin' sweat. Due to the fact that she had him by his legs. I couldn't see his face, but as I stepped around her. I noticed the Lexus seemed unscratched. Not a dent—scratch—not a bullet-hole. That shoulda been my first indication. The second warning should have been when I noticed the absence of blood. Suddenly the Mexican bitch dropped the man's legs.

"Damn, nigga, you not gonna help or what?" She flipped on me.

I noticed the accent was long gone. Then the strangest thing happened, homeboy sat up like the wrestler, *'The Undertaker'*, after he'd been beaten. What—the—fuuuck? Soon as our eyes met, I realized my first mistake. I should have never trusted these hoes! I slowly backed towards the car, homie began laughing maniacally. My adrenaline was at full speed, truth be told, I was damn near 'bout to turn and run, but the cold steel against the back of my head deaded all of that. Tessa spoke to Playboy as if they'd been doin' this shit their whole lives.

"Baby let me do this nigga with his own gun—pweese, bae?" she begged.

Homie looked at me with a satisfying smirk. "What you think, homie, choose your poison? You fell for the oldest trick in the book. Boys never learn pussy kills mo' niggaz than the streets."

***

As I stepped into the dimly lit room, I couldn't stop my heart from hurting. Ever since she told us about her condition, life didn't seem so colorful. A man can acquire all the money in the world, fuck some of the baddest women, and pop every typa bottle known to man. But, at the end of each day, his balance was found in the people that will love him without all that shit. In this day and age, love and loyalty was just as materialistically important as a car, and clothes. Mu'fuckas will love you and pledge their loyalty for just as long as you whippin' the hottest whip and allowed them to share in the riches you took penitentiary chances fa.

Soon as yo' time expires, the love becomes spite, and the loyalty becomes betrayal. As I stood here and allowed my eyes to take in the condition of Lovey for the millionth time in my life. I wondered if there was such a thing as God? If so, why he let certain shit happen? Just because a person could bear certain shit didn't mean it wouldn't fuck them up to a point that they'd be betta off dead. I never respected the cliché of *'God may not come when you want Him, but He's always on time'* because all I'd witnessed in this life made me ask, on time for what?

Yet and still, I wanted to believe in the homie. It's just hard! I made my way over to my Queen, slowly. It crushed my soul to see how feeble she looked as she slept. I'd never seen her down or weak—never. There's so much I needed to tell her—too much love to return. My eyes blurred without my consent. As I stood over the woman who's loved me beyond the loot—the materialistic shit, I closed my wet eyes and did something I ain't did since Shy was murked. I did the only thing I could do for her—I talked to the O.G.

"If there was a different portion of my life captured within every tear, I've shed maybe the people that question my belief and perspectives could see the why's instead of the animal in me. But since it's not, I know you understand! O.G., I don't know if you're up there, or if I'm talking to myself, but for this woman, that's laying here fighting for her life. I'm coming to you earnestly. Life ain't ever been good to me, my nigga. I can't remember a time that I've ever been truly happy. Yet, as I reflect on the shit I've experienced in life, I see Lovey there, O.G. I guess she's my happiness, my air, God.

You snatched my moms from me when I was fourteen, dawg, stole the heart of a gangsta. If you knew everything that's gonna happen before it happens, then why you let that go down when you know she was the best part of me, fam? You left me with the worst of me—my regrets—my anger—but most of all—this pain! It's raining right—here, dawg—" I used a clenched fist to tap my chest, where my heart was 'pose to be. "It's storming inside of me, O.G., and it's dark. I need you to hear me, God—hear me, mann!

Shy gone—Moose gone—I ain't got shit to give you God—just a few dollas stained with blood, a couple punk hoes that may not last, and a soul that's so black I'm ashamed to offer it to you, but I'll trade it all for this woman to live. Please, God, I don't know if you can see me in the crowd of so many that's needing you, right now, but—" I reached in my pockets and pulled out a lighter. I flicked it once—twice—three times, then—fire. A small flame danced from the octane filled container.

I glanced over at Armani, she stared at me with eyes of confusion, but also respect. She didn't know the story of when I was little and set the couch on fire to get Gods attention, but she was smart enough to know this flame meant something. "God, I need you to see these tears in my eyes—this hurricane that's stirring inside me. I'm not asking you to intervene with this beef that's on its way. I'm not asking you to forgive me for my iniquities. I'm asking you not to take, Lovey, God—please—"

The lakes in my eyes overflowed, as I waved the flame around the room. I slowly opened my eyes—the flame flickered, then died. I need God to see—need him to. So, I flicked the lighter as a flood submerged my face. The sound of me trying to strike the lighter was loud as a Congo drum in the silence of this room. At least to me, it seemed that way. *Zzzp—zzzp*—it sounded off, as I continued to try to bring the flame back. God must've felt a nigga cause an angel called to me from somewhere outside of this bubble of rain, I'd trapped myself in.

"Satta, Baby, that you?" Lovey whispered.

I leaned down and began placing kisses all over her face until it was baptized with my lip prints and tears.

"Yea, mama—it's me—I've been here trying to get God's attention, Lovey, but him won't listen." I cried, as I tried again to make the flame dance.

I need him to see me! *Zzzzp—zzzzp—zzzzp*—fire! I smiled through the tears as the flame danced as if He finally saw me.

***

~Detective Winslet~

I hadn't been to work since the bank heist, so there was much to be done now that I was back at the office. As soon as, I entered officers applauded as if I'd won a Grammy or something. I was quite speechless as I stood in the middle of this room, surrounded by Fort Worth's finest. It was honestly a cultural shock to be surrounded by so many cops after being in the company of so much money—so many gangstas. Truth be told, it felt good! This was me. This was what made my father, who was a cop for thirty years before being murdered on duty, proud of me.

This was his dream. I knew he must've been turning over in his grave for the things I'd been doing. I regretted so much, yet what use was regrets? The only thing I could find peace in was Hunter's blood. He was a threat, he knew my deepest secrets. Secrets that could ruin me! Secrets that I was willing to do anything to keep buried. So, to go along with Goose's plan was easy, yet I couldn't seem to shake the images of what happened to Tony. He was a good man—a husband—a father! He didn't deserve to die like that. Murdered by the hands that he risked his life to help, and for that my hate for Goose and his brothers had begun to fester!

"Winslet, my office—now," my captain screamed from his office door.

Before I headed in that direction, Johnson, the only other female detective in the homicide division grabbed my arm.

"I need to speak with you before you go in there," she stated.

The intensity in her eyes piqued my interest. I stole a quick glance at the captain's office and saw him slipped back inside. I stepped over to her desk, watching as she fidgeted with her hands as she took a quick look around. I assumed she was content with her observation, cause she rocked my world.

"Look, Kamika, I know you don't know me, but with us being the only women here in this man's world—black women at that, we gotta look out for each other. Now, I don't know what's been going on around here, but I have ears. Girl, these white folks are dirty, they ain't for us, Winslet. It's been talk about you being a rogue cop. The rumor is that you had a hand in Hunter's death, and now Tony has come up missing. His wife is a wreck! Right now, as we speak, there's some Fed boys waiting for you in that office. I'm not sure what's going on, but I feel you're a good woman. I know what they're saying about you is pure bullshit, but be careful girl, they—"

"Winslet! I don't have all day, bring your ass, now," Captain Kastle screamed. "Johnson, try to use your mouth for more than girlfriend gossip. Get to work before you find yourself doing security detail down at Dunbar!"

My mind was overflowing with what if's as I dragged my feet in his direction. A quick glance behind me confirmed my suspicions. All eyes were on me, sharks awaited the scent of blood. It was evident that the same fellow officers that just showed so much love at my entrance, wouldn't hesitate to be the first to slap cuffs on me in an instant if the order was called down. I entered the office and as soon as I passed the threshold, the door closed behind me.

Captain Kastle had an indifferent look on his face as he gestured to one of the empty seats at his desk. Turning to take my seat, I came face to face with Agent Harrison, the F.B.I Agent assigned to head the bank heist investigation. He sat behind Kastle's desk with his feet kicked up on it. In a chair to his left, a semi-grey-haired man sat stoically with a pair of deep-set eyes fixated on me. Without changing position, Harrison turned his electric gaze to Kastle.

"No offense, Captain, but can you give us a moment, please?" Kastle seemed disrespected.

"Now wait one damn minute, this is my office! I want to know why the boys have a high up need to talk to my detective. Also, if you don't mind could you please take your damn feet off of my desk?" he fumed.

"Captain, this is a federal investigation. You agreed to cooperate, and we greatly appreciate it, but there's such thing as compromising interest and being as though your division has had an officer murdered under your noses, and another one missing. It shows that there's someone on the inside working with the bad guys. So, that tells me it could be a conflict of interest to divulge any information from our office until we smoke out the rogue. Now unless you're trying to protect them, then have to explain to your superiors how you breached command, I'll ask again—can you please give us a moment?"

They stared each other down for what seemed like forever, but Kastle knew he was outranked.

"Twenty minutes—that's it! Twenty minutes, and I want you and your partner here out of my station," he demanded as he turned and left the room.

There was a tense silence as me and Harrison had a stare down.

"Do I need my lawyer?" I asked.

"Well—that depends," Harrison stated.

"On?"

"It depends on what you're trying to hide, or better yet if you want to explain to him how ballistics show that the killing shot that took your partner out was the one that entered through the right side of his cranium, three inches from his temple. That means the shot had to come from the direction of the right, the passenger seat," he smirked. "And before you say that's merely circumstantial, wait—there's more!"

I'm assuming this was his way of introducing his partner because the second man in the room flipped out his I.D.

"Special Agent Forrest—D.E.A!" He opened a folder and took out a stack of papers of some sort then handed them to me.

It turned out to be pictures and indictments. There were pictures of Goose and his entourage at various events. Me and Goose walking into a warehouse, me and Hunter talking in his car at different times, then—the picture of us all at the abandoned building. The last page was an indictment with my name on it! The charges read, conspiracy to commit murder of an officer in alliance with the bureau, a participant in a CCE *(Continuing Criminal Enterprise)*, and several other charges that spelled out *'life'* in prison, and or the death penalty.

My resolve cracked a little and my hands began to shake. I watched through blurry vision, as Harrison stood and came around the desk. He leaned on the edge and came in for the kill.

"Now, I don't have to tell you how serious these charges are, Ms. Winslet. I'm sure you already know, but what you don't know is that there's a way to save yourself. Now, I'm not saying you won't have to do a little time, because that's almost close to impossible, but—two or three years are much better options than life imprisonment, or worse—death! Yes, these crimes are easily worthy of the death penalty, and as you know, our great state is very much in favor of it. So, what do you say, officer, you want to go down for this scum that nine times out of ten will leave you for dead in the thick of things or are you ready to come back over to our side?" he proposed.

My eyes searched his for the joke. I knew that it was no way they would let me off with merely a slap on the wrist. He sensed my hesitation—my skepticism.

"Listen, Detective Winslet, we know you're just a young girl that fell for this nice guy, right? We also know of the illegal undercover assignment you and your partner conducted in order to get him back in the good graces of the commissioner," he said, with a knowing smile at the shocked look on my face. "You'd be surprised how far our reach is, Detective. So, yes, we know how you went undercover to assist to take down the Kreek Organization, but somewhere along the lines of duty, the line became blurry. It happens all the time, you know. That lifestyle is very enticing if I must say so myself. This is what the Bureau and Drug Enforcement Agency is willing to do for you. We're willing to make a deal with you, that will ensure at the end of this madness, you'll leave with less than a slap on the wrist considering your crimes."

"Get to the point, Agent Harrison, what do you want from me?" I lost patience.

He merely smiled before replying. "From this day forward, you work for us! Every detail you know about these sleazeballs, we want to know! No bullshit, we want the good stuff. From now on, whenever you're in the company of Mr. Trice, you wear a wire. Plain and simple, we want Bennie 'Goose' Trice, Dunte 'Pain' McDaniels, and Assata Lamar all the way down—"

"What if I can give you not only them but also someone bigger? Will that exonerate me—keep my badge?"

The skeptical looks on their faces told me that would be as he said, close to impossible, but they don't know the bomb I'm about to drop on them.

So, I smiled like the cat that swallowed the canary when the D.E.A Agent said, "Well, that all depends on your *'someone bigger'.*"

"How big is David 'Ice-Berg' Swanson, the man that's now number nine of America's Most Wanted?" I played my hand.

"Get—the—fuck—out—of here," the D.E.A boy said, loosening his tie.

I guess the prick was ready to play let's make a deal now. Cocksucker!

Chapter Nineteen

The Tiger
~Assata~

"Boy stop fussing over me." Lovey swatted at me weakly. Then turned her gaze to Armani, I saw the wheels spinning in her head, so I made the introduction.

"Lovey, this is a blessing that I found in the midst of the storm. Her name is Armani, Armani, this is my surrogate moms, Lovey. She is the only person that can make me eat spinach!"

They both laughed at my realism, but I was a hunnid percent fa real!

"Come here chile, let me look at those pretty eyes of yours," Lovey called to her.

I can tell that lil' one was as nervous as a child at a new school, asked to stand up and introduce themselves to the class. Yet, she did as she was told. Lovey stared so deep into her eyes that the girl actually blushed. I knew she wanted Lovey to like her, but I also knew Lovey liked, Jazmina. Yet, like always, she surprised me.

"You know what they say about the eyes don't you, chile?" Armani smiled as she shook her head no.

Lovey continued to stare without smiling, but her look was as gentle as a breeze in spring. "They say that a person's eyes will tell you things that their tongue conceals. Through a person's eyes, you can see clear through their pain—happiness—and desires."

I grinned at Armani, as she listened to my Queens knowledge. "Through your eyes, Armani, I see a deep pain that you've yet to let go of. I also see the love that you have for my son."

Armani was at a loss for words. Her eyes studied Lovey's from a surprised expression. Now, I was wondering 'bout shit Armani has obviously been through.

"Assata has had a hard life, Armani. For some people, it may be hard to love a person of his nature because he won't open up enough to allow anyone to help heal his wounds, but for some reason, I think you're different." Lovey turned her eyes to me, "You have a new shine to your handsomeness."

As she observed me, I saw her eyes landed on my neck, the new tattoo of the lion's head. Due to the fact that I was standing at the end of the bed, she couldn't see it clearly, but before she even opened her mouth, I already knew what she was gonna say.

"Chile, what I tell you about putting all that devil's work on your skin? What you get now?" she fussed.

I knew how the lady was about tats. When she used to come visit me while I was in prison. I'd show her my newest work and she'd fuss and rant 'bout how God said to treasure your body, and it was his temple, blah-blah-blah. She loved me nevertheless, and we didn't keep secrets. So, I walked over to the side of the bed and showed her my neck.

She stared at it with wide-eyed awe. At least that what I thought the expression was, but then fear became unmistakable. It looked as if she was having a nightmare, even though she was wide awake. Something was wrong with my Queen!

"Lovey, you okay? Armani go find the doctor and tell them that—"

"No—no, chile—" Lovey waved me off. "Nothing wrong with me, but Assata, you need to explain to me what that lion stands for."

I stared at her perplexed. "Lovey it's only a tattoo. It symbolized that I've become the king of my destiny. Nothing more and nothing less. Now, I know, you don't like tattoos, baby, but I just needed to complete my artwork. If you want me to, I'll try and get it removed, mama. It's nothing!"

Lovey smiled at me. "No, no, don't be silly, it's just that I've been having this reoccurring dream about a lion squaring off with this giant tiger. It always ends with the tiger defeating the lion. I— I." Lovey couldn't bring herself to finish her statement, yet I already knew the rest. I leaned down to kiss her forehead. I knew she was always worried 'bout me.

"Stop worrying ya self so much, young lady. My karma ain't that bad that a tiger would escape from the zoo just to find me and bite my arm off for having a lion tattooed on my neck. At least I hope not," I said as we shared a laugh.

***

~Goose~

Fresh out the shower, I felt rejuvenated. All morning I had this feeling in my gut that something ugly was about to happen, but don't ask me where it came from because I didn't know. What I did know was this situation with these Russians boys had me off balanced. After Assata sat me down and explained the entire situation, we had a heated argument because he knew betta! He not only put his own life in jeopardy but all of ours as well. I vowed to God, that after that bank bidness, I'd lay my tools down. How could I honor that when my people's lives were lost in the balance?

I was 'pose to be back in San Antonio weeks ago, but I ain't built to turn my back on my fam. As I dried my dreads, my mind was conflicted. I was so lost in my thoughts that I barely registered that someone was knocking at the door. Lovey's spot ain't that big, so it didn't take me no time to get to the living room, with my tool in hand, I stood to the side of the door.

"What's up?" There was nothing but silence, my blood began to heat up. "Who is it?" I asked again, but after this, it was gonna be straight trigga play.

"It's me, baby—open the door, it's nippy out here." Kamika's sweet voice made love to my ears.

I released a whooshing breath and unlocked the door, as well as loosened my grip on the Nina Ross. Lil' mama couldn't know how close to the reaper she just was. I swung the door open, October's breath kissed my skin. It was chilly out there. As she stepped in, she pecked me on the lips before gliding past. I stepped out for a brief moment, eyes alert—sensitive to every moment and sound. I didn't know too much 'bout them Russians, but I knew that them boys were 'bout their business.

I wouldn't allow them to catch me with my pants down. Content that there was no threat, I eased back into the spot and locked the door. I came down here to this lil' country ass city to aid my baby brother and wound up in mo' shit than I'd ever been in.

"Baby, what's wrong?" Kamika asked as I enter the room, her eyes glued to the nine in my hand. Using the tip of it, I massaged my temple.

"I'm good, ma, just—"

"Don't lie, Bennie," she said, as she walked up to me and peeled my fingers from around the burna.

She took it by the barrel and walked over to her purse. I watched as she placed it inside and found her way back in front of me.

"We won't start a relationship with lies." The look on my face must have made her feel self-conscious because she rolled her eyes and corrected that shit.

"Yes, Bennie, I came into this with ulterior motives, but that was before I knew you. It wasn't my intentions to fall for you, baby. I honestly wanted nothing to do with the investigation, but that cocksucker that you made me kill forced me into it. You know what? I'm glad I did because if I would have followed my first impulse, we wouldn't be standing here, right now. Baby, you're going through something, and I've noticed it ever since you came back from the hospital from visiting your moms. Look at you baby, you're so out of it, you're walking around with a dirty pistol. A pistol that has the blood of a Detective on it." Her eyes were gentle— searching, yet right.

"Yea, you're right, ma. It's just-just a lot of shit a nigga gotta deal with, right now," I admitted, as I pulled her in my arms.

She wrapped her arms around my neck before using her teeth to seductively nip at my bottom lip.

"Let me make you feel better." She kissed my neck, *muah*— "Take—*muah*—all—*muah*—your—" her hand tugged on the elastic of my sweats, she reached inside and took a hold of my power. As she stroked me to an erection, she kissed her way down my bare chest, freeing my lil' man as she continued. "Stress—*muah*— *muah*— she squatted down until she was face to face with my one-eyed monster, then her eyes looked up into mine. "Away, baby." Then she sucked the tip of me into her mouth.

"Hisss," I growled, as she bathed me with her tongue and mouth.

214

Shawty had me so gone that I forget to ask, why the fuck she put my tool in her purse, but most of all, fuck she know my government? I ain't never told her that!

***

~Ice-Berg~

Cigar smoke rose from the tip of my cigar as my cold greys held Bella's stare.

"So, you mean to tell me that Russia's punk ass has sent assassins to do his dirty work, huh? Tell me more about this Tiger cat you speak of," I proposed.

We stood out by her manmade pond. Her spot was rare in its opulence. It was my first time being there, but the beauty of it didn't surprise me. Only Belle would think of having a house built out here in Lake Dallas. It was a majestic mansion that sat up on a hill allowing you to see Dallas, Fort. Worth in all its glory. The waters of the freshwater pond rippled as the cool breeze blew from the East. Me, her, and my boy Pablo, the head of the El Salva Trucha that's been aiding me in my pursuits of solidifying the streets were putting our heads together to see how we were gonna play this spin of events with the Russians.

"Chu mas not underestimate, mi husband."

A sharp look from me gave her pause, even gentle laughter as she turned her eyes back to the beautiful pond. She scratched the shaggy coat of the maine coon cat, she cradled in her arms.

"Such insecurity, cute! Nevertheless, as I was saying, tat man kills for fun. You can't underestimate, mi husband, David, he's not so successful for being ignorant. He's vedy efficient when he wants to be. Now, mi sources tell me tot he's sent two members from his black mamba syndicate here to the states. These two killers are of the highest order, especially '*The Tiger*'. He's the serpent that actually personifies the definition of an actual black mamba. He's known to kill with such reptiles. He's a huge fan of snakes, especially those of the elapid species."

The frown on my face must have been her clue, I didn't know what the fuck elap—elapid meant cause she smiled and looked at Pablo for elaboration as if he too was a fan of reptiles. Nevertheless, he added his input.

"The elapid species are highly poisonous snakes of the Elapidae family. The cobras, mambas, and coral snakes. I familiar with tis mamba mafia, Berg, and tese sons-of-bitches have no honor code in war, especially, *'The Tiger'*! I've heard of a few of his jobs, and all involved the green or black mamba snake. They're his signature! Me know chu no scared, and chu can hold chu own, ba don underestimate teese guys, mi friend. We mas go at them with calculated savagery," he proposed, as he emphasized his point by smacking a closed fist in the palm of his hand.

Belle continued to stare out at the rippled water as she nuzzled the furball under her chin. The feline meowed in affection. I laughed, as I tried to understand how a woman as vicious as her could become so gentle—seem so—so normal?

"I'm going back to mi country for a few days, but mi wan chu to be extremely careful and remember chu pledge to the saint. Time is up, David—we must have his blood. The Tiger is—"

"Fuck the Tiger, bitch! If you respect the fool that much, fuck him. Suck his—"

Before I could finish my rant, a slight string pricked my neck, the cat shrieked as it was tossed in the air, and an impact to my chest flipped me onto my back. Disorientation was my companion as I tried to figure out what the fuck had just happened. My first thought was that Pablo took disrespect at me talking to his cousin like that. But, as my mind cleared, and my eyes regain focused, they landed on the figure standing before me, clutching what looked to be a sharp ass dagger. Instinctively, I put my hand to my neck, pulling it away, and looked at it, the blood that tainted it infuriated me. The feel of the cut told me it was only a flesh wound, but I ain't ever let a mu'fucka spill my blood and get away with it. I owe her one, bet breath on that!

"Don ever speak to me in tis fashion. I respect tu and chu will repay me in kind or else," she seethed.

My head was inches from the water. Pablo stuck his hand out to help me up, but my anger caused me to shove his hand away aggressively. He laughed, as I picked myself up off the ground, and dusted myself off. I entertained the thought of pulling the burna off my waist and airing both their asses out but rationally was pure, as I choose the lesser of the two evils. I'd use them to benefit me and my squad, then I'd whack them and whomever this *'Angel of Death'* was!

"Say, if you ever in your life put your hands on me again, I'll kill you," I growled.

She placed the cat back in her hand and snickered like she doubted my 'G'. Then, as if to punctuate how crazy she was, the silly bitch tossed the cat far off into the rippling pond. It shrieked in midair, clawing the atmosphere trying to prevent gravity from pulling it down into the watery depths. Never taking my eyes off it, Belle turned to walk away, but not before leaving me with something to think about.

"Death is promised to us all, my dear, Ice-Berg, but chu don knows the different stages of it until you've met the likes of the Tiger. Oh, respect is a mas in mi country. Men have been castrated for the lack of it." As she walked away, the cat screamed a horrible sound as it was snatched under the surface.

Seconds later, it emerged bloodied and fighting an unseen foe, yet to no avail. It went under a second time. I wait—ten seconds—twenty! Then bubbles rose to the surface, tainted with blood and patches of fur. A strange sound ensued from the water. It could be mistaken for a form of chattering, but more like, "cha-cha-cha-cha-cha," in rapid successions.

I looked at Pablo, he shook his head with a strange look on his face. "Piranha's, mi friend. The pond is filled with the little devils. Come, mi friend let's prepare for our enemies."

***

~Assata~
Hours Later

"You sure you don't need any company, bae? You know, I don't mind." Armani offered, but I needed to be alone, so I declined with a soft kiss.

Yeah, I fucks with her, but you just couldn't let anyone know about your place of comfort. Mama seemed sincere in her feelings, but so did Jazzy and I've known her my whole life. After bidding lil' mama a safe trip home. I made way to the front door of my castle. The strap was gripped tightly in my hands as I unlocked my door and took a studious glance around to ensure nothin' was stalkin'— just waiting to take my piece off the board. If them Russian's think they'd have an easy win fuckin' with the kid, they'd be more careful the next time they underestimated a boss!

***

~2 a.m.~

As Lovey slept, she dreamed that Assata was in grave danger. She tried to warn him, but for some reason, it seemed as if he couldn't hear her.

"Assata—Assata, baby look behind you,' she screamed.

Assata continued to smile at her, oblivious to the panic in her screams. The dream began to get even stranger as someone in the distance called her name.

"Lovey—mi der, Lovey," he called.

Lovey tried to see who the stranger was, but he was too far off. She fought against the nagging feeling that it was a thin line between reality and subconscious state. The shadow behind Assata was upon him, yet he merely stared at her with a big smile on his face still unaware.

"Baby—look—behind you," she screamed and pointed.

"Lovey—the beautiful Lovey," An accented voice beckoned to her.

Lovey's eyes cracked open slightly, realizing that the dream had followed her into consciousness, she forced her eyes to focus. Two figures stood next to her bed, both in doctor's coats, but neither had the license to practice medicine. The one closest to her was the one that sent her blood pressure through the roof. He was sun-kissed brown, bald, but most notably, his entire head and face was tattooed. That's not what sent the machines she was hooked up to into hysteria, they were tribal designs that intricately covered his skin, jagged tiger stripes that gave him his namesake. His partner began to snatch the plugs from the wall until peace and quiet made love to the room.

"Much better, you tink, hmm?" he smiled evilly.

"Hi, Ms. Lovey, mi name tis, Te Tiger. We both seem to have a codmon interest, wouldn't you say. Now, mind you we're not here for you, but tings get quite ugly, hmm. Where te fuck is you son, Assata?" he screamed at the top of his lungs.

***

~Assata~
2:20 a.m.

My eyes popped open at the constant ringing of my doorbell. I feel asleep with the Mac .90, and I recently reached for her out of instinct. Yet I was sure whoever it was leaning on my shit like that wasn't here to harm me, cause one thang—two thangs for sho, death didn't ring no doorbells! Yet, the constant ring of my doorbell irritated the hell out of me. Through groggy eyes, I glanced at the clock, 2:30 a.m. Who the fuck could be this bold? It could only be three or four people, Goose, Pain, Lovey or Armani.

No matter the perpetrator, every one of them mu'fucka's knew how I felt 'bout being disturbed after one o'clock in the a.m. A nigga could only be doing a few things after one at home—burying himself inside something wet, about to bury himself in something wet or sleep. All three possibilities deserved the proper amount of attention. Besides, the first three has a key so if it was either one of them, I was liable to shoot 'em in the big toe for playing games! Well, maybe not Lovey, with familiarity, I slid through the darkness of my castle, with the mac clutched to my side just in case it was the angel of death at my front door, the odds will be even.

Without announcing my presence, I peeped out the peephole. A slow, yet heavy breath escaped me. Mere inches away—on the other side of my oak door, trouble leaned on my doorbell like she could give two fucks about my nine o'clock rule.

"Assata," she whispered as if she could detect my presence.

Easing my grip on the tool, I began to unlatch the bolts that secured my domain. Before the door opened completely, I tried to conceal the burna behind my back, no woman wanted to be greeted at gunpoint, but this big ole bitch couldn't be hidden. As the door opened, my eyes anticipated hers. My blood heated up and my dick began to rise in anticipation.

***

~Freedom~

"Assata," I whispered.

I'd been out her ringing this doorbell for about all of thirty minutes. It was late—it was cold—and my heart had finally gotten the best of me. It has been almost a month since he showed up at my job impersonating Obama. I must know—why? Why did he do what he did? Why—did he love me? Trust me to keep his secret?

"Free, fuck you leaning on my shit like you're the doorbell tester woman for?" he demanded.

Once the door opened, I couldn't help it. In spite of the seriousness of the situation. I giggled at this king's appearance. The mug on his face only tickled me even more.

"What the fuck is so funny, Free?"

I couldn't help but laugh. Obviously, he didn't know that he was missing one sock, and he had caked up drool on the side of his mouth. His black ass musta been in a deep slumber. As my eyes took in the nature of his man portions or this creature—the slope of his chest—the roughness of his aura—the sharp lines of his face—and umm, the—the hardness of him that saluted me through his boxers.

"I'm up here," he interrupted my assessment.

Embarrassed, I said, "Huh?"

I assumed it was his turn to laugh because that's exactly what he did. Blood rushed to my cheeks, yet I'm a grown woman, and if he felt comfortable enough to answer the door in his boxers, hell—who am I not to take notice?

"Happy to see me, Assata?"

"What do you want, Free, it's almost three in the morning. You're acting like just showin' up to my spot announced is cool, but it's not! What if I had company?"

I don't know why he said that, but for some reason, my mind overflowed with reasons of why I slapped him as hard as I could—the bank robbery—making me miss him so deeply—him-him—my heart—him—it all came down upon me. Fire ignited in his eyes as the animal inside him clawed its way to the surface. He reached out with the speed of light and tapped my chin with his fist—not with all his might. I could tell but just enough to let me know he believed if his woman stepped outta line, he'd remind her of her place. He grabbed a handful of my hair, snatched me into his lion's den, and slammed the door with his foot. I didn't notice the big gun until he dropped it to the floor and slammed me into the wall with so much force I lost my breath.

"Fuck wrong with you, ma, why you putting yo hands on me?" he fumed.

I got my breath back. "Fuck you, Assata, what's wrong with me? Naw, nigga, what's up with you, yo?" The big apple in me revealed its ugly face. "You fuckin' come to my job and pull some John Dillinger shit and think I should be cool with it, huh?" My emotions refused to stay harnessed. Tears blurred my vision. "You profess to be so righteous, but you're just like my brother!"

That slipped, but Assata seemed to be more in tune with the storm that fell from my eyes. The animal in him retreated, and the king did the least expected thing I'd imagine, he began to lick my tears as they fell.

Renta

Chapter Twenty

Who Shot Ya
~Detective Winslet~
3:30 a.m.

I slipped out of the bed and eased my way to the living room in the dark. I went straight for my purse. Now, that I had the gun that killed Hunter. I could not only clear my name but take down one of the most dangerous men in the city, right now. His fingerprints were all over this gun. I'd hide it somewhere here, and when the time was right. I'd send the boys straight to it, but first, taking out my phone. I made sure that it recorded the whole conversation me and Goose had earlier with me saying he made me kill Hunter.

This was just leverage just in case these fed boys tried to double cross. I'd play the victim in front of a jury and present the evidence I had. No jury in this world would convict a cop that had been held at gunpoint! At least that will be my story! As I searched for a perfect spot to stash the pistol, I wiped the barrel where I touched it, careful not to smudge Goose's prints. Where could I stash this where it wouldn't be found until I wanted it to be found? My eyes searched the darkened room, and as if some unseen force spoke to me. I headed for the old floor model tv that looked as if it hadn't been moved in centuries.

There was no reason for Goose to move it nor look behind it. So, I got down on my hands and knees and reached as far behind the outdated television as I could and wedged the pistol between it and the wall. Now that, that's out the way, I retrieved my phone and made a call to another vital part of my plan. As soon as he answered—

"What's up, ma? Fuck you up at three in the morning on the phone?" Goose said from the darkness.

***

~Assata~

I laid in the dimness of my room, and I watched as the shadows danced over the silhouettes of our tangled bodies. The drapes to my window were pulled open to allow the moon to watch over us, and I could tell from the light snores coming from shawty that I had put it down. She'd been out for the count for 'bout an hour now, but my thoughts wouldn't let me find the Sandman. It has been months since I'd rose from my coma, I still didn't know who tried to whack me. I still didn't know who murked Gusto's bitch ass.

"Who shot ya, bitch nigga? I want to find 'em and fry their cabbage for robbing us of the showdown we was meant to have," I whispered to the night as if he sucka ass nigga could give me the answers to the questions that plagued me, and as if the pussy could read my mind.

Jazzy's letter popped into my mind. *"I need you to go to the mountain. Follow your heart!"*—fuck was she—then it hit me! The mountain—the story of how Elijah Mohammad went to the mountains to pray—to find himself. Then, the reason I told her the story! Fuck, could it be? Am I overthinking shit? I slipped from underneath Free's warm body. I went to the dresser that I stashed the letter in. Opening the top drawer, I lifted my folded boxers and pulled the letter out. Silently, I made my way to the living room. I turned on the lamp on the nightstand and began to read.

I read and reread the missive about five times until I was sure I wasn't trippin'—I'm not—I'm sure of it! My baby been callin' me for this whole time, but my eyes have been blindfolded! I know I'm missing a lot, but I'm fa sho' I'd find what I was searching fa when I found, Jazz—but fuck I'ma do that? My mind was in a million places, and in the middle of the tornado of thoughts, my horn vibrated on the table where I discarded it when I made it home. I walked over to it and picked it up without looking at the screen.

"Hello, may I speak to, Assata Lamar?" I didn't recognize her voice, but to call my government out means she gotta know me.

"Yea, this he, who this?"

"Um, this is Dr. Nicola, and we need you to get down to the hospital as soon as possible, something happened to your mother and—"

That's as far as she got before I Tom Brady the phone against the wall. It shattered into a million pieces just like my heart did when the words penetrated it. There was no need to listen to the rest or ask any questions. I knew she was gone—I could feel it! Niagara Falls exploded from my eyes at the same time, that an animalist sound clawed it's way up my lungs until it burst out of my mouth. I fell to my knees not noticing Free stood before me naked as the day she came into this world. Her face was stained with confusion and fear as she took in the devastation around her.

The phone in a million pieces, and a gangsta in agony—she did the only thing she knew to do, she rushed over to me, and wrapped me into her embrace. She wanted to absorb a niggaz pain and studied me. Our eyes connected in a cosmo of madness. My eyes, two oceans—hers, dryland. My soul tried to swim onto it, but the waters were too deep to wade through. So, I merely stopped trying and allowed myself to sink to the bottom of this emotional sea. I knew now that it was a possibility for a man to walk on water because my tears stained the floor, and I hadn't sunk yet.

"They—they took her from me, Free—my air—they—they took my reason to live, ma." I found the only words I could formulate. "Why, though, why God let that happen? Huh, why, Free?"

Water filled her eyes as she shook her head like she was telling me no to something, and truthfully, she was. She was tellin' me she didn't know why. She just couldn't seem to find the words to formulate that truth. Maybe God—or even the devil wanted to answer because not even ten seconds later, my picture window exploded, and a small canister flew into the room. It spun to a stop—Free stared at it, but I tackled her and covered her with my body. The flash was ultra-bright, but the gas that ensued fucked us both up. In seconds the house was filled with smoke. Vomit rushed up my throat and spilled over Free as she clawed at her throat, trying to get to her knees. I snatched her back down, gas was like heat—it rose!

I remembered some advice an old school gave me while I was in TDC—" the main objective is not to panic, youngsta. Breathe out ya nose—slow as you can, and don't panic. That gas is all mind." I tried my best to get my breath, I used the little energy I had to pull

Free towards the back. She was weak, but she crawled with me. Right as we got to the hallway, another gas grenade flew through the window. By now, I could breathe a little, and I wasn't trying to fade that shit no more. We made it to the room, Free was actin' like she was 'bout to die, and shid, I didn't blame her. That bidness was crucial, but this wasn't the time for dying. Mustering all my strength, I pulled her to her feet.

"Listen, Free—I need you to listen! I don't know who these people are, but you can bet life on it that they're here for blood. I need you to climb out this window and go through the backyard. It leads to some woods, but if you want to live, you, betta swallow your fear of the dark! Once you get there, run into the woods and hide until you see daylight. Once the sun is—"

My spill was cut short by the sound of the front door caving in. Out of time, I pushed her toward the window. She followed instructions until she was halfway out, but the silly girl stopped and turned around.

"Why can't you come with me? Come with me, Assata, don't let them kill you, baby," she cried.

I damn near punched her in the face. I kissed her hard and pushed her dumb ass out the window. Then I spun around, my intent was to make it to my closet where I kept my tools, but the door to the room flew off the hinges and two gas masked gunmen rushed in—fuck it. I turned towards the window, I was about to see if that shit they be doing in them movies was real. I made it four steps before something sharp wedge its self in my neck. Two more steps, I was a foot away from the window seal, but suddenly I was super tired. My legs got rubbery, and my energy spilled from me like water from a hole in a fish tank.

I reached to the back of my neck and yanked out whatever the object was that rocked me to bed. I put it in front of my eyes, and to my surprise, it was a dart of some sort. I laughed out loud at the irony. These lil' mu'fuckas real—it's not some T.V. shit! As my vision faded to black, the only comfort I had was that whomever these mu'fuckas was, they wanted me alive, if not, they woulda sent bullets instead of a tranquilizer. I'd have a chance to murk they dumb ass for being so arrogant as to give the devil a nap instead of death. Somebody wanted me alive for a reason!

To Be Continued...
Who Shot Ya 3
Coming Soon

Submission Guideline

Submit the first three chapters of your completed manuscript to ldpsubmissions@gmail.com, subject line: Your book's title. The manuscript must be in a .doc file and sent as an attachment. Document should be in Times New Roman, double spaced and in size 12 font. Also, provide your synopsis and full contact information. If sending multiple submissions, they must each be in a separate email.

Have a story but no way to send it electronically? You can still submit to LDP/Ca$h Presents. Send in the first three chapters, written or typed, of your completed manuscript to:

LDP: Submissions Dept
Po Box 870494
Mesquite, Tx 75187

DO NOT send original manuscript. Must be a duplicate.

Provide your synopsis and a cover letter containing your full contact information.

Thanks for considering LDP and Ca$h Presents.

Coming Soon from Lock Down Publications/Ca$h Presents

BOW DOWN TO MY GANGSTA

By **Ca$h**

TORN BETWEEN TWO

By **Coffee**

BLOOD STAINS OF A SHOTTA **III**

By **Jamaica**

STEADY MOBBIN II

By **Marcellus Allen**

BLOOD OF A BOSS **V**

By **Askari**

LOYAL TO THE GAME **IV**

By **T.J. & Jelissa**

A DOPEBOY'S PRAYER **II**

By **Eddie "Wolf" Lee**

IF LOVING YOU IS WRONG... **III**

LOVE ME EVEN WHEN IT HURTS

By **Jelissa**

TRUE SAVAGE **V**

By **Chris Green**

BLAST FOR ME **III**

ROTTEN TO THE CORE **III**

By **Ghost**

ADDICTIED TO THE DRAMA **III**

By **Jamila Mathis**

LIPSTICK KILLAH **III**

CRIME OF PASSION **II**

By **Mimi**

WHAT BAD BITCHES DO **III**

By **Aryanna**

THE COST OF LOYALTY **II**

By **Kweli**

SHE FELL IN LOVE WITH A REAL ONE **II**

By **Tamara Butler**

LOVE SHOULDN'T HURT **III**

By **Meesha**

CORRUPTED BY A GANGSTA **III**

By **Destiny Skai**

A GANGSTER'S CODE III

By **J-Blunt**

KING OF NEW YORK II

By **T.J. Edwards**

CUM FOR ME **IV**

By **Ca$h & Company**

Available Now

RESTRAINING ORDER **I & II**

By **CA$H & Coffee**

LOVE KNOWS NO BOUNDARIES **I II & III**

By **Coffee**

RAISED AS A GOON I, II, III & IV

BRED BY THE SLUMS I, II, III

BLAST FOR ME I & II

ROTTEN TO THE CORE I II

By **Ghost**

LAY IT DOWN **I & II**

LAST OF A DYING BREED

BLOOD STAINS OF A SHOTTA I & II

By **Jamaica**

LOYAL TO THE GAME

LOYAL TO THE GAME II

LOYAL TO THE GAME III

By **TJ & Jelissa**

BLOODY COMMAS I & II

SKI MASK CARTEL I II & III

KING OF NEW YORK

By **T.J. Edwards**

IF LOVING HIM IS WRONG…I & II

By **Jelissa**

WHEN THE STREETS CLAP BACK I & II III

By **Jibril Williams**

A DISTINGUISHED THUG STOLE MY HEART I II & III

LOVE SHOULDN'T HURT I II

By **Meesha**

A GANGSTER'S CODE I & II

By J-Blunt

PUSH IT TO THE LIMIT

By **Bre' Hayes**

BLOOD OF A BOSS **I, II, III & IV**

By **Askari**

THE STREETS BLEED MURDER **I, II & III**

THE HEART OF A GANGSTA I II& III

By **Jerry Jackson**

CUM FOR ME

CUM FOR ME 2

CUM FOR ME 3

An **LDP Erotica Collaboration**

BRIDE OF A HUSTLA **I II & II**

THE FETTI GIRLS **I, II& III**

CORRUPTED BY A GANGSTA I & II

By **Destiny Skai**

WHEN A GOOD GIRL GOES BAD

By **Adrienne**

A GANGSTER'S REVENGE **I II III & IV**

THE BOSS MAN'S DAUGHTERS

THE BOSS MAN'S DAUGHTERS II

THE BOSSMAN'S DAUGHTERS III

THE BOSSMAN'S DAUGHTERS IV

THE BOSS MAN'S DAUGHTERS **V**

A SAVAGE LOVE **I & II**

BAE BELONGS TO ME

A HUSTLER'S DECEIT I, II

WHAT BAD BITCHES DO I, II

By **Aryanna**

A KINGPIN'S AMBITON

A KINGPIN'S AMBITION **II**

I MURDER FOR THE DOUGH

By **Ambitious**

TRUE SAVAGE

TRUE SAVAGE II

TRUE SAVAGE **III**

TRUE SAVAGE **IV**

By **Chris Green**

A DOPEBOY'S PRAYER

By **Eddie "Wolf" Lee**

THE KING CARTEL **I, II & III**

By **Frank Gresham**

THESE NIGGAS AIN'T LOYAL **I, II & III**

By **Nikki Tee**

GANGSTA SHYT **I II &III**

By **CATO**

THE ULTIMATE BETRAYAL

By **Phoenix**

BOSS'N UP **I , II & III**

By **Royal Nicole**

I LOVE YOU TO DEATH

By Destiny J

I RIDE FOR MY HITTA

I STILL RIDE FOR MY HITTA

By **Misty Holt**

LOVE & CHASIN' PAPER

By **Qay Crockett**

TO DIE IN VAIN

By **ASAD**

BROOKLYN HUSTLAZ

By **Boogsy Morina**

BROOKLYN ON LOCK I & II

By **Sonovia**

GANGSTA CITY

By **Teddy Duke**

A DRUG KING AND HIS DIAMOND I & II III

A DOPEMAN'S RICHES

By Nicole Goosby

TRAPHOUSE KING **I II & III**

By **Hood Rich**

LIPSTICK KILLAH **I, II**

CRIME OF PASSION

By **Mimi**

STEADY MOBBN'

By **Marcellus Allen**

WHO SHOT YA **I, II**

Renta

BOOKS BY LDP'S CEO, CA$H

TRUST IN NO MAN

TRUST IN NO MAN 2

TRUST IN NO MAN 3

BONDED BY BLOOD

SHORTY GOT A THUG

THUGS CRY

THUGS CRY 2

THUGS CRY 3

TRUST NO BITCH

TRUST NO BITCH 2

TRUST NO BITCH 3

TIL MY CASKET DROPS

RESTRAINING ORDER

RESTRAINING ORDER 2

IN LOVE WITH A CONVICT

Coming Soon

BONDED BY BLOOD 2

BOW DOWN TO MY GANGSTA

Renta